SEX

BY THE
BOOK

MW00446661

SEX

BY THE
BOOK

Gay Men's Tales
of Lit & Lust

Edited by
Kevin Bentley

GREEN CANDY PRESS

Sex by the Book: Gay Men's Tales of Lit and Lust
edited by Kevin Bentley
ISBN 10: 1-931160-52-X
ISBN 13: 978-1-931160-52-0
Published by Green Candy Press
www.greencandypress.com

Copyright ©2007 by Kevin Bentley. All rights reserved. No part of this
book may be reproduced in any form without written permission from
the publisher, except by a reviewer, who may quote brief passages in a
review where appropriate credit is given; nor may any part of this book
be reproduced, stored in a retrieval system, or transmitted in any form
or by any means—electronic, photocopying, recording, or other—without specific written permission from the publisher.

Cover and interior design: Ian Phillips
Cover photograph: Tom Blanchard
Model: Sean Ling

"Coming of Age in the Worlds of 'If'" by Richard Labonté, originally
appeared in a slightly different version in *The Future Is Queer: A Science Fiction
Anthology,* edited by Richard Labonté and Lawrence Schimel (Arsenal
Pulp Press, 2006). "Something about Wittgenstein" by Van Scott, originally appeared in Velvet Mafia, issue 15.

Authors retain copyright to their individual pieces of work.

The majority of the selections in this volume are fiction, and any names
characters, places, and incidents are either the product of the authors'
imaginations or are used fictitiously, and any resemblance to actual
persons, living or dead, is entirely coincidental. In the five personal
essays, proper names and descriptive details have been changed to protect the privacy of any living individuals.

Printed in Canada by Transcontinental Printing Inc.

For Paul, whose love speaks volumes

Contents

Secret Shoppers
Lou Dellaguzzo

"I could kill people who look at me like I don't belong here."

The man's rasping voice hisses along the cookbook alcove on the second floor. He springs off his chair, tossing an old newspaper in the air. Pages scatter around him.

Freddie doesn't know what to do. The college sophomore only looked for a moment. When he realized the bearded, smelly guy was arguing with a comic strip, it was too late. He got caught gawking.

"This is fucking harassment against the homeless," the grungy man says. "I know my goddamn rights." He struts around like a rooster, bragging about his famous karate skills—and how he's not afraid to use them. He tries to demonstrate a kick and almost falls to the floor.

His wild behavior petrifies Freddie nonetheless. He wants to walk away but is afraid to. What if the crazy guy follows him out of the store and there's a fight? Who'd get hurt? And who'd get blamed for causing it?

His imagination careens through different scenarios. Somehow he gets arrested. No. Only the guy gets arrested. Worse yet, they *both* get arrested and share the same jail cell because the cops don't believe he's innocent. Anyway, there'll be a trial. His parents will have a fit. They'll haul him back to Minnesota, back to the small-town college he pleaded to escape with promises of good behavior. And better grades. How he'd like to be home now.

Where'd everybody go, anyway? he wonders, still unable to move or speak.

If Freddie could turn around, he'd see a tall man in his late twenties

Secret Shoppers

dressed in a pale gray suit.

Jack stares at the belligerent wacko to get his attention. With a flourish, he pulls a cell phone from his vest pocket. He presses three numbers in slow motion so his squinting audience of one can count.

"Fuck you, motherfucker," the guy says. He spits on the floor, careens past Freddie, and makes a wobbly beeline for the escalator. "I'm the victim of discrimination," he chants on his slow descent. Only a few shoppers pay attention before moving on.

His voice ricochets around the cavernous store—and in Freddie's ears.

Jack puts away his phone. No need to cancel his complaint. All he'd gotten from 911 was a steady ring. He watches the angry man stomp past magazine racks and out of the store.

Meanwhile Freddie still can't turn around, start walking. During the incident, he felt completely alone. Now he expects to see many eyes staring at him in judgment. At a kid who wants to be invisible.

One floor above the mortified boy, deep in the fiction department, Jack holds a problematic book in his hand. Somehow the incident—and his inventive response to it—encourages him to buy the volume he looks at whenever he browses lately, but always shelves at the last minute. Surely now he can buy whatever he wants without feeling too self-conscious.

"Surely," he murmurs.

He turns to his favorite page, reads the passionate scene between a skilled lover and his shy but eager acolyte. It's a scene he knows by heart.

"Can I help you with something, sir?" the clerk says.

She shouldn't have crept up on him like that.

"No thanks. Just browsing." He keeps his hand over the book's title.

The clerk leaves, Jack sighs, and sunshine pours through lofty windows. Sunshine that always looks brighter on Fridays. His short day at work. A luminous outline runs along his sculpted nose, his high forehead and square chin. He opens the book, chooses a page at random. It describes a sex scene he doesn't much like. Still, the collection is meant to gratify diverse tastes—something he's learned to appreciate.

I really have to get out more, he thinks. *Not make excuses for staying in. Maybe meet a nice guy. Or try to, anyway.*

Before he heads to the checkout, he considers buying another book, a serious text, to offset his racier purchase. Instead, he decides to brave it out, save the weightier tome for another visit. But he definitely won't use a credit card.

There's nothing but junk on the first floor. Some fancy office supplies and lots of bargain books no one wants. Jack examines a suede file box. *Suede?* he thinks, puzzled by the lavish material. He spots Freddie standing at the end of the checkout line. When did he get there? An older gentleman—dapper in his safari hat and camel-hair jacket—makes his way to the attractive boy, but then a transparent mechanical clock with a loud ticking distracts him.

Enough time for Jack to reach his goal.

Now what does he do?

If only he'd introduced himself earlier. But it was better just to back away, not embarrass the kid even more.

Gazing at Freddie up close, Jack stops thinking about an opportunity lost. The boy's auburn hair is slicked back. He has a square-shaped nose, full lips. His dark blue eyes blink often—he probably wears contacts.

Some acne marks his tawny cheeks and robust jaw. Bits of flesh-colored medication cover the small eruptions.

Jack wants to kiss the boy, reassure him about his great looks, say they'll only improve with age. It takes a few seconds to realize his gaze is returned. He smiles, tries not to appear overeager.

Here's where things often break down. Where he loses his nerve, says awkward things.

Freddie wonders why the man next to him keeps grinning at him so oddly. Maybe he's a store employee working undercover. Maybe he's one of those secret shoppers who follow people around.

People who've caused trouble.

To keep from getting totally paranoid, he focuses on his selections.

Secret Shoppers

The small book is about bread baking. The second one—a hefty volume on Italian cuisine—promises to reveal the secrets of a master chef. His dad better like these birthday gifts, considering all the hassle.

While the boy browses, Jack works up the nerve to stop hiding the title of his own purchase—*The Mammoth Book of Gay Erotica*—so that the boy might see it. The cover has a big photo of two young, athletic men. They reach toward each other, their embrace eternally—annoyingly—deferred. Jack gazes at the image and feels lecherous.

How long can he stare at this damn picture without appearing obsessed?

"Oh shit, man," Freddie says.

The heavier book he was browsing tumbles to the floor. When he bends to retrieve it, the straps on his backpack slip down his elbows, binding his arms. Squatting, he tries to adjust the straps, but his effort fails. Instead, he falls backward, unbalanced by the heavy weight.

Jack kneels to retrieve the book. And Freddie as well.

He rights the backpack and pushes the boy forward so he can stand. Left on the floor is his own book, front side up.

Freddie stares at the erotic cover with discomfort and interest. He reaches for the challenging text, wanting to return the man's kindness—and get a closer look.

"No, don't," Jack says. "You might get stuck again."

He means to be funny. Break the ice. But the boy's face is blossoming red.

Jack quickly retrieves his book.

Two clerks working side by side request the next customers in line. Freddie and Jack.

This is getting ridiculous, Jack thinks, *a real burlesque.* He compares the store scene with his imaginary encounters, where he appears socially adept, easily achieving seduction and lasting friendship. Both goals he considers important. Often, like right now, he can't believe he's twenty-seven. He really should be better at this.

But he'll worry later.

Time to enjoy a last look at Freddie, still fumbling with his books at the sales counter.

Then, a minor miracle. The boy meets his gaze with unreadable blue eyes.

At least there's no hostility, Jack thinks.

He braces for the loneliness that will hit him on his way home, carrying a book about the sexy encounters of guys who don't exist.

Stuck with a slow clerk, Freddie watches the helpful stranger leave. He elides his reason for looking. He won't admit the handsome stranger, so eager and friendly, made his stomach tighten, his crotch swell. He only knows he wants to follow the guy. But when he catches up at the entrance, he pushes the door too hard, and it slams against the wall.

The loud noise startles Jack. He looks at the boy with puzzled eyes.

Angry with himself, with his clumsiness, Freddie rushes past, swearing under his breath.

Shrug it off, Jack tells himself, wondering what he did wrong.

Yet he can't.

Freddie stands on a breezy corner, watches the man cross the street. Feeling dumb, his skin tingling, he decides to pursue Jack, somehow strike up a conversation. But he keeps getting cold feet. How can he talk to the guy if he can't catch up to him? What would he say anyway? And now he's got a long red light against him.

But he can't stop thinking about the man's black hair. His smooth, pale skin. And what about the sexy green of his deep-set eyes?

When Jack turns around, hoping for a final glimpse, the boy tries to smile.

But he can't.

The WALK sign changes twice. Both guys feign interest in the street choreography that swirls around them.

An impasse.

Freddie pretends he's unsure which way he should go. He knows where he'd *like* to go, but he can't get his feet to move. His eyes jump from a matronly shopper—whose bag brushes against his leg—to a group of college kids laughing at a shared joke. Never does his sight veer too far from his real interest. Now and then, his eyes connect

Secret Shoppers

with Jack's, but he can't summon enough nerve to hold his gaze.

Clouds drift above. Afternoon light enfolds the boy in pale gold.

Jack resolves to take action. Something's going on. He doesn't know what yet, but he's determined to find out, even if it means a crushing rebuff that makes him not want to look at another guy until spring. He shivers, recalling last winter. All those lonely nights spent at home—with a book—after he talked himself out of going to some noisy, crowded bar. It's not the kind of place he likes.

Crossing the busy street against the light, he walks to Freddie.

The boy's resolve fizzles. He's ready to bolt.

"This weather's kind of cold to stand around in," Jack says. He waits a beat or two and gets nothing. Not even a blink. Unless he counts the pained expression. "I'm Jack, by the way." He pulls off his glove and extends his hand in a make-or-break move. It would be downright rude not to return the gesture. He braces for an icy rejection.

"I'm Freddie. I mean, Fred."

"Ouch!" Jack wasn't prepared for the strong grip, undiminished by a thick, blue mitten. Despite his pain, he thinks the mittens are charming.

"Jeez, I'm really sorry. I didn't mean it on purpose." Only last week, Freddie's political science teacher had the same response to an overeager handshake. The slight man had scowled at him, made the boy think about switching his major.

"I can do it better," he says. And he takes Jack's hand to prove his point.

Freddie looks onto a balcony filled with bushy perennials. He sips his lemon-flavored seltzer water. He avoids sweet drinks, thinking that sugar causes pimples. The angry ones. He catches his reflection on the glass door.

What a mess, he thinks.

But he doesn't notice how the double glazing distorts his lovely features and pliant skin.

Meanwhile Jack stands in his bathroom, taking a whiz. He obsesses about the stilted conversation so far. His job as the editor of an environmental newsletter seemed to impress Freddie. But then he rambled on about offshore drilling and the boy shut down. Probably oil spills don't make for great small talk.

Still, Freddie does seem mercurial. Either he's friendly and talkative, or he clams up—looking like he'd rather be in hell than with you. Perhaps it's Religious Guilt that makes him waver. After all, he attends Catholic University. And he definitely is Irish.

"Maybe I should go," Freddie says when Jack enters the living room. His skin tingles. A sure sign that fresh pimples are budding everywhere. His fantasy of getting fucked seems impossible now.

Even if he hid his face in a pillow, there'd be the same mess on his back. Who'd want to see that?

"Please don't leave." Jack holds the boy by his shoulders, looks into blue eyes that sparkle in the clear November sunshine. The topaz month. And then he kisses Freddie's cheek. The more blemished one.

The boy pulls away.

"Let me," Jack whispers. "Just once more. This time on the mouth. Then you can say if you want me to stop."

His lips feel moist and cool.

Freddie's first real kiss, from a guy at any rate. It's not like the passionate, even rough kisses he thinks about when he masturbates. But it's a good one nonetheless. One that excites him.

"You looked so good when I came in," Jack says. "I couldn't wait."

Freddie yields to the embrace. He smells the floury warmth, wants to admit his inexperience but worries it will be a turn-off.

"Are you a kisser?" Jack asks. He rephrases the question. "Is it okay to kiss you again?" Freddie's eyes widen. He'd like to back away and start all over again. Maybe.

If he had more experience with shy guys, Jack would know what to do next. Since he doesn't, he goes by intuition—and the more assertive protagonists he's read about in erotic stories. With a firmer hand, he draws the boy to his lips, presses hard until a sigh resonates against his cheek.

He's a bit surer how to proceed. But with care. More a gesture

Secret Shoppers

toward roughness than the real thing. He doesn't want that, and hopes Freddie feels the same. His tongue explores the yielding mouth, where he discovers a slice of fresh chewing gum. Mint flavored.

"You better get rid of the gum." He pulls a tissue from his pocket. "Don't want you choking on it."

Freddie tries to remove the piece with his tongue, but it sticks to one of his fillings. "Damn." He turns away so he can pick the stuff out.

"Guess I assumed a lot, haven't I?" Jack says.

"Wha da ya mah?" (Freddie still has a finger in his mouth.)

"That you've been with a guy before."

The boy shrugs, his face blotched with crimson. He doesn't want to hear what they're doing put into words.

Jack scowls playfully. "You're not a boy genius, are you?"

Freddie spits the gum into the tissue, shoves it in his pocket. "A boy what?"

"You know. One of those kids who graduate high school early and get a BA before they're eighteen."

No response.

"I just want to know how old you are, make sure you're not too young for...you know, this."

"Twenty," Freddie says. "I'm twenty. I lost a year in high school."

He runs two bony fingers along his temple. "For a while, my concentration got messed up, I guess." A memory of adolescent misery grabs his shoulders, constricts his breath. His parents' disappointment. The smirks from other kids who labeled him and his best friend Dumb and Dumber.

"I'm barely a C student." He wonders why he even offers the information. "Can we drop the subject now that you know I'm dull normal?" He rubs a blemish on his chin.

What a skilled romancer you are, Jack thinks. *Now you're losing him. You have to say something good. Something Freddie can believe about himself. Or at least about you.*

"Back in the bookstore," he says, "I wanted to speak with you when I first saw you. Before that crazy guy hassled you."

The boy looks as if someone had struck him.

"I was standing close behind you all the while," Jack admits. "I stared at the guy to get his attention, so he could watch me dial nine-one-one on my cell." He caresses the boy's chin to stop him from picking at it. "The guy caught on real fast. And if he hadn't, I would've helped you if he became a real threat, instead of the loopy windbag I took him for."

Freddie stares down at his large red sneakers. One's untied. Part flattered, part mortified, he musses his auburn hair. His square nose catches late afternoon sunlight. "That guy," he says, shaking his head. "I mean. It wasn't me who bothered him. Not at first. He was arguing with comic strips! I only looked at him for a few seconds at most. And then he went nuts on *me*. I was so embarrassed, and kind of scared, when he started talking about karate. Man, I just didn't know what to do. Something like that never happened to me before. Not even close."

Jack could kick himself. Now he's upset the poor kid all over again. "Look. I don't know how to make you feel comfortable with me. Maybe that won't ever happen. But I do know I like you, and wouldn't have left you to defend yourself in that predicament."

He embraces the boy, kneading his tense back.

"There's nothing to worry about anymore. You're with me, in my place, where it's safe. Where you can feel at home." He fights the urge to kiss again. "If you need to go slow, or if you decide you only want to be friends, either way it's okay."

Easing his lips against Freddie's neck, he inhales the warm, pearlike aroma. They remain silent, not moving. Time goes elsewhere, burned away by the growing heat between them.

The boy runs his hand along Jack's bottom. He squeezes flesh and muscle. Yet all the while, he thinks only about the man's crotch.

Surprised by the move, Jack adjusts the scenario playing in his head. He imagines the erotic shift from fucking to getting fucked. He's never done that before. The handful of pretty guys he's slept with wanted only one thing.

And it wasn't his rump.

Gently he takes hold of Freddie's ass. The boy's baggy pants

Secret Shoppers

have been hiding two generous mounds.

"You're amazing," he whispers.

Freddie tightens his grip on Jack's backside. He kisses the man's face, lets his mouth wander everywhere but those waiting lips. Jack forces the issue. As they kiss, he tries to redirect the boy's hand to his crotch, but fails.

"Guess we have a little problem," he says in a muffled voice.

"What?" Freddie's mind is somewhere else. On a bed, face down—he *must* be face down—the skin on his back all clear, his pliant ass, ready for the taking.

Jack holds the boy at arms' length. "I like to fuck," he says. "I like to fuck"—again, for emphasis, to reclaim that dreamy gaze. "I do it safely. Patiently. But it's what I like, Freddie. I'd be happy to, you know, make love to you—jerk you off while I'm still inside you. That'd be great. Really. But I..."

He has to stop. He's angry with himself, his own stubborn limitations—but not nearly enough to breech them. Better to know now, anyway. Forget about the sex part; just focus on a possible friendship. He ruffles the boy's hair, studies his worried face. What a sweet guy. So hapless. His passion rises again, despite the gloomy prospect.

"Sorry," he says. "I'm not very versatile. My fault, not yours."

"That's not what I want," Freddie says.

"I know." Jack's startled by the volume. "I've figured out as much." He's feeling a little defensive.

"No." Freddie says.

"What?" It's hard to unravel the boy's thoughts.

"I mean *that's* not what I want." Freddie imagines fucking Jack—a picture he's yet to relate. He grabs hold of the man's waist, then jumps back, not sure what to do.

"Calm down, now." Jack embraces the boy, gives his ass a playful whack. "Start at the beginning, and tell me what's on your mind. Only this time, don't skip the antecedent."

"The what?" Freddie says.

When the moment finally arrives, the moment to live his sexual fantasy, Freddie starts to shiver. His teeth chatter. They sound like heavy rain on dry grass.

Intermittent panic. The mysterious sounds behind him. Still mysterious, even though Jack describes everything he does: Unwrapping the condom. Unraveling it around his cock. Applying lubricant to the taut, latex sheath—and to Freddie's clenched, resistant ass.

Caressing him, Jack kisses the boy's long neck, his ear. He strokes twitching muscles, waits for the trembling to stop.

But it only worsens.

And his frustration mounts. He can't get himself to enter—no matter how patiently—while Freddie shivers and chatters beneath him. The act would seem more like torture than pleasure.

Something has to change.

"You've got to turn around," he says. "Look at me. Then you can see how careful I'll be with you."

Freddie shrugs—although it's hard to tell with all his trembling. "I don't know. Why do I have to look at you? I mean, I like to look at you. You look *great*. But…maybe not while…"

Ambivalence hangs in the air. The pimples on his back itch. He feels more undesirable than he did after he undressed, revealing a body that—to his admirer—seemed angelic, a contrast of light and hardness.

Then the trembling began.

"Please," Jack says, "you have to trust me just a little more. You've come this far. Don't change your mind; don't make me think it was a mistake bringing you home, wanting to do this. You did say you really wanted to."

He rubs Freddie's back, stroking rigid muscles. "I'm not a jerk. I won't brush you off. You know, afterward. You're someone I want to be friends with, Freddie. I like you."

Then, more hesitant, afraid to provoke the unwanted outcome. "I'll like you no matter what we do. Or *don't* do. But give me a chance first. Okay?"

Time passes. Its measure is distorted by frustration and growing embarrassment.

Jack takes the long silence for a no. Freddie probably wants to be

Secret Shoppers

alone. To dress. Maybe to leave furtively, or after a quick good-bye. He pats the boy's thigh, draws his fingers across reddish down, the tawny skin he's admired there, has kissed and tasted.

"Think I'll wash up." He slides off the bed, slouches into the dark hallway without looking back.

"Yeah. It's better, I guess." Freddie rests his calves on the man's opalescent shoulders. The boy shrugs. Then goes silent.

After he shouted out for Jack to return, it took more convincing, and a lot of patience, to get him into this position. Face-to-face.

"Slow and careful," Jack whispers. He rubs the tight ass with his sheathed dick, the very tip. He eases his way inside. Whenever the boy winces, he stops his progress, murmurs reassurance. He tells his yielding partner how good it feels holding him—holding an armful of hapless, beguiling Freddie.

He makes love to the shapely calves that frame his face. He doesn't want to pump yet. The boy's muscles tighten around his cock.

All movement ceases.

Jack wants his partner to relax, elude discomfort, give in to the pleasure he can see awakening in Freddie's eyes, his arching dick.

A gyrating movement, repeated a few times, signals it's okay.

And Jack begins.

Long thrusts, nearly suspended. More like slow gliding.

Freddie lets pleasure overtake him. He delights in Jack's heated smell, gets lost in the gentle face. When they open, green eyes capture the twilight. And Freddie's heart. He looks deeper, deeper into those smiling eyes. Flecks of yellow seem to welcome him.

Library Hours
Don Shewey

My sexual education began by reading books. Sleuthing down sex stories as an adolescent in the 1960s took some work, but I was an expert bookworm. And the pickings were so slim, I was satisfied with very little. The dictionary would do. *Homosexual. Penis.* Seeing the words in print would raise my temperature. Looking up *homosexuality* in the card catalogue at the library became the equivalent of checking myself in the mirror—yep, I exist. I practically made a fetish object out of a dry medical manual called *The Sexually Adequate Male* I found on the paperback rack of a grade-Z five-and-dime store at a shopping center in Denver. No one bought this book the whole year I lived there, so whenever I was in the vicinity I got to pick it up and turn to the chapter on Perversions, the only place in the book where homosexuality was discussed. It had to do.

On my sex-ed reading list, the most arousing if not quite practical texts were the novels of Jean Genet. I came across *Our Lady of the Flowers* in the Aurora Public Library at the age of thirteen. I read this book a chapter at a time, crouched in the aisle on the gray linoleum to hide the boners I got reading about French queers in prison sniffing each other's farts. Later, it was creepy William Burroughs titles on yet another rack of paperbacks that never seemed to change, where I would scan *The Soft Machine* for the page about ass-fucking in the bathroom of a railroad train or the mention of the famous dildo Steely Dan in *Naked Lunch*.

Did I read in some pulpy novel a reference to sex in bathrooms? Or was it a sixth sense that drew me to the basement men's room of the campus library?

Library Hours

This was a world unto itself. Two stalls and two urinals completely surrounded by salacious graffiti. Men who travel as much as I had by the time I was nineteen have used a lot of public toilets. Somewhere along the way I'd picked up the idea that *Show hard for blow job* was the way it worked. I was more interested in seeing hard cocks and taking them in my mouth than getting blow jobs, though. All it took to get initiated into this quiet, forbidden, secret world was one episode of going into a stall, reading all the graffiti, and waiting fifteen minutes.

If my initial tentative gropings and suckings with my roommate Sandy in the bedroom of our off-campus apartment were my innocent introduction to sex, the basement men's room at the Rice University library was my first experience of adult sexuality. Nothing innocent here. Desperate men having perverted sex in public a few feet from unsuspecting straight folks—heigh-ho, that's the life for me.

The graffiti in the bathroom had obviously been there for some time, possibly for years. The bathroom was surely cleaned and maintained every day or two by a custodian who mopped the floors and replenished the toilet paper. Did he ignore the graffiti out of shame and embarrassment, avert his gaze, do his job, and leave? Did he report the defacement and the signs of homo sex activity to some authority? Did he try to scrub away the scribbling in Magic Marker and ballpoint pen but find himself thwarted? Were bathroom cleansers not strong enough in those days to cut through ink? Or did the custodian enjoy the alluring self-descriptions, the carefully dated advertisements of availability, the phallic iconography, the succinct and astonishingly literate capsule reviews of assignations posted for toilet-seat reading? Perhaps he got off on it, his sphincter tightening as he confronted the range of sexual possibilities this tapestry of handwriting samples revealed.

Like any temple where many people have prayed, this bathroom had a distinct aura to it, even when no one else was there but me. It was cool and quiet. The air stood thick with sexual memory and possibility. When I entered this sanctum, all my senses changed and became more attuned, as if I were back in church, stepping into the confessional, preparing to receive the sacrament. I slowed down (everything but my heart, which leapt and raced until I thought it might pop out my ears and bounce against the walls). From the basement stacks, you entered the men's room through a door with a handle. That door opened onto a tiny vestibule. To get to the toilets, you had to walk through a second, swinging door. The double-door configuration was crucial. It made all the difference between an ordinary lavatory and a prime meeting ground for anonymous sex.

What thickened the air was the presence of two levels of realities, the sexual and the nonsexual. The nonsexual reality had to be maintained at all times, at any cost. If anyone walked into the men's room, by the time he was through the second door, he had to be greeted by the appearance of nothing more remarkable than men going about the mundane business of relieving their bladders, moving their bowels, washing their hands, or combing their hair. Any number of things could happen between two men standing at the urinals or, more commonly, in the toilet stalls, but they had to be simple enough acts to be hastily concluded at the two-second warning of the outer door—the mechanical revolution of the doorknob, the whoosh of air breaking the vacuum seal of the closed quarters, the thump of a hand on the swinging door.

The first time I took a stall in the men's room, I dropped my pants, sat on the toilet, and waited. I didn't know what would happen. I looked around at the graffiti. My eyes wanted to gobble it all up at once. In my memory all three surfaces I could see were covered with writing as dense as a Chinese story painting, from knee-level to the top of the stall. I needed this information. I needed to know that other men had desires for other men and that it was possible to satisfy those desires. I needed to know that satisfying those desires could take place in a location within my reach, not some other time and place. I couldn't wait for it to happen to me.

How did this game work? There were no active indications, no positive steps to take. The overriding rule was: don't get caught. But how do you connect in this underworld? How do you know the difference between the guy who interrupted his chemistry homework to

Library Hours

take a dump and the guy who right this minute is fondling a thick boner you'd like to be tasting? Sitting in the toilet stall was like being in a prison cell, in isolation, fantasizing about another prisoner, whom you could hear cough, breathe, whistle, hum, tap, fart, but you could not see. You had to imagine who he was, what he looked like, what he wanted, if he knew the scene, if he wanted to blow or be blown. All of this took time. But in this furtive public space requiring constant vigilance for trouble or danger, time got compressed. A minute of waiting to determine the intentions of the guy who just stepped into the next stall felt like eternity. How long could I spend in this limbo? I was in a trance. I was under a spell. From the moment I knew I was going to the tearoom—which might have been in my dorm room; or walking across campus; or in the middle of Latin class; or when I walked through the front door of the library, flashing my student ID card; or while reading the newspaper; or when I felt the urge to pee—the spell would descend. I would not speak. I would switch from a verbal input-output mode to sensory mode: alert for danger, sex-vibe radar flipped on.

I forgot to mention an essential flavor of the gumbo-like atmosphere in the men's room: guilt. I felt crushed with guilt till I could barely breathe, walking into that men's room looking for sex. Nowhere else on campus was there any indication that men might want to get together for sex. This was 1973. There was no gay students' league yet. The Rice Players, the extracurricular theater company with whom I spent every spare minute, and the architecture department were hotbeds of closet cases. I took the only women's studies course offered on campus, where we read smart feminist texts like Shulamith Firestone's *The Dialectic of Sex* and *Toward a Recognition of Androgyny* by Carolyn Heilbrun. Ten years later, a course like that would be a haven for brainy queers; back then I was the only guy in the class.

The only open appearance of homosexuality on campus occurred in Sociology 102, the first-year second-semester course commonly referred to as "Nuts and Sluts." Each year the instructor would bring in a gay person to speak to the class. It was usually the first time any of the students had come face-to-face with someone willing to admit to being homosexual. I wasn't enrolled for the class, but my roommate was, and I went with him on The Day of the Homosexual. The specimen on display was a friendly, attractive, bearded young man who bravely weathered the awed and ignorant questions the class put to him. I remember that he said, "I don't spend all day thinking, 'I'm gay, I'm gay, I'm gay.' "

The guest slot in Nuts and Sluts class, along with my avid reading, satisfied my intellectual curiosity about the existence of other homosexuals. But homosexuality in action was still a mystery. My brief, one-sided grapplings with Sandy didn't really count. What did men do who wanted to have sex with each other? Again, this was 1973. Home video didn't exist. Pornography must have been available somewhere in Houston but as a nineteen-year-old college student, I'd never laid eyes on any gay porn.

All I knew were the cryptic, largely imagined movements of the denizens of the library bathroom. The nondescript man with dark-framed glasses and navy blue windbreaker looking over his shoulder repeatedly while standing at the urinal, for instance. I could see him through the crack between the door and the doorframe of the toilet stall. Was he looking at me? Could he see me? What did he want? What do I do? Should I open the door and say "Right this way"? I want something to happen. I'm not exactly turned on. In fact, I'm so scared my hands are shaking, and I don't think I could even stand up. My dick is not hard. If he wanted to come into the stall, I'd be curious to see what would happen. How is he supposed to signal that to me? I intuit that he wants something to happen, too, but he's just as frustrated as I am. He doesn't know how to make it happen, either. So he leaves.

Most of my experiences in the library bathroom were like that. It took a rare brave soul to connect. One day I sat in the stall next to another occupied stall. I tuned in to my radar and determined that we were on the same wavelength. We'd edged our shoes close enough to the marble divider between us so they were nearly touching. My right-foot white sneaker cruised his left black loafer. Suddenly a

Library Hours

hand appeared under the divider. I took it in my hand. That felt really ridiculous, holding hands under a marble wall between toilet stalls like Pyramus and Thisbe. I was a smart boy, fifth in my high school class, in the top one percent of intelligence tests. I figured out that the hand wasn't looking for my hand.

I slid halfway off the toilet seat so the hand straining up from under the wall could grip my now erect penis. The hand communicated to me wordlessly that I should kneel next to the wall and slide the lower half of my body underneath the divider, as if I were doing the limbo. There I was, lying on the cold tile floor, my pants around my ankles, leaning back on my elbows. It was as if I had volunteered for some strange magic act, strapped into a box in order to be sawed in half. The unseen bottom half of my body was completely naked. The magician on the other side of the divider quickly made my cock disappear into his mouth. I couldn't see anything. I could only feel it.

I'd never felt anything like this before. It felt silky, his smooth mouth descending onto my cock. The attention he paid to the few inches between my legs flooded my body with unprecedented sensations. The isolation of the sex organ from every other stimulus—visual, verbal, manual, the coordination of other muscles—heightened the intense sensation in my groin.

He hadn't taken more than two or three good sucks when suddenly the hinge on the outside door squeaked. Faster than Elizabeth Montgomery could wrinkle her nose on *Bewitched*, I was back on my side of the wall, perched on the toilet seat, my heart pounding, hoping we hadn't been discovered. The intruder went about his piddly business—tinkle, flush, zip, adjust, running water, splash splash, screech of the faucet, silent preening—which gave me time to catch my breath.

As soon as he exited, the hand motioned underneath the divider. Without hesitation I assumed the position once more. The silky sucking wetness ministered to my pulsing phallus, shocked and ravenous for this kind of attention. I felt a lock of his hair brush against my belly as he skillfully swabbed me with his tongue. Our interruption had slightly diminished the fierceness of my erection, yet it had also underscored the preciousness of every second. It couldn't have been more than a minute or two before I exploded into his mouth. I slid back into my stall. I don't remember if there was an opportunity to reciprocate on my part, or even a desire. I fastened my pants and left the men's room in a daze of complete ecstasy, joy, wish-fulfillment, and an exquisite feeling of shame that assured me that I could not speak of this experience to anyone on earth.

In the few months I spent at Rice after discovering the men's room in the library basement, I must have revisited this chapel to pray for sex twenty or thirty times. *Bless me, Father, for I have sinned. It has been two weeks since my last confession.* I almost never succeeded in connecting with someone there. I clearly remember only one other occasion. It was a rare face-to-face encounter. A handsome, craggy-faced man with dirty blond hair and thick fingers—I decided he must have been Scandinavian—accepted an invitation into my stall for a few frenzied moments of wordless groping, kissing, and relief. The other times may have left me sick to my stomach with nervousness, fear, unmet desire, and shame but still they fed me in some way. They were opportunities to practice my homosexuality. You know, practice makes perfect.

Whatever guilt and shame my bathroom exploits brought me, they also triggered a kind of cocky pride. Leaving the library, I would look around at the other students walking through the quad and think, *How many of these people can say they've just had an orgasm at two thirty-five on a Wednesday afternoon? Ha! None of them!* I got a kick out of belonging to a secret brotherhood, an underworld. I liked the exclusivity of it, much as it had thrilled me as an altar boy to hang out "backstage" with the priest before and after the show, I mean, the Mass. I enjoyed the radicalness of my library basement adventures and the freedom of choice that I got to exercise. No one gave me permission to suck cock in a library bathroom. I seized the opportunity myself. I knew that most people didn't behave this way. I didn't mind. I didn't want to be like most people. Most people didn't study Latin and Greek. Most people didn't read Beckett and Joyce for fun. Most people didn't listen to the Incredible String Band and Van Dyke

Library Hours

Parks and Ry Cooder. My aesthetic temperament developed at the same time and along the same less-well-trod path as my sexuality.

Looking back now, I think, *That's it? Fumbling around with terrified strangers, contorting myself in toilet stalls, investing all that emotion for a two-minute stand-up hand job? Is that the Joy of Gay Sex?* It seems sad to me, and paltry. I'd been listening religiously to pop music for ten years, eavesdropping on 150 flavors of boy-girl romance. John Lennon and Paul McCartney, Diana Ross and the Supremes, smooth Smokey Robinson, and those bad bad Rolling Stones had drilled my generation of teenagers with chapter and verse from the Book of Love— how to date and how to flirt, how good it feels to kiss for the first time and how rotten it feels to break up. I'd been going to the movies for the same amount of time and watching TV shows even longer. I'd seen dozens of cute and tortured love stories. I'd never seen two guys kiss. I'd never been handed the first clue about how to act on desire for another guy. I certainly identified with the swoony yearning of boy-girl romance, but I couldn't see where I fit in. I wasn't Wally Cleaver borrowing Ward's car for a date, and I wasn't Little Miss What's Her Name on *Father Knows Best* flouncing her ponytail down the stairs whenever the doorbell rang. I didn't have any images to guide me or suggest there was any other way to be gay besides the world I stumbled upon in the library basement.

It was in some ways sordid, smelly, and unpleasant, like the inevitable bookends of *perversion* and *deviance* that bracketed the mention of homosexuality in *The Sexually Adequate Male* and other pop-psych paperbacks of the time. But like the word *homosexuality* in the dictionary, those graffiti-covered stalls were a granite-and-Magic-Marker mirror that allowed me to see my existence as a sexual being, to experience it, and to accept it.

Abducting Frodo
Jeff Mann

for S.

He's even handsomer than I remember, striding out of Roanoke Airport's security area with his luggage. Lean, rangy, shorter than me by several inches, younger than me by a decade. Boyish, with big, wide, shy eyes and a head of black curls. "My hobbit," and "Boy Frodo" I've called him for months, because of his amazing resemblance to Elijah Wood in *The Lord of the Rings* film trilogy. Just the sort to bring out the Top in me something fierce.

As he moves closer and closer, as the distance between us dwindles now to inches and the months apart shrink to seconds, I'm trying to look calm, in control, trying to hide the welling exhilaration I feel. Tonight his sweet young body has moved hundreds of miles through dark sky to me, from Manhattan, his home, and his husband; high over ocean and Pennsylvania earth; in and out of Dulles, and into these mountains at last. It's been a good long while since I've topped a boy this desirable, this smart and talented, this eager to be tied.

"Howdy," I mutter, gripping his shoulder in welcome. "Hey," he whispers, squeezing my forearm. I'd hug him, but, despite months of e-mail flirtation, up to now we've just been writer and reader, men with mutual friends. We've never before been together like this—as soon-to-be lovers, as Top and bottom. Our movements are still careful, tentative. The hard hugs, the deep kisses, they'll come later, after I have him home, stripped, collared, and bound.

"The beard looks real good," I say, studying his smile, the angles of his face, the new stubble darkening his cheeks. That little patch of

Abducting Frodo

silver on his chin makes me want to kiss him hard right here, in the middle of the airport, under the disapproving, pious eyes of Southwest Virginia, but I don't have time for fisticuffs with homophobes. I want us on the road and on the way to Hanging Rock Park and then on down the interstate to Pulaski as soon as possible.

We've been planning this weekend for a long time, plotting the details of his abduction, the way we'll meet, the ways he'll be restrained, what I'll do with him once he's my prisoner. It's been like composing erotica together. I've ordered him not to shave or use deodorant for days, because I love beard shadow, facial hair, and armpit musk. I've told him to wear his scruffiest jeans and, beneath them, a jockstrap. In my truck, as promised, wait the collar, the cuffs, the hunting knife, the tape, the bandana.

Our time is finally here. He grins up at me, and the difference in our heights maddens me, makes me want to rope and gag and fuck him, hold him and protect him from the world, which is, of course, exactly what he's come so far for. He studies me for a long moment, assessing the man he will soon submit to. In about fifteen minutes, for the first time he'll be exactly as he wants to be—completely helpless, a big man's captive—and I'm sure he's still a little nervous. I'm a little nervous too. He's come a long way, and I want to be the perfect Top, the perfect Southern host. I want to insure that all his fantasies, the many scenes we've discussed so long on e-mail, come true without a flaw.

Novelty, anxiety, and anticipation: the combination's a true aphrodisiac.

What does he see? A tall, beefy guy with a close-cropped silvering beard, a black biker jacket, a black leather-flag baseball cap, faded jeans, and black cowboy boots. Would have worn the black cowboy hat, but it was too windy today. The mountaineer queer, I call myself. Too much of a country boy to tolerate cities, so I've had to make peace with my Appalachian hills, with the way they've shaped me. Luckily, I'm fierce enough to defend myself and my kind, if need be, from local fundamentalists and conservatives. Two hundred pounds and regular gym visits help.

I grab the larger of his two bags and nod toward the exit. "This way." It's eleven p.m., and I want us home as soon as possible.

"Good to be here, Strider," he says, following me toward the escalator. "Let me visit the restroom, and we can be on our way. No other luggage to collect."

Strider. I love it when he calls me that. Wish I resembled handsome Viggo Mortensen's Aragorn as much as my boy resembles adorable Elijah Wood's Frodo, but he calls me by Aragorn's nickname anyway. He knows that Aragorn is a major role model of mine, that the ring I'm wearing tonight—silver dragons wrapped around a green stone—is a copy of Aragorn's, that I have replicas of Aragorn's ranger sword and elven hunting knife hanging on the walls at home. Surely he knows the name makes me feel strong, protective, a warrior of sorts. The kind of man I want to be: ruthless to enemies, tender and caring with friends and kin. Pretty much the kind of man I already am, after years of conflict and self-shaping. Surely he knows that he's entirely safe here, that a boy who submits to me will be shielded from the hateful orcs of this world, protected from all pain except whatever abuse he begs for.

On the escalator, a little polite chat. "How was your flight?" "What's the weather been like down here? Any snow predicted?" In the restroom, we stand at urinals side by side. Then we're out in the darkness together, heading across the huge parking lot toward my pickup truck. The wind gnaws at our necks. A few dead leaves scuttle by. One day I'll be decrepit, but I'll have this night to remember. I'll have written what I could to retain what I can.

Six months since we met by that pool in New Orleans, introduced by mutual friends at Saints and Sinners, the LGBT literary festival. Five months since our e-mail correspondence began, after he'd read my *Masters of Midnight* vampire novella *Devoured* and some of my other BDSM-themed work. He was particularly excited by a short story I'd published in the online magazine *Velvet Mafia*. "Captive" is about a young Southern man who gets picked up, overpowered, bound, gagged, and used by a Yankee biker and loves it so much he eventually decides to become the man's full-time slave. *How much of*

Abducting Frodo

that story was true? Frodo asked. *How often do you live what you write? Have you ever been part of a consensual kidnapping? Have you ever kept a guy bound and gagged for hours? After reading "Captive," I really want to submit to a man that way. Do you know any trustworthy New York City Tops who might introduce me to bondage?*

Perpetual Southern altruist, I offered my kidnapping services, agreeing to play out with him some version of "Captive," if he could ever get out of that noisy Northern city and down to my mountains for what we soon began dubbing "A Wilderness Bondage Weekend." His husband gave reluctant permission and took to calling me "Wilderness Daddy." Mockery, perhaps, but it was a title I gladly embraced. My husband bought me both Aragorn and Frodo bookmarks, and he plans to return from a business trip tomorrow in time to join us and help create a Hobbit Sandwich.

Months of sweet planning, and now here we are. I shove Frodo's luggage into the truck's extended cab, then turn to him in the dim parking-lot light. I have to touch him now—I'm tired of waiting—so, awkwardly, briefly, I stroke his curly head. So soft. I can't wait to feel his mouth on my cock, taste his nipples between my teeth.

"Look what I wore for you," he says abruptly, pulling up his knit sweater long enough to show me his T-shirt. BOY is printed across his chest. "Very good," I say, chuckling but secretly touched. I open the passenger door, he slips in, I close the door behind him. We both know that this is where it really begins.

Behind the wheel now, looking around the parking lot to see who's within eyesight. A fat middle-aged man—well, about my age, I guess—trundles by with his rolling suitcase, so I wait till he moves off before I look Frodo in the eyes and say, "Ready?"

"Yes," he whispers, meeting my gaze for a second, then dropping his eyes.

My beat-up old black-leather backpack is behind the seat. I pull it into my lap, unzip it, and begin sorting through what's necessary.

The collar first: a short length of heavy chain to circle his neck and then padlock together just below his clavicles. The metal's chilly, but soon enough his young heat will lend it warmth. The molecules will speed up the way my heart is speeding now.

"Looks good," I say, stroking his hair. "You're mine now, right?" As we've agreed, he'll remain collared till I return him to this same airport three days from now.

"Yes," he says, looking up at me long enough to nod, then lowering his gaze back into submission. How much I love a boy's submission. Nothing gets me harder.

Well, I guess one thing gets me harder: restraining and gagging a boy. The gag, unfortunately, has to wait. Right now, we both know, it's time for the cuffs. Eagerly, without waiting for my order, he holds out his hands before him, and I snap the black metal around his wrists. I'd prefer to cuff his hands behind his back, but he's a novice at all this, and it's a good hour to Pulaski. I want him powerless but not hurting. Not yet, anyway.

That's all for now, simply because I have to pay for parking first. I toss the extra sweatshirt I've brought for this purpose across Frodo's lap, concealing his cuffed hands. I tuck the slave collar under his sweater. I drop the backpack on the floor between his feet.

"All right?" I ask. He nods. I start the truck, turn off the blaring country-music radio—107.1 FM, my favorite station for back road driving—let the engine warm up for about half a minute, then head for the brightly lit booth on the lot's far edge.

"How you?" I ask, passing the elderly attendant a dollar. "Jus' fine," he replies. "Not a bad November we're havin'." He and I have to shoot the shit briefly—we mountain folk make a short social chat out of every interaction. His accent is about the same as mine, and I'm guessing he likes the same kind of music and food I do—Toby Keith and Reba McIntire, brown beans and cornbread—but I'm also guessing his values are otherwise pretty different. This is the sort of queer juxtaposition I love. I look and sound and sometimes pretty much act like just another local redneck in a pickup truck, and in many ways I am just that. But of course I have a leather-flag sticker on my rear window and, this blessed night, a handsome young man from New York City collared and cuffed in the passenger seat. I guess I've become the kind of wildly contradictory and complex man I've always been attracted to and I've always wanted to be: good baker

Abducting Frodo

of biscuits, collector of cowboy boots and hats, aficionado of four-wheel-drives, adept user of cuffs and ball gags, deft maker of knots. When you're butch enough to blend in, you can get away with a hell of a lot in this region, despite the stupid fuckers that compose the Religious Right and run most of Virginia.

So, on out to 481, then Interstate 81, with nothing much said. Another five minutes down the interstate, and we're in the tiny park beneath Hanging Rock Mountain, the place I've picked out well in advance for its darkness and isolation.

I pull into the gravel lot, gratified to see that no one else is parked there. As I'd hoped, it's a little too late, a little too cold, for teenagers to be necking. Nothing to see but the looming blackness of mountains, a hillside of bare trees across the road. No sound save for the distant, just-audible purl of a creek. A Civil War battle raged here a long time ago, men fighting for power. No fight tonight. One man's more than ready to give up power, one man's keen to take it.

"Ready for Part Two, boy?"

Frodo nods. Since midsummer I have been waiting for, dreaming of, jacking off to the thought of what I'm about to do next.

The Case XX knife was a gift from my high school biology teacher, the lesbian godsend who helped me come out. She presented it to me just before my first deer-hunting foray with Mike, my hot straight buddy, whose hairy chest and black beard I so quietly admired, whose easy mountain masculinity I tried to emulate. Tonight, after decades of whittling the occasional twig and otherwise lying unused in my series of pickup trucks, ready to threaten or slice any assailant if necessary, it serves a rich purpose.

I slide the blade out of its black sheath and hold it up in the starlight. Frodo stares at it, I stare at him. At the same time that he knows I would never harm him, I hope he's sweating just a little. Later, when he's naked and hog-tied and ball-gagged on my bed, I may have to run the knife ever so carefully over his nipples, neck, belly, and cock, just to hear him gulp and whimper.

The edge is a mite dull, got to admit—will have to sharpen it later. But, with just a little effort, it slices clean through the black bondage tape I ordered from San Francisco's Mr. S. With one hand, I carefully slide the knife back into its sheath; with the other, I hold the segment of tape, about eight inches' worth, a lustrous cross section of darkness, by one end in the air between us. "Keep still," I say. Frodo gazes quietly at me, then nods, closes his eyes, and settles back into his seat. Slowly, gently, I center the tape over his mouth, then smooth it across his face.

"Fuck," I grunt, sitting back to admire him. My cock, fairly hard since I first saw Frodo in the airport, is swelling considerably larger in my jeans. "I have been wanting to see you this way ever since I met you," I can't help but groan. "Nothing prettier than a good-looking boy with his hands bound and his mouth taped shut." I reach over, press the tape against his face a little closer, study the indentation of his lips beneath the shiny black, savor the contrast between the smooth gag and the rough stubble on his cheek.

These are my aesthetics. These are the sights and sensations I live for. Don't know why, don't care why. Why question blessing?

Blindfold next. I pull the black bandana from the backpack, my last prop before we get home to the big bed and the heavy bag of toys I'll be lavishing on Frodo all weekend. His dark hair's so thick I fumble a little, but finally his eyes are covered and the cloth's knotted behind his head. He leans back again into helplessness. I've taken away his speech and his sight and the easy use of his hands. All he can do now is relax into the darkness. All he can do is relinquish.

"My little kidnap victim," I growl, patting his knee. "You look so fucking fine. You're looking as sweet as that poor little boy who got all roped up in 'Captive.' You set?"

Frodo takes a deep breath and slowly nods.

"You like this? You like being bound and gagged?"

Another nod. Palpable enthusiasm.

"Cuffs not hurting you?"

Unhesitating shake of the head.

Some bottoms might prefer a less solicitous Top, and I can be brutal, callous, and indifferent if they want that, but my natural tendency's to check on a captive's comfort with great regularity. When a

Abducting Frodo

boy's given up his will to me, that means his fate and his fantasy are in my hands, and I want to make sure he's where he wants to be at all times. Part of the code of Southern hospitality, I guess.

I study Frodo for half a minute, listening to that distant creek, exulting in how hot and handsome he looks with metal around his wrists and tape across his mouth, wanting to memorize what details I can to cup like water in the face of any future drought. Now I'm unbuttoning the fly of his jeans, and, yes, as promised, there's the pale gleam of white jock, the feel of its coarse fabric beneath my fingers. That's our luck, his and mine, that hard lump I grip and squeeze gently inside the jock and knead till my boy groans. I lean over, gratefully kiss his forehead, then pull up his T-shirt, slide my hands over his smooth, flat belly; up to the little hillock-swells of his chest, to the few curls of hair between and around his nipples, to the nipples themselves, just about my favorite part of a man, soft and hard at the same time.

"These are gonna be sore as hell by the time you leave. You want that, right? I'm gonna be sucking and tugging on these all weekend. I'm gonna worry 'em like a dog."

"Ummm mmm." Frodo nods, arching his chest against my fingers, then begins a soft little moan as I dig my fingernails in just a bit. Goddamn, how I cherish the whimpers a boy makes against a tight gag.

I give his right nipple a final pinch, then start the engine, slip in a CD for the hour's drive south, and turn back toward the interstate.

We're not a mile down 81 before Frodo lifts his cuffed hands over his head and slips them behind his headrest as if I'd bound them there, then slides down in his seat till his arms are stretched tautly above him. Note for future reference: this boy, unlike many nervous novices, might relish a little discomfort and might benefit from very secure restraint. Later, after I've stripped him down to his jock, I'll have to rope his wrists good and tight to the headboard while I eat his ass. Maybe buck and gag him while I fix us breakfast tomorrow. He's young and lean enough to endure a few lengthy sessions and challenging positions, and he's going to look mighty pretty

28

Jeff Mann

drooling around a fat black ball or thick bit.

Almost midnight now. The dark hills and pastures are streaming by, the lights of trucks are blurring past. I wonder if the sight of a man being kidnapped is giving any of these high-seated truckers huge hard-ons. For a moment, I worry that someone with a cell phone might call the cops, then mutter "Fuck it" and turn the music up louder. I'm forty-six: *Carpe diem* is a timely motto.

The CD's one of the latest by hot, handsome, hairy, goateed Tim McGraw, my favorite country-music star. Talk about a man I'd give my soul to kidnap, strip, rope and gag tight, then keep captive and top continually, with alternating brutality and tenderness, for about six months to a decade. In his plaintive tenor, Tim's singing "Set This Circus Down," and I'm pounding out the song's rhythms on Frodo's knee, quietly exuberant, delighting in the rasp of fiddle and dwelling on all the previously-agreed-upon pleasures to come.

It will be so sweet to finally get my boy naked. How fine his armpits will smell and taste; it'll be a fucking rapture to rope his hands behind him, spread his legs and eat his hole; wake him up, after a drowse together, with my cock up his ass, ride him on his side, on his belly, my big bear weight growling on top of him. I can tell I'm going to be entirely besotted by his ass. On his back then, his legs over my shoulders, our eyes interlocked while I ride him hard. So many varieties of tit clamps and gags to use, the music of muffled pleas, and tape across his chest, pinning his arms tight to his sides, layers of tape around his wrists and ankles. Pissing over his head and shoulders in the shower, knotting a piss-soaked sock in his mouth. Cooking him barbeque tomorrow, getting him good and drunk, tying him to a chair and feeding him with my fingers, cornbread and coleslaw and bourbon-barbeque ribs; letting him lick sauce off my fingers and my beard.

In his mute and blind cocoon, Frodo, I suspect, is dreaming of the same things, all we've promised one another. That quiet young stranger by the guesthouse pool last May, chatting with his husband on a cell phone, looking up at me with an interested smile—who would have guessed how desire's electric language and serendipitous switchbacks would lead him here? What a gift, when greed meets greed and one man's longing completes another's.

The CD's ended. I drive awhile in silence, occasionally looking over at him stretched out in his seat, slender and curly-headed as a captive Bacchus.

"Comfortable?" I ask. He's so still I wonder if he's dozing.

"Ummm mmm," is his quiet reply. I recognize the serene tones of complete surrender, the ripe calm of orchards before harvest, of high-grass pastures before the scythe; the calm of appetites certain to be sated.

"We'll be home in just a little while," I say, squeezing the hard jock, tracing the imprint of his cockhead with the side of my thumb. We're hurtling along at seventy miles an hour, the hard, deadly pavement and the hillside's rocky soil only feet from us, but I have to touch him, his lean and fragile body, again and again and again. Soon enough our weekend will be over, our long-awaited idyll will be ended. So, keeping careful eyes reluctantly on the road, I stroke his belly, play with a nipple. I fondle that endearingly silver-stubbled chin, caress the curls on his temple, rub his mouth's glossy seal. Tenderly I trace his eyebrows, the line of his jaw, then rest my hand soothingly on his thigh. For the time being, his life is mine, his warmth pulses beneath my palm. Tonight, our fates and brief bodies move together, intertwined through autumn and the dark. Tonight, one hand on his body, one hand on the wheel, I'm threading black hills with consummate care.

Mustang
Tulsa Brown

"I collect orphans," he said.

I nodded blankly and smiled, eyes darting, looking for escape. Fruitcake. Nutcase. These events always brought the crazies out of the woodwork, disguised as would-be writers or gushing author groupies, convinced that pumping your arm brought them one step closer to fucking John Grisham. Or Hemingway.

But the man wasn't shaking my hand, he simply held it, clenched my bear's paw in his cool, knobby grip. He wasn't *overtly* scary: thirtyish, in a bad brown suit, long and thin as an afternoon shadow, dark hair that should have been cut a month ago. Harmless.

Except for the eyes. They were watery-blue, slightly magnified by the large lenses of his glasses and rimmed red with passion. I'd been to enough Meet the Author nights to know the worst danger wasn't the tin-tasting salmon canapés.

"Well, it was nice to meet you but I really should be— "

"I have almost three hundred of yours," he blurted.

"Pardon?"

"Your orphans. Mostly remaindered copies, but some I found in secondhand bookstores or at garage sales. I hit the jackpot at the hospital fundraiser—a whole cardboard box of Jack Vigoreaux! I got it for a song. I was the only bidder."

Knife wound. I remembered giving the hospital those copies for their library, the fluttery, chirping gratitude of the old hens. *Oh, thank you, thank you, Mr. Vigoreaux.*

The man's eyes were luminous at the remembered triumph. My stomach threatened to drop onto the carpet. I wriggled out of his

Mustang

grip, my voice cold.

"I'm very...flattered to meet such a fan." I was still murmuring my excuses, pulling away, when lightning struck and spun me. "Any copies of *Every Little Kiss?*"

"Sixty-seven."

"That many! The print run was less than a thousand."

"Three-Legged Press," he recited proudly. "I was so sorry when they went under in ninety-six." His face softened. For an instant he was beautiful—reverent eyes and ruddy, velvet mouth. "*Kiss* is my favorite book."

"Mine, too," I croaked. A terrible faux pas. An author never admits he *has* a favorite book, let alone his own. Or his first. In that instant we were the only two people in the room, bridged by a secret, shameful love of the imperfect.

I'd squandered my own copies, passed them out with reckless abandon to men I loved or lusted after, anyone I'd wanted to impress. It was my resume, my calling card, a cocky hello or a lacerated, bleeding good-bye. Now, twelve years and three novels later, the only copy left for me was in my mother's sunroom, pristine and unopened, wedged between the Bible and *Funk & Wagnalls.*

"Are any of them autographed?"

He nodded. "More than half."

I reeled, dizzy with fresh pain. *Thanks, Jack! I'm honored. I'll never forget you.*

"Do you want to see them?"

See the betrayal in black and white, written by my own hand? Know for certain the names of the men who'd discarded me, probably before the sheets were cold?

"Yes."

We slipped out of the bookstore. I wouldn't be missed in the ensemble: the bug-eyed children's author, the screechy poetess, the blustery ex-captain who'd built an entire writing career around the battle of Vimy Ridge. Local authors. We knew each other's shtick like second-string vaudevillians.

The collector's name was Laurence. With a battered sheepskin bomber over his suit he looked younger, a careless, dreamy Perpetual

Student. Ironic, because I was in my professor uniform, tweed and turtleneck, autumn beard. I hailed a cab and we crawled into the close darkness of the backseat, the ancient springs giving way to slide us together, thigh to thigh. The firm length of his muscular leg was a pleasant surprise. He smelled nice too: unpretentious soap and the warm, animal musk of his wooly collar. It was like huddling beside a friendly llama.

We started the journey in silence. I was still shell-shocked, but the first blaze of treachery had burned off. Spider fingers of a different grief stole into my clothes.

There is no book like your first. It's what you write when you don't know any better, raw and clumsy, painfully real. Other novels are just ideas you lasso and reel in, polish up with a thesaurus and send out to trot in the ring. Trick ponies.

Every Little Kiss had been the mustang of my body, bucking, snorting, pawing at the dirt for thirty years before it broke the traces and thundered out. It was *my* story, the lean, hungry sinews of sex and desire; my bare flank turned bravely to a ravenous unknown. That book told the world I was gay, in stilted, stiff-legged prose that shamed me now.

It was also the truest thing I would ever write. The gust of emotion was ferocious, possessive. I wanted them back, all sixty-seven, signed or not.

"...it started. With his copy."

I flinched, awake and guilty. "Oh," I said pleasantly.

The cab pulled onto a narrow street, traveled past a long row of boxy wartime houses. It stopped at one that zigzagged in front, the strange toothy grin of a wheelchair ramp.

Laurence smiled as we trudged up the slope. "I know it's an eyesore—sure makes it easy to get a dolly into the house, though."

A dolly! How many books did he have?

Walls full. I stood in the doorway and gazed at the tiny living and dining rooms, each paneled floor to ceiling in a colorful patchwork of spines. I was agog.

"I finished my masters in England." Laurence shrugged off his

Mustang

bomber and suit jacket in one quick thrust. "Lived down the street from a rare book store. Didn't come back with a dime," he said cheerfully. "Here, this is your section."

Can you be prepared to see a whole wall of yourself, your name queued up in row after row? My face prickled and my stomach swayed, queasy with sudden embarrassment. It was as if my secret writer's jerk-off fantasy had materialized for the scrutiny of the world.

But there—the shelf of narrow blue spines. *Kiss.* I pulled one out, heart thumping. I was startled by the condition: torn cover, dog-eared pages, soft with wear. This book had been *read.* Devoured. I kept flipping through in wonder, avoiding the half title page, where I would have signed. Whoever had owned this copy, I forgave him.

Laurence slipped in beside me. He'd tugged off his tie and unbuttoned the collar of his white shirt, his bare neck ruddy by contrast.

"This isn't all of them," he said. "Some are on loan to Harbor Lights."

He noticed my quizzical look. "The hospice. They were so good to us."

Us. My eyes moved carefully, surreptitiously around the room for the first time. Photographs. A handsome, scholarly man fading by degrees, the continuation of the story I should have been listening to in the cab. I realized this six-shelf tribute wasn't to me, but to someone who'd enjoyed me. A memorial.

"How long?"

"Four years ago." Laurence smiled ruefully. "Long enough that I should've torn down that ramp."

"But you need it for the book dolly."

He laughed, we both did. I was suddenly light with relief, effervescent, a marble statue returned to flesh.

Laurence tilted his head, shy eyes smoldering blue. "Do you know which scene is my favorite? The bus station."

"Funny—I hardly remember it."

He reached for the tattered book in my hands. "I'll show you."

"Why don't you read it to me?"

Laurence was a wonderful reader. Sitting together on the couch, he entranced me with the spare, famished voice of my younger self.

"I wanted to smell him in the blunt, probing animal way a dog wound around into the tail of another. I wanted to lap up the sour days on his skin, just to shock my mouth."

I pressed my knuckles against the side of Laurence's leg. He clasped my hand and moved it on top of his thigh. Long, thrilling muscles. I stroked him hard, polyester crackling, threatening to ignite. His breath thickened, the story slowed. I crept into his crotch, teased the tight plum of his balls gathered by the fabric, cleaved by the seam.

"Oh." He put the book down and *Kiss* became the real thing. Our mouths twisted like grappling wrestlers, tongues plunging; my beard bristled against his late-night stubble. I rose up and straddled him awkwardly on my knees, my erection straining in its cramped quarters. Laurence unzipped me and my pants opened in a hot fissure. He groped me through my underwear, murmuring happily, then pulled away, lips gleaming, glasses smudged and tilted.

"Let's do the bus station."

The sweet shorthand tingled with wickedness; my life had become someone's fantasy. He hadn't finished reading the scene but it came back to me now in a hot stripe of memory and lust. Only this time I wouldn't be me.

"All right. But you have to take your clothes off."

The drapes were already closed. The living room lamp gave an intimate yellow cast to the room, not the stark, blue-edged glare of fluorescent, but it would do. I pulled off my sweater and left my pants on, unzipped, as if I'd just stepped away from a urinal.

Laurence's naked body was austere, swirled with a layer of dark hair. He had the stretched, unfinished look of a much younger man, knobby at the wrists and knees, meaty between the legs. There the helmet of his cockhead bobbed, trembling. Had I looked so alluring twenty years ago?

I remembered the words. "You want it, boy? Come on."

He stepped close and leaned his face into my wooly chest, rubbed one cheek against it, then the other. I closed my fist in the back of his thick hair and he inhaled sharply, ready. I forced him to

Mustang

his knees and pressed his face against the tent of me. The pressure and sight of him sent me sailing. I smelled that day again: acrid, unapologetic sex, raw current flowing without wires. Or strings.

Laurence began to gnaw me through my underwear, a leisurely, drunken mouthing that blew hot swells against my balls. I ground against his teeth, riding the knife-edged pleasure. Oh, damn—too good, and it had been too long. I brought him to his feet.

"Lube?" I asked.

He leaned forward, bracing himself against the back of the couch while I oiled him. Each of my hands was in love with a different landscape: one caressed his firm, fleshy pillar; the other luxuriated in his scalding crevice. My erection bumped his thigh impatiently like the muzzle of a fractious horse. Mustang.

He moaned softly when I entered him. For an instant I was transfixed by the velvet squeeze, pulsing in sweetness that latex couldn't dim. Then instinct seized my loins. I began to buck—mindless, plunging strokes and slapping flesh. I fumbled beneath our bodies and gripped him, let him thrust into my hand. But all the world was my own cock and the bent-over burn of my rutting, the unstoppable drive into his core, the center of animal triumph.

Triumphant, I brayed my relief.

It was almost two a.m. when I called the cab. Dressed again, my clothes nettled me, the chafe of civilization. Laurence wore a burgundy bathrobe, his wiry, masculine frame overwhelmed by the rich folds. He looked like an orphan himself, bundled for rescue.

He gestured at his collection of me. "Do you want any of them?"

I hesitated. The sight of the tall shelf was strange now, like discovering one of my old suits in the closet, the one with the wide lapels and shiny weave. It was a dead thing and I was alive. Stirring.

I kissed his cheek, then his lips. "They're better off with you, even if you give them away. Besides, you could always read to me."

Laurence smiled.

I slipped out into the early morning feeling light, quick, in the mood to run.

White Punk
Shane Allison

Can't keep myself focused on the book I'm reading. Bukowski's *Ham on Rye*. Just started taking an interest in his work after learning of his life from a documentary that was on the tube last week. The students are back for another semester to wreak havoc on this college town. The campus bookstore is packed with boys dressed to the nines in their Abercrombie & Fitch tees, cargo shorts and flip-flops. But these preppy clones don't do it for me. I like 'em grungy and punkish like Adam, covered from head to toe in tats and piercings. He works every Thursday round this time. Admire him from the corners of bookshelves; worship that hint of gluteus flesh that peeks from the waistline that sags past his ass as he places periodicals. We got Multicultural Lit together. Adam sits directly in front of me where I can see the crack of his butt between the grooves of the desk chair. Spend the entire fifty minutes doodling in the margins of my notebook; sketch him with a dick in his mouth, me dipping my tongue in the pocket of that elastic where his ass begins. Thirsty for the sweat that arises from the trench. Stare at the tat of skull and crossbones emblazoned on the nape of his neck. He's the only guy in class, maybe on this whole campus, that has tattoos running across his skin, rings piercing through the flesh of ears and eyebrows, through the bottom of a cherry-red lip. I'm not much for the Lacrosse poster boys; I like men cloaked in tattered, black cut-offs, sporting Goth-rock tees. Boys with the scum of the earth under their nails and smegma around the rings of their dickheads that I can lick clean. So refreshing to see boys like Adam here on this campus where Ann Coulter cult followers roam the scholarly halls.

Dick thickens in my britches. I attempt to keep it calm, to keep

White Punk

the randiness in me at bay, but it's no use when your dick's got a
mind of its own. Saunter past shelves of textbooks, clearance sale
tables strewn with calendars, leather-clad day planners and rows of
football paraphernalia with GO NOLES inscribed, in my attempt to
make it to the bathroom. Haven't jacked off all week and it's high
time for some hand-to-hand combat. My dick continues to twitch
between my legs as I study Adam's milk-white skin through ripped,
poker-chip-sized holes in his jeans. As he stoops in front of a rack
of CliffsNotes, a smidgen of his crease is exposed. Waves of dark hair
bloom from his butt, cheeks I want to plant myself between. Look to
see if anyone's watching me watch Adam, if they notice from those
crystal ball cameras that I'm pulling at my crotch in an attempt to
give my dick the growing room that it needs. Adam is my favorite out
of all these bookish boys with his Kool-Aid-red Mohawk and black
argyles in battered sneaks.

"Excuse me," I whisper, "but can you tell me where the bathroom is?"

He extends his tattooed arm and points past the college football
merchandise to the book buyback section. I watch the ring in that
voluptuous lip bob as directions tumble out of his mouth.

"Thanks," I tell him. As I walk, I can almost feel his eyes on me,
his heat on my neck.

I could eat every boy at this school alive, suck the meat from their
bones until there is nothing left. As I push open the door to the shit-
ter, the stench of piss and air freshener permeates throughout, gorg-
ing my lungs. The melancholy sound of Enya leaks from the speakers
above. This toilet isn't as infamous as some others, barely a blip on
the radar of Cruisingforsex.com. Yet it is fast becoming a hotbed of
tricks and trade. Still gotta watch your ass with store security and all.
I've been cruising here since '98 and haven't been busted yet. Sure
there were a couple of close calls, but nothing I couldn't handle. I
always like to take the larger, handicapped stall at the far end of the
bathroom. The smaller ones barely give me enough room to wipe my
ass, and I like to stretch. The glory hole's been sealed off again with
another metal plate. By this time next week, it'll be pried off by Tim,

a friend of mine. Says he uses a screwdriver. Not much in the way of graffiti here. Just your run-of-the-mill propositions for blow jobs followed by cell numbers and e-mail addresses scribbled along the stall walls in ballpoint ink. The drawings of cocks being inserted in asses are enough to keep me hot and hard. It gets so that sometimes I don't know how I make it to class with all the boys to be had around here. If there was such a thing as a bachelor's degree in dick and ass, it would be my major. There's nothing quite as nice as dropping to my knees at the flip-flopped feet of anonymous men and worshipping at their bulges. Funny. They don't have a clue when they're being checked out by other dudes like they check out chicks, tongues hung out and watering over sorority tits.

This particular bookstore bathroom is the one I love the most 'cause of the handicapped stall with the mirror in front of the toilet where I can watch myself jacking off. I've got a swell dick. Not as big as I would like it to be, but I don't get any complaints.

"You're the perfect size," they say. As I give myself a workover, toying with the foreskin between my fingers, I hear someone walk in. Rise up off my commode, peek through the slit of the door. It's Adam, my punk rock star. My belt buckle clatters across the floor as I shuffle my feet slightly. Study his sneakers, which don't give me a sign. Hike my shirt over my belly, above my nipples. Tug a bit at my dick. It's hard, ready for anything. Dim lights gleam above us. The sweet sound of piss splattering in Adam's toilet really gets me going. Stand off my toilet again; cup my hand under the dispenser of liquid soap—another handicapped stall extra—and press its white thickness into my palm. Slather it on my dick. It's cold as I massage it in thoroughly, keeping an eye on the tattered, black All-Stars. The soap forms a slick lather. I smear a second helping onto my cock. Stuff makes for the best lubricant. Right up there with baby oil, hair grease, butter, cooking oil and pancake syrup.

The sound of skin slapping against skin is within earshot of Adam. Stoop below the stall to check for any signs of movement, but only hairy, thick calves are exposed. Bite down on my lip as I stroke myself, staring at the toilet art that defaces the wall. Can see him suddenly

White Punk

from my peripheral vision, his head bows down, those eyes pry in on my actions. Pretend like I don't know he's watching. Push my boots off; slide them against the wall with my feet. Pull off my underwear; fold the Makaveli jeans neatly next to the stacks of books for my other three classes: Truman Capote topping Toni Morrison, Morrison topping Harriet Beecher Stowe, Ralph Ellison and Gabriel Garcia Márquez bottoming to Stowe. Peel myself out of my shirt. Stuff it between the plaster and the metal railing. Leave on my cotton socks, brown and soiled on the bottoms. Study myself in the mirror—the dark pouch of skin, my gaping thighs, my dick that damn near comes up to my belly button—when all the while he watches me put on a show exclusively for him. When I reach over to dispense more soap, I let him know that I'm in on him. He doesn't move.

"That's hot," he whispers. *Hot* being the word of the Paris Hilton generation.

Turn on my toilet to give him a look, only to be interrupted by guys taking a leak, bitching about the store not having the books they need. Adam and I keep our wits about us until they leave. Funny how Adam's Mohawk sweeps along the floor. His face blushes red as blood rushes to his head. Stand up, crouch, and shove myself under and into his domain. His hand is a dream around my dick. A pleasant sensation other than my own for once. Adam's touch sends shock waves of ecstasy through me; those nubby, gritty fingers imprison my dick. Forelegs are ablaze as I press my hard-on further under his partition. Claw at the stall when I feel his lips around it, the heat of his tongue warming me.

With each scream of the bathroom door's hinges, we jerk ourselves back into our respective positions. Adam's spit dries cold on my dick as we wait. Knees burn due to broken skin. Write a note to Adam telling him that there's too much traffic. *It will slow,* he scribbles back. And so it does. The bookstore bathroom is quiet again. Just as I'm about to shove myself back beneath his stall, he beats me to the punch by sticking his own sex under the wall. Adam's dick is thicker than a porn novel, longer than a bookmark, circumcised, pale pink. Our knees kiss as I take his dick in my hand. Run my finger along his sticky slit slathered with what is to come. Can hear him on the other side of me sighing sounds of satisfaction. Reach under his balls and fingers coast along a grungy ass. I press in. His backside eats my finger. Stretch and twist with discomfort to take him into my mouth. Look up at him sideways as he gawks down at me giving him head. Adam's dick swells in my mouth. He doesn't let me in on the fact that he's coming. Streams of semen are immediately across my face and glasses. Adam milks the rest in my hair. We lift ourselves off that filthy floor. I take some tissues and clean Adam off me. Hear him rustling about, pulling on clothes.

"Come over here." Pull the latch of my door open inviting him in. He stands and watches me with those punk rocker eyes, his head-set still on. Every part of him is covered in ink; several piercings line the cartilage of both ears. Adam moves closer, taking me in his hand. Adam speaks to me like a porn novel as I watch him from the mirror in front of me working his magic. He asks if I'm about to come. All I can do is nod my head. I almost get Adam in the face, but he won't let up. Then, when he feels that I'm done, he washes his hands under the tongue of water as I lie there in an exhausted slump with stars in my eyes. Manage to pull myself together. I want to exchange numbers, e-mails, something, but suddenly I'm not there, a ghost he can't see. Adam lets himself out of the men's room without any care that I'm still in the midst of getting dressed.

The next day, Adam is M.I.A. in Multi. Lit. Someone else has taken his place. Someone who isn't as cute as him, who isn't dark and edgy underneath. I return to the bookstore only to be informed that he has found employment elsewhere. But I know this ain't the end— that in this tiny little college town, I will see him again.

Like a Virus
Sam. J. Miller

I think we ought to only read the kind of books that wound and stab us. If the book we are reading doesn't wake us up with a blow on the head, what are we reading it for? A book must be the axe for the frozen sea inside us.
—*Franz Kafka*

"For me, books were always a safe place," Steve said. Seven minutes after orgasm, he picked up the conversation precisely where we had left it. "As much shit as I was dealing with at home, at school, whatever, I could go to a book and that was a place where I fit in, where I could find other people who thought like me."

"Hmm." I burrowed my face into his armpit. By staying silent, maybe I could squash this debate before it started. I valued Steve's intellectual *and* sexual insatiability, but I preferred to take them on one at a time.

"That's why I like the existentialists so much. That whole worldview makes a lot of sense to me. A lot of people think the existentialists are bleak, but I don't think so. I think they're about embracing life for what it is. Seeing through all the bullshit."

"Yeah," I said.

Steve's room, on the fifth floor of the Honors Dorm, had been transformed into a honeymoon suite. Ninety-nine-cent-store candles flickered on every shelf and surface. Mozart piano sonatas tinkled harmlessly from his computer speakers. Our arch-nemesis Ryan the Roommate was out of town, so we could actually try our hand at lovemaking, instead of our usual hasty fuck sessions.

Our first five weeks at college had turned us into quickie experts.

Like a Virus

We ate dinner at odd times, so that we could have a half hour of privacy while our roommates were at the cafeteria. We skipped classes, but that did not work so well because we were freshmen and everyone else skipped classes too. I sucked him off in bathroom stalls, and in the study lounge at three in the morning. One night, a hand job was interrupted by an unimaginative cop who could not think of anything besides drug use to explain why two gorgeous young men with no car would be huddled together in the middle of the night on the top level of the Rutgers parking garage. These risky public trysts were fun for me, but they freaked Steve out. He was a candles-and-clean-sheets sort of guy.

"I mean, if you rely on books for self-affirmation and a sense of security, I respect that," I said, "but I feel like that approach turns literature into...an opiate. Like sitcoms, dance music, stuff like that. It's pretty, it's nice, and you listen to it and you feel like everything is all right in the world. I like the stuff that shakes me up, scares the shit out of me, shows me something that makes me rethink everything I know. I learned more from *Naked Lunch* than from any of Kerouac's stupid shit about how nice it is to wander around with no responsibilities."

On the Road was Steve's favorite book. He watched me, his rebuttal just about bursting from his mouth.

"I like a good story and fun characters as much as anybody else," I continued. "But I want more than that. I want something where when I finish it, I'm practically shivering, because in some way it's totally freaked me out. It doesn't have to be something that makes you question everything you're living for, or changes your mind about some political issue. When I read *Ulysses*, I could hardly breathe when I finished it. Because it totally changed my whole understanding of what a novel could be."

"I see that," he said, although, honestly, I suspected he couldn't. *Ulysses* was "too messy" for him. He was the sort who read Gogol for the satire on government bureaucracy, and totally missed the contortions of language and narrative that terrify and delight to the point where, like the hero of "The Overcoat," you become confused as to whether you're in the middle of the street or the middle of the sentence.

"I want something that's going to get under my skin and make me sweat, disturb my sleep, break me open like bullet smashing a Ming vase. Infect my body like a virus."

I yanked the sheet away, to expose his sweat-damp body. He tensed up—even with the doors locked and the curtains drawn, Steve felt uncomfortable fucking above the sheets. Not until my nose was firmly nestled in the hair four inches below his belly button, and his cock was pressing against the back of my throat, did he loosen up, but even then he didn't get into it. His hands remained pressed to the sheets at his sides, and he was still and reverent as a corpse. Only his mouth and toes moved.

"I'm coming," he whispered. I leaned back and watched it spurt out onto his belly. Then he pulled me up, sucked the taste of himself out of my mouth, and wiggled down to return the favor. Steve was a very fair-minded man, very concerned with giving as much as he got, which I always found rather boring.

I made a mess of my own, and Steve covered my belly and then my chest and then my neck and then my face with little love-pecks.

"I've got to go," I said. I sat up. That night my shift was from eight to midnight, putting books back on the shelves in Alexander Library.

"It's only seven thirty," Steve said. "We have a little more time."

"I have to get in a little early tonight," I said. Steve waited for more explanation, watched me pick up the pieces of my grungy outfit. Tattered socks and patched jeans and a hooded sweatshirt, standard Salvation Army-issue college stuff, scattered across the floor of his room.

"I'll come right back when I'm done," I said.

Steve shrugged. When he feigned apathy he looked gorgeous.

"I'm sorry I had to work on the night of our first sleepover," I said. I pinched his nipple a teeny bit too hard.

"Ouch," he said, and pushed my hand away, but his face softened, and he kissed me good night like any needy boyfriend.

The night was cold, even for late October. Everyone was inside

Like a Virus

studying, or more probably, partying. Tall crowded dorms looked down at me. Behind their windows were rooms packed with happy students. Smart kids, rich kids, kids bound for bright futures. I felt very Dostoevskian—the outcast hero, slinking out at night to avoid running into his friends, stomping his feet to keep them warm, torn between wild love and desperate terror at the sight of every single person he passes.

I'll be honest: in the safety of Steve's bed, or surrounded by sympathetic friends at parties, I was Mr. Proud Liberated Homo. Out in the open, I was scared. Call it lingering small-town paranoia, call it a reflex reaction from years of bullying, but every time some straight thug or stern waitress looked me in the eye I panicked. In class, in the cafeteria, I stiffened when Steve stuck his tongue in my ear. And not just in the predictable way. Even in the quiet halls of our dorm, he would grab my hand in his and I'd look around to see if anyone was watching. If I got off on fucking in public spaces, it was precisely because it scared the shit out of me. The week before, someone scrawled DIE FAGGOT in indelible marker on my friend Chin's dry-erase board. So on my walk to work I kept expecting thuggish frat jocks to burst out of the shadows and beat me to death.

Alexander Library is one of the twenty-five biggest university libraries in the country. Within its walls were more than two million books and a million government documents, and they wouldn't return them*selves* to the shelves, so there were always plenty of jobs for poorer kids in need of work-study assignments. The big building loomed up in front of me, its windows full of light and books and absolutely no people. It was a Friday, after all, and finals were a month away. The library was my favorite place on campus, possibly my favorite place in the world.

In Intermediate Existentialism Steve was getting his worldview reaffirmed by Jean-Paul Sartre; meanwhile I was having my whole understanding of gay sexual identity shaken by David Wojnarowicz. We read *Close to the Knives* in Queer Lit, and I was on fire to find out more about New York queer life in the days before AIDS and gentrification. It was like learning about some crazy free amusement park that burned down just before you were born. To hook up with random men at the piers! To fuck on subway platforms, in abandoned buildings, in seedy hotel rooms where the sheets were still damp from the guests before you! To wander the highways with a thumb out and a hard-on, having all kinds of wild sexual adventures!

I felt cheated. Monogamy felt like a harsh sentence, imposed on me by AIDS. Call me coldhearted, call me a victim of internalized homophobia, but I didn't want tender pecks on the cheek and cozy evenings watching Jean-Luc Godard with my erudite friends. Call me a contrarian, call me stupid, but I didn't want a college education and a successful middle-class life. I wanted to be out there experiencing the horror and misery and wild dirty disturbing joy that is America.

"What's up," said some overworked Library Studies student serving as a librarian, when I came around the counter.

"Not much." I signed for a cart of books bound for floor 2B.

"Later."

At Alexander, no one knew anybody else.

"Later."

None of the work-study kids ever did a damn bit of work. We'd sign for our carts and bring them up to the appropriate floor, and then we'd either sit down somewhere and do homework, sit down somewhere and go to sleep, or go home and go to sleep. It took me a little while to catch on. For the first few weeks I actually shelved the books I was supposed to shelve! How lame.

In the inner pocket of my hooded sweatshirt, I had brought *Close to the Knives*. I read it in the elevator. I smiled at David's rage at people who say "...we shouldn't *think* about anything other than monogamous or safer sex. At least in my ungoverned imagination I can fuck somebody without a rubber, or I can, in the privacy of my own skull, douse Helms with a bucket of gasoline and set his putrid ass on fire."

Let me be clear: I'm a bottom, and my sexual pleasure is the same whether or not there's a rubber on the cock in my ass, and I have no sympathy for silly faggots who hate to use condoms. My empathy with Mr. Wojnarowicz was not based on any shared frustration with the

Like a Virus

prohibition of fucking without a rubber. What I hated was the expectation that everything we did had to be sterile and unthreatening, and safe, safe, safe. *Ding!* said the elevator, opening its doors on a tableau of endless desolate stacks.

Floor 2B was my favorite: Russian Literature *and* Cinema Studies! My two favorite subjects, a mere three aisles apart. Plus, hardly anyone ever went up there. People went to study or socialize in the basement, or on floor 1, or on floor 2, or even floor 2A, but no one went to 2B unless he had a mission in mind: finding a particular book or a hookup. All sorts of crazy shit could happen there. Every week the work-study kids traded rumors of arrests made in the men's room, ugly messes found on the floor, funny smells lingering in the air. Lots of times I'd find sperm-soaked tissues nestled provocatively on the shelves. At work, walking between the rows, the hairs on my arms would stand up and tingle with the conviction that frenzied masturbation and filthy perverted sex was happening all around me.

Floor 2B also had the best graffiti. The windowsills and study tables were positively covered in painstakingly scrawled pictures and text. Spread legs and close-up vaginas; cocks and balls; long detailed descriptions of the sex acts those poor frustrated boys wished they were engaged in. Phone numbers of ex-girlfriends, accompanied by glowing recommendations of their bedroom skills. Song lyrics. Fortune cookie quotes.

Incredible, the sexual frustration that builds up in someone surrounded by books! To make matters worse—or better—every frat required its men to spend seven hours a week studying, some kind of agreement the Greek societies had with the university. I hated the frat houses, and I hated the frat boys who came to Alexander to pretend to study, and I was helplessly, absurdly attracted to them. That night I made a complete circuit of the floor and I only saw one guy, and it happened to be someone I knew, someone from my Expository Writing and Argument class. A surly fine young man named Jeff, who week after week refused to even attempt to understand what *epistemology* meant.

At work I would stroll past those boys, those *men,* and quiver with desire and terror at the proximity of so much machismo. Fear kept me moving, even when I felt sure I could have had sex if I wanted it. On this particular night it was only my frustration, and my boredom with Steve, and the book in the pocket of my hoodie, that gave me the courage to make eye contact. I stopped a few feet away from Jeff, and pretended to inspect the shelf in front of me. Twelve books about Tchaikovsky's libretti. I turned my head, and Jeff was looking at me.

"What's up," he said.

"Not much."

"You work here?"

"How'd you know?" I asked.

"I saw you come out of the elevator pushing a cart."

"Yeah, I work here." I shifted my weight to one foot, and did my best to look as bored and aloof as he was.

Jeff smirked and leaned forward. "You know, one of the guys in our class said some horrible things about you."

"Oh yeah?"

"Yeah."

He watched me, waited until I asked, "What'd he say?"

"He said you were a faggot."

"That's not horrible," I said.

"No?" He raised an eyebrow.

How often did hate crimes get committed in university libraries?

"I don't think it's horrible either," he said. He swiveled the chair around, sat with his legs spread far apart. The crotch of his pants was swelled invitingly. "How'd you like to help out a hard-up brother?"

Simple as that. Behind me, the aisle extended the length of a full city block. On each side of us, dozens of desks sat empty. It was late, and it was a Friday, but any one of Rutgers' forty thousand students could step into the frame at any second. I dropped to my knees and looked up at him, then wriggled over to nestle my face between his legs.

Jeff was short, and his feet were not remarkably large, but for some reason I had been imagining a foot-long cock cradled in those jeans. Most likely it was because I saw him as a consummate man, virile and

Like a Virus

athletic and crude and mean, with a consummately manly package to match. Instead, when I'd unzipped his pants, the thing that sprang from his boxer shorts was your standard six-incher, albeit disturbingly thick and kinda ugly. In a flash my mouth was on it. I gagged, struggling to adapt my mouth to the width.

"What's the matter with you?" Jeff growled. "I thought y'all were supposed to be born cocksuckers."

The question was rhetorical. I couldn't have given an articulate answer if I wanted to. The hand at the back of my neck pulled me further onto him.

"That's it," he said, as I inched forward a centimeter at a time. "Nice and slow for starters."

I made a choking noise and tried to pull back, but the hand was as firm as a noose. He brought his other hand around to hold me firm. "Calm down," he said. "Just relax."

After what seemed an eternity, my lips were flush with the base of his cock. "See?" he said. He pulled himself out slightly, then pushed back in.

"That's right," he said, smiling at the sight of my red sweaty face. "That's a good faggot." And he began to push himself in and out of my mouth, picking up speed as he went.

At one point, a few aisles down, a woman turned the corner and saw us. She stopped, watched for a second, then turned and left. Would she fetch security? Would she sneak back with a camera, and run the pictures on the first page of tomorrow's *Daily Targum*? I was too excited to slow the bobbing of my head.

She had happened to walk into my very limited field of vision. Who knew how many other boys and girls strolled by in the course of that blow job, in search of something on D.W. Griffith, or *Anna Karenina*, and stopped to watch this spectacle of enthusiastic degradation?

"Look at me," he said.

His face, from that steep angle, seemed godlike, like something out of a silent film. A Greek statue was fucking my face. His lip was curled, maybe from pleasure and maybe in a sneer, but there was no contempt in his eyes. They were almost affectionate. Sweat began to well up on his forehead. "You doing okay?"

I nodded to the best of my ability; my head's motion was not under my control. After that I tranced out on the rhythm of it, the ache of the friction and the smell of his ball sweat, his grunts and dirty talk and the unrelenting hands holding me, the proximity of so much great literature. I had half a dozen epiphanies in the time I was muzzled with Jeff, among them *all literature is born in sex.*

"I'm gonna shoot," he said, and tried to pull me off. "Come on, watch out!" Instead I sped up. I had never swallowed a load before—Steve was strict about safe sex—and the prospect excited me, but Jeff yanked his cock from my mouth as I was on the upstroke and an instant later was spraying a mediocre volume of come that dribbled down to pool in his pubic hair. A lone drop hit my chin.

"Nice," he said after a minute or two. "What'd you think?"

I nodded my head. I was breathing heavy, so when I said "Nice," it sounded like a whisper.

"What a mess," he said, pointing to his crotch, which was splattered with phlegm and sperm. His smile was all gratitude.

"Sorry," I said.

"No worries."

He tore out the bottom half of a page from his Sociology textbook. "Take this," he said, scribbling on it. "Call me sometime."

"Yeah?" I said.

"Yeah."

"What would your frat brothers say about this if they knew?"

He shrugged. "They know. They don't care."

"Really?"

"Really. Have a nice night, Simon." He tore out the other half of the page, and used it to mop himself up. He left the crumpled soggy paper on the desk.

Two hours were left on my shift. If I had had any sense, any real spark of rebellion, I would have walked out of Alexander Library right then and there. But then I would have gone back to Steve, and for reasons both obvious and not-so-obvious I was in no hurry for that. So I decided to do my duty by the federal government that was

Like a Virus

so generously and begrudgingly funding the education that would enable me to spend the rest of my life trying to destroy it, and stay until midnight.

Jeff and Steve were just different branches of the same tree. The same white Jersey upbringing, the same level of socioeconomic security, the same trajectory in terms of the income range they'd have upon emerging from college. Only a slightly different relationship with the straight world separated them. My heart still thudded, from arousal and fear and the excitement of being faced with a thousand and one amazing possibilities. I got the same shivery sensation when I stood in the Media Basement, standing before a rack of canisters of movies on 16mm, these rare beautiful films by Carl-Theodore Dreyer and Sergei Eisenstein and Roberto Rossellini.

A huge factor in my decision to drop to my knees had been frustration with Steve, but now the only thing swelling up in front of my face was reality. Consequences. Decisions. What if I broke it off with Steve? What if I stuck with Steve and never saw Jeff again except in class? What if I kept seeing both of them, balancing my affection for sweet sincere Steve with my naked need for bossy brutal Jeff? What if we had a three-way? What if I turned my back on both of them?

I spent the next two hours curled up with some Foucault shit I barely understood. Wind battered the sturdy walls of the old building. I cradled the ache where my jaw, like my mind, had been pushed past what's comfortable.

Coming of Age in the Worlds of "If"
Richard Labonté

I can't recall the first science fiction book I read. I know I was reading science fiction by the time I was seven or eight, when I was
already bored by the Hardy Boys, the Bobbsey Twins, the Rover
Boys, Nancy Drew, Brains Benton, and Tom Swift, whose spacey
adventures were my favorite for reading more than once—though I
had a thing for those Hardy boys and their hearty comradeship,
too. Perhaps my first time with the worlds of "if" was when I read
one of the non-Tarzan books by Edgar Rice Burroughs. I may have
been escaping from the world with *The Chessmen of Mars,* or exploring
forgotten worlds *At the Earth's Core.* I was living then in Paris, a military brat, borrowing English-language books from my father's
enlisted men friends—my parents didn't read much beyond the
daily newspaper.

But I can recall my first queer erotic moment—and it was all
about books, a large shelf of Burroughs paperbacks, mostly the
Tarzan titles with a brawny man on the cover, but a couple of the
outer-space titles as well, in our neighbor's living room. I also recall
how I liked to wrestle with our neighbor, a single corporal, probably
ten years older than me—though he seemed as old as my parents.
Our roughhousing was physically innocent but, more in memory
than in the moment, wonderfully erotic.

When I was ten, my father was transferred to Mont Apica, a now-
shuttered Pine Tree Line radar station in the isolated middle of Parc
Laurentide in Quebec. The base was small, eight hundred or so residents, about forty miles from the nearest small town, a self-contained
village, really: I was able to deliver the daily newspaper bused in from

Coming of Age in the Worlds of "If"

Montreal to about eighty homes during my school lunch break—six-days-a-week work that started with lugging a delivery bag stuffed with forty and more pounds of newspapers up a hill so steep it was tobog-gan central come winter. I was a muscular lad, thanks to that climb. And that newsprint was my happy connection to easy sex.

After school, I loaded up another thirty or forty papers to deliver to the barracks where the single enlisted men and the bache-lor officers were quartered. I was a hunky youngster, I was horny, most of the men were barely out of their teens, and sometimes they were alone in their rooms. Hanky-panky ensued—clothes-on wrestling, quick masturbation, occasional blow jobs. I had the sex-with-older-men thing figured out at a pretty young age.

Meanwhile, there were so few kids my age, boys and girls together, that grades seven, eight, and nine—families were trans-ferred when their children graduated grade nine—sat in the same classroom, maybe a dozen of us. Add in the kids from the Catholic school across the playground, and we managed to cobble together two softball teams in the summer, three or four hockey teams in the winter. I was athletic, but not really a team player; I was the catcher in softball, the goalie in hockey, ready to head home to a book when the game was over.

The book at home came from a small base library, tucked into the basement of the recreation hall between a two-lane bowling alley on one side and the room where our Boy Scout troop met once a week to tie knots. It's a cliché, I know: I learned to do more than tie knots with a few of the boys in my scout patrol. It was an early, untroubled queer sexual initiation.

I set pins in the bowling alley most weekends and some week-nights, sometimes handling both lanes myself, more often paired with a French-Canadian boy a year or two older than me, twelve or thirteen: Gilles, taller than me, not as stocky, blessed with red hair and a large nose...the look of a man that so many decades later still catches my eye. We perched side by side while waiting for pins to fall, sweaty in the stuffy air, sometimes with our shirts off, bump-ing shoulders and thighs and feeling up each other's biceps. Boy

Scouts and bowling: young lust. Our work didn't end when the last bowler left; with the alley closed and the door locked—I was entrusted with a key—and after we'd swept the cigarette-butt strewn floor (this was the '60s, remember, when anyone could smoke anywhere) and polished the lanes and racked all the balls, Gilles and I would jack each other off, or trade blow jobs, or just masturbate ourselves. Gilles wasn't gay, as far as I know (his family was transferred about a year after we started having sex); or if he was, he couldn't articulate it, didn't have the language for it, or didn't really care what he was. He just liked the orgasms, and my company. We weren't in love. Not even in crush. But I had the sex-with-male-peers thing figured out as well.

The library next door was where I fell in love. At first, with Robert A. Heinlein, Andre Norton, Jack Williamson, A. E. van Vogt, Murray Leinster, E. E. "Doc" Smith, Manly Wade Wellman, and Jack Vance, among many—a universe of imaginations conjuring a wealth of universes and endless escape. This was in 1960, and it was the first time, but not the last, that I lost myself in a room full of books. It wasn't a large room: there were perhaps five thousand volumes, every one donated by families and bachelor officers and young, not-yet-married enlisted men. I remember an awful lot of *Reader's Digest* condensed editions. A lot of mysteries, but they weren't of interest to me then. And a lot of science fiction, enough to keep me reading for a year, until one day a card fell out of a newer book, an invitation to join the Science Fiction Book Club. Which I did, in 1961. I was twelve by then. And for the next seventeen or so years, until I moved to Los Angeles in 1979 to help open the first branch of A Different Light Bookstore, I ordered every book, every month—except for the Edgar Rice Burroughs titles: his stories were for little kids....

So there I was, a practicing fag by the time I was twelve, and reading four or five science fiction books a week. My future was certainly going to be queer.

My future also became more homosexual, thanks to that same small base library. That's where, as I browsed the stacks, I found—

Coming of Age in the Worlds of "If"

again, I can't recall My First Literary Time; as I age, I regret I never kept an adolescent diary or an adult journal—a book by Gore Vidal or Tennessee Williams or Mary Renault. And just as I found my physical queer self in the hushed, musty bowling alley, back where the lights were dim, I found my literary queer self in that cramped, fusty library with its bright lights. I discovered a daisy chain of writers writing about people like me. Vidal led me to Williams, Williams led me to James Baldwin, Baldwin led me to Truman Capote, Capote led me to Paul Bowles, Bowles led me to William Burroughs, and Mary Renault taught me about both lesbians and lithe Spartan lads: all part of a covert coven of queer writers who blurbed each other's books.

There were probably, in all, about twenty books, thirty at most, that whispered *Gay boy, read me* as I went through that library, shelf by shelf and book by book. And remember: military families and single men who rotated through Mont Apica every two or three years had donated them all. Obviously, there were homos among them—John Rechy's *City of Night* popped out of a dusty box in 1963!—though it was certainly possible that a well-read family's personal library would include novels by Capote or Baldwin or Renault.

Ronald Firbank was in there, too, and John Horne Burns, and Paul Goodman, and Fritz Peters, and Christopher Isherwood. That's where I learned the language of being queer, where I discerned that what I was *doing* with the young men in their barracks and with the boy in the next bowling lane—and with Jack, who'd come by to neck with me while I was babysitting; and with Daniel, another French-Canadian, who loved to sleep over; and with Martin, who'd lie under the trees in the summer heat and listen to the allure of rock and folk from faraway WBZ in Boston, one of the few radio stations that reached, in those pre-satellite days, into our mountain-surrounded little village—wasn't an isolated, inchoate pleasure: our adolescent sexual fumbling had an intellectual underpinning and a philosophical basis for existence. My physical pleasure had literary cachet. Books gave me the words and the ideas with which to express my young gay self, without guilt.

Richard Labonté

By the time my father was transferred, late in the same year that Rechy steamed a young boy's glasses (my mother was awfully lenient about the books I brought home from the library, and had in fact given the woman who ran the place a letter saying I had permission to read anything I wanted, though *City of Night* was one book I hid from prying eyes), I was a practicing homosexual, an avid SF fan and unusually well-read, for a young teenager, in the classical homosexual *oeuvre*. I've stayed that way for the forty years since. Well-read, that is, not a teenager.

The Skater and the Punk
Joel A. Nichols

Noah was bent over the coffee table when I opened the door. Half-inked squares lay on big white sheets all around him on the floor and the table. He looked up at the noise and smiled at me. Two black fingerprint smudges kissed his lips where he'd been biting his nails. He slid the sheet he'd been working on away from him with the edges of his fingertips. The apartment was dark except for the bright oblong pool of light cast by an elbow-joint lamp clamped on the edge of the coffee table, its helix cord stretching toward the outlet tucked into the flaking exposed bricks. The electrician had mortared it in crooked.

"You already smudged it." I stooped to kiss him on the back of his head and he shook it like a wet puppy. His hair stunk. "Did you take a shower today?"

"I'm trying to concentrate." He pulled the ashtray toward himself and slipped a cigarette between his inky lips. "I promised I'd have this page done when you got home." I ruffled his greasy hair, looked over his shoulder, and picked up the top sketch on the pile.

"You also promised you wouldn't smoke," I said as I walked across the room. I kicked off my work shoes, narrow, shiny ugly loafers. I'd worn sneakers every day the week I started as Georgia's assistant. On day four, I got a dress code memo: no sneakers, even for the boy with no responsibility and no room for advancement. I tugged loose my tie and poured a glass of water.

The sketch I'd grabbed was pieces of what would be the cover. The Skater stood on the right, his heel kicking up his board. A burst of light shone from the end of the skateboard. The large framed

The Skater and the Punk

print of Noah's original cover for the first comic hanging over our couch had the same pose and a similar light effect. Before that art was due to the publisher, Noah had been reworking his chin for days and it still had not been quite right: too pointed, with a false shadow that made our hero's face look dirty. But somehow, in the last hour before the courier got there, Noah had gotten it exactly right.

Now we were pushing up against a deadline again. Although Noah drew every day, we hadn't made much progress because I'd barely had any time to work out the story.

Noah stubbed out the cigarette. He licked his lips. "What do you think of it?" He hadn't shaved in a month, and ruddy hair grew all over his cheeks and chin. It was thick and gave me shivers when it scratched me. I'd asked him to draw the Skater with a beard like his, but he refused. Heroes don't have beards, he had said.

"I love the starburst—the light shooting from the board. It's exactly like I pictured. And his sneakers look hot—but they should be green. Aren't you going to make them green?"

He scratched his chin and shrugged. "I was kind of hoping the color would change from time to time. Nobody wants to wear the same color sneakers forever."

"You said that about his T-shirt, too. But we can't have a hero that changes clothes.... You heard what they said: we need him in a uniform. Even if it's not spandex, his clothes have to make a uniform." *They* were Rebecca and Steven, acquisitions editors who'd given us a thousand dollars to finish the project. Their company had brought out the first *The Skater* comic and still believed in us enough to publish the second even though the first hadn't sold that well other than at gay comic cons.

"Trust me," Noah said as he stood up and walked over to where I was standing. He leaned one hand on the kitchen counter next to mine and kissed my ear, then the corner of my jawbone. "I know how to draw the Skater. Trust me." I leaned against him, felt his scraggly beard against the back of my neck and his left hand holding my bicep. He was my inspiration for the character, but I knew that he didn't think he was drawing himself.

60

"I know," I muttered as I melted into him. "I know." He held me for a minute, then let go and grabbed a bag of chips. The top half of the bag was curled under the bottom and as Noah held it in his palm, the oily plastic looked alive as he dug around for a whole chip in a sea of crumbs. He reached out to me, pointing with the open maw of the chips. I shook my head no, and started unbuttoning my shirt.

"How was work? Did you have time to work on the story?" I cringed thinking about the number of times Georgia, my boss, had bellowed my name. Bellowed. Shouted. Hissed. Whispered, if she was on the phone with *her* boss. And each time it was to tell me to do something useless: pull a file from one of the cabinets well within her arm's reach; walk her through how to attach a document to an e-mail; take her empty cardboard coffee cup to the lunchroom so the grumpy Hungarian janitor wouldn't give her dirty looks for food waste in the office. And that was all before ten.

"Georgia was being Georgia," I said, snaking my tie off my neck and slinging my shirt over the back of a chair. I hunted around for my backpack and crossed the room to where I'd left it leaning up against the side of the couch. "Three freelancers won't speak to Georgia at all anymore...and all three are horribly past deadline." I bent down and rummaged for my notebook. "But I did get to work on the story a little bit in the afternoon. I hid it underneath the ad sales reports whenever I heard someone walking toward my cube. I figured out how the Skater and the Punk are going to join up. How we're going to get them from enemies to mistrusting allies."

Crumbs stuck in his beard. He wiped his mouth with the back of his hand and set down the empty and misshapen packaging. His sketchpad and pencils were closer to me, on the coffee table. I sat down on the couch and motioned for him to come over. "Mistrusting allies," he repeated. Noah took up his sketchpad and started drawing as I told him what I'd worked out.

"We know that the Skater got his powers when he missed the land-ing and the bus hit him, in volume one. But what about the Punk? You're not just bitten by a radioactive Mohawk, right? I think it must have something to do with the bus, too. Not sure what yet." Noah

The Skater and the Punk

never looked up once when he was in this mode, just cocked his ear in my direction and stared at the pages. It was now that I got to stare at him like I always wanted to stare at him without him feeling self-conscious. There was a little scar above his eyebrow—the same little pink knot that everybody has on their eyebrow from a childhood injury—where I liked to start. His was the same little pink knot, but it was more. I knew it was from when he and his sister were jumping on the bed playing Superman and Wonder Woman, and Noah'd taken too big a jump and knocked his head against the bedpost.

"By the end of volume one, the Skater and the Punk have faced off in the courtyard of City Hall, and we've diffused the bomb that was going to kill the mayor. In the fight, the Punk has stabbed Benjy with one of his spikes. We ended with the Skater planning an assault, to avenge his wounded boyfriend and all that. We've already decided to open with Benjy crumpled on the floor in a gray hoodie that's soaked in blood. The Punk's spike is still lodged in his side. So he's splayed out, bleeding, and pleading with the Skater not to go back. 'Jason,' he whispers because that's all the strength he has left and he's using the Skater's real name for the first time since the bus accident, 'don't. You can't risk yourself again. He's going to try it again,' and so on, when Grand Slam and Free Throw come rushing in. Free Throw bounces her basketball off the TV and it snaps on. The Mayor's there, pale but hard faced, declaring martial law."

Noah's smile drooped lopsidedly and he started chewing on the ink stain. His eyes were big and bright but trained on the page so I couldn't really see them, all ruddy brown like his beard but marbled with streaks of green lightning. They weren't the first thing I noticed about him, but once I had noticed them I couldn't stop looking. I leaned in to peer at what he was drawing and he choked up on the sketchpad, pulling it closer to his chest. Sometimes he did that, wouldn't let me see what he was making until he was done. I pictured the Mayor as my high school principal; Noah pictured him as his uncle. His pencil bit into the sheet of paper. His eyebrow—the one with the scar—arched but he didn't look up. "Martial law?"

"Yeah," I said. "The Mayor announces martial law and says that the city police force will be assisted by PleuriCorp's security forces. And that they're going to start clearing the streets, enforcing a curfew."

Noah reached across the coffee table and fished a cigarette from his pack. He flattened the sketchpad against his chest. As he reached up to light the cigarette, his T-shirt rode up his stomach. His slight round belly rested in between the two sharp Vs of his hip joints. It was furry, covered with brown silk. I couldn't quite see his belly button because he exhaled in smoke rings and scrunched down his shirt and pulled up the waistband of his boxers. I stood up and pulled open the window.

From this angle I could see the bulge of his crotch pointing down the left leg of his gray corduroys. He flipped over a page of his sketchbook, and I saw our hero's feet on his board, flying through and over a crowd of people and cars. When we wrote the first volume of *The Skater*, I thought up a story line. And sat while Noah created all the images—images that my words never would have assembled. Noah made action out of nothing, and then I filled in words around his pictures. Captions.

"The Skater knows that unchecked, PleuriCorp will start their homeless and poor roundups. And so he sends Free Throw and Grand Slam to approach the Punk, while he gets Benjy to the hospital." I described their scuffle with the Punks as they crossed the line into their territory.

Noah put down the pencil. "You really think he should send Free Throw and Grand Slam? Don't you remember that fanblog that said that whenever we use those two as the Skater's sidekicks, we weaken their credibility as superheroes. And Rebecca agrees..."

I looked down at the notes I'd made on the story at work.

"A fanblogger? Who cares? Free Throw and Grand Slam do function as his sidekicks. But they aren't his sidekicks." *You're my sidekick,* I thought.

"I'm your sidekick," he said. I laughed, and then kissed him. The sketches that had lain on his knees slid to the floor as he leaned into me and kissed me full and hard. His beard scraped my face as he slid his tongue across my lips and into my mouth. I met his

The Skater and the Punk

tongue with mine, and then nibbled at the ink stain on his bottom lip. He grabbed my hip and squeezed, and slid his other hand up my side, massaging my ribs. I tilted my head back and his tongue tumbled out of my mouth. His lips grazed my chin, following the line of my jawbone down my neck. I tingled from knees to elbows and up and down the length of my back.

I reclined on the couch and Noah climbed on top of me. He pressed himself against me, grinding his chest into mine and holding my hips. "Don't we have to finish a couple of pages tonight? Rebecca called today but I didn't pick up," he said.

"Yeah, we do. But we can afford a short diversion." I wished that he hadn't told me that Rebecca had called. Or had told me before. But that was Noah.

"I don't know," he said, still squeezing my hip with one hand and grinding himself into me. "I know you, though," he whispered in my ear. Then he let go of my shoulder. "You'll get pissed at me later, if this isn't done."

"Okay. Let's talk about the story then. I've been thinking about what's going to happen once the Skater and the Punk have beaten PleuriCorp's forces and freed the streets." Noah was straddling me. He set his fingertips down on my chest, tapping a light trail on my collarbone. I felt the fingertips of his other hand on my stomach, underneath my T-shirt, tracing the patches of hair on my stomach and the trail leading up my chest. "You're tickling me," I said but he didn't stop.

"I think they should fuck," Noah said. "Our heroes should screw."

I grabbed his chin and looked into his eyes. "You know what Rebecca and Steven will say to that. What they've already said to that." Noah's beard was roughed up, sticking up against the grain of his face from where he'd been rubbing his chin and neck on me. His lips were parted just a little, like he wanted to say more. He flicked out his tongue and wet the corners of his mouth. "Do you think you could draw that? The two of them fucking?"

Noah nodded yes. He grabbed at the top of my waistband. My cock was getting hard. I knew that Noah could feel the tension in my

64

shorts as he tugged at the flap covering my zipper. He squeezed me through the fabric and leaned in again to kiss my neck. "What would it look like? What would I have to draw?" Noah whispered against my chest. I felt him getting hard against my belly, too.

"It would be after the battle. And Benjy is dead. The city is on fire, but our good guys have won. Benjy survived the Punk's spike to the stomach, but he had to sacrifice himself in the final battle—throwing himself on a bomb meant for the Skater. The Skater even tried to throw himself on top of Benjy on top of the bomb, but the Punk held him back. Out the window flames lick the skyline, and the Skater is punching the walls, destroying whatever he can lay his hands on. The Punk seizes his shoulders, and holds him tight to his chest. After a pane of wracking sobs, the Skater looks up into the Punk's eyes, and they kiss long and slow."

Noah pushed his dick into me and laid his palm flat over me. He was nuzzling my chest, his beard prickling me through the thin worn cotton of my undershirt. "And the Skater starts unbuttoning the Punk's jacket, and pulls off their shirts, like this," I said as I pulled Noah's shirt off him inside out. I lifted my arms and Noah peeled mine off. His skin was warm—almost burning me where our bellies and chests were touching. The soft hair covering him from his belly button to above his nipples was driving me crazy. My dick was throbbing as he crushed his body into mine, pointing the tip of his dick under my ribs.

"They kiss long and deep, and the Punk starts tonguing his mouth and holding the sides of his face. The Skater moans, and pulls the Punk down on top of him, on the floor of the Punk's squat. He yanks down his skinny black jeans by the chains and the Punk gropes at the hard dick bulging in the Skater's pants. His board is in the corner of the frame, tipped up against the wall."

Making the Skater a skater had been my idea—because of Noah. His wide, reinforced sneakers, big pants, and the sight of his T-shirt riding up over his belly when he lifted his arms to balance a jump had given me a hard-on. The character had been my desire for him taking shape. It took shape because of his drawing it, creating the images. And as he created those fantasy images of my desire, my love,

The Skater and the Punk

my hunger for him had grown.

"I want you," I whispered. "Right now." I pressed back with my hips, tearing at his pants. He wore them big enough that I could yank them down without fussing with the button or belt, and in a second his boxers were tented in my face. With his pants tangled around his knees, he pulled open my zipper and reached through to squeeze my cock.

"Is that what the Skater is going to say to the Punk?" he said. "I want you?"

"No way," I said, cupping his asscheeks with my hands and pushing his cock, the head of which was now jutting through his gaping fly and dripping a spidersilk of pre-cum. "He says, 'I want you to fuck me. I want you in me.'" Noah cocked a crooked smile, and bent in to kiss me again, deeper and harder. We both knew it was something the Skater probably wouldn't tell the Punk, so soon after Benjy's death. But it didn't matter at that point. I let Noah feed his dick into my mouth. When I tasted the salt of his pre-cum my own dick started leaking and the tension in my ass and balls started releasing, relaxing, opening up. He grabbed the back of my head and thrust into my mouth. He leaned to the right awkwardly to reach my dick, licking his fingers and squeezing me, mixing his spit and my pre-cum and rubbing it around the tip of my cock. I moaned and then he moaned with his dick buried inside my throat. As his balls hit my chin I closed my eyes and felt desire wash through my whole body.

He was working my cock with his hand, holding the head on his thumb joint, like the butt of a beer bottle, rubbing down the shaft with the pad of his thumb and curling his fingers around me. I spit out his cock and pulled him down to kiss me. He devoured my mouth with his tongue again, and reached down with both of his hands, one cupping my balls and tugging at them gently, the other jerking me in slow, wet rhythm. I pushed down at him with my ass, and spread apart my legs. Holding his dick at the base, I shoved my tongue into his mouth, pressing at the inside of his lips and his tongue. He tasted ashy. He started to buck his hips, fucking my fist.

I leaned back so our dicks would touch, and he took both of them in his left fist. He coated my head with more of his pre-cum and my

66

spit, and started pumping our cocks against each other. With his other hand, Noah went for my balls again, pulling and squeezing. He cupped my asscheeks, and slid two of his fingers up my crack, toward my ass. I opened my legs wider, trying to pull him toward me, and thrust back at him with my hips. His cock felt hot and long and heavy against mine. I was flat on the seat of the couch now, with my neck bent awkwardly and my head jutting into the seat back.

Noah mumbled something I couldn't understand because my ear was pressed into the couch cushion, and he spit into his hand. I felt one of his fingers pressing on the outside of my ass, felt him point his fingertip into me. His finger felt hot and wet and hard, and I burned for him. I bore down on his finger as it slid into the ring of my ass. My balls felt so full and so tight. "Fuck me. Quick, Noah, before I blow."

He spit on his hand again and slicked the head of his dick. I felt it at my hole and I opened up again for Noah, my super Noah. His cock was huge and throbbing, and he stabbed into me with a sharp and quick thrust. I gasped, and reached around to grab Noah's ass again. I pulled him in deeper, I wanted him as far inside me as I could get him, and bright light flashed at the corners of my eyes as I felt Noah filling me up. I tried to say "I'm coming," but was too far gone to find my breath, to vibrate my throat. Instead my dick exploded, spraying my stomach and chest. Drops hit my shoulder and face and the couch cushion, and it felt like I was flying as Noah let go inside of me.

He collapsed on top of me. My fingers and toes tingled as I tried to catch my breath. I hugged Noah and felt the slick of sweat on his back. "You're crushing me," I said and he shifted his weight, rolling onto the cushion next to me. His dick hung big still as he flopped down. I wiped myself with his boxers and handed them to Noah so he could clean up. I was thirsty, and as I stood up to get another glass of water, I said, "Come on, supercock. We've got pages to finish."

Sleeping at the Feet of the Prince
Joseph Manera

I could eat bananas, toast, and little else. Protein and fat were pro-
hibited. I could drink water and tea. I was told that, if my health
improved, I would probably be able to manage a peach smoothie in
a week or so.

I put two slices of bread in the toaster and sat down. In another
minute, I'd have to stand up again. *Shit,* I thought. That would take
a lot of energy, lifting myself out of the chair. I had to begin thinking about these things, these tiny movements. I thought about how
exhausting it would be to walk from the kitchen to my bedroom and
wondered if I should have just remained standing.

The austerity of my existence rattled me. A few weeks before, I
was bounding up stairs at my job and zipping through the city with
energy to spare. Suddenly, I had to take the bus everywhere. I missed
walking. The city looks completely different when you travel on foot.
I missed the sense of possibility that San Francisco provides when
you walk its streets.

"You'll feel this way every now and then," the nurse said casually. "About every six months. That's Hep B for you—assuming
that's what you have." When I heard this, I was lying on a cot in St.
Mary's emergency room with a fever. My skin looked as resinous
and pale as a cucumber candle. I wondered what a lifetime of this
dragging feeling would be like. "You know, I think the mom from
the Judds has it," the nurse added, somewhat excitedly. I wondered
if I was supposed to be pleased by this, to be in celebrity company
with my hepatitis.

"This could be an acute seroconversion to HIV," the doctor's assistant said a week later. "Everything else is coming back negative. You're a sexually active gay male, so we should definitely test for it." I began to doubt my memory and judgment. I was always safe in bed, right? I wondered if I had ever had a cut in my mouth or on my tongue, something that could have provided an entry point for infection. Maybe I had, and ran it across an open, bloody sore. I should have thought more about those things, those tiny movements.

I knew this was unlikely, but knowing and feeling are not always the best of friends, and sometimes they go long periods of time without speaking to each other. I looked around the office. The doctor, an athletic blond man in his forties with alarmingly white teeth, had pictures of himself and his two smiling little boys on the desk in his office. I wondered what their lives were like. They looked rudely healthy.

"You have two sons," I said. "That's nice."

I looked around my kitchen and noticed how filthy it got when no one bothered to clean it. Piles of dirty dishes crowded the sink. They had remained unwashed for so long that the remnants of food covering them appeared to have hardened into glue. A smell so putrid and funky emanated from the area that I expected the dinnerware to march across the kitchen counter in protest. "Don't you see us?" they'd ask. "We deserve better."

My toast popped up. I poured myself a glass of water and sat back down. I thought about how my life might change. *You'll feel like this every now and then...about every six months.* I was supposed to begin a doctoral program in clinical psychology in one month's time. How would I manage all of my future responsibilities while feeling so lousy? I thought about what other people survive, what they bear. I felt a twinge of shame and wondered if I was surrendering to self-pitying victimhood.

My thoughts turned to the men I had been with. I reflected on my sexual experiences, but surprisingly my mind did not linger there. I started to think about romantic love, and how I always seemed to run toward doors that were closing and push on them too hard, for too long. I'd meet men who were about to move out of town or who were on trial separations from long-term boyfriends. It would begin and end quickly, and then it would begin and end again with someone else. Sometimes I'd think about it, the difficulty of starting all over again, that crawl out of the tar pit, the dark stickiness and terror of it. Too often, I confused letting go with failure. When you set up your life as winning or losing, you lose a lot.

I was reading Rilke's *Letters to a Young Poet* at the time and underlined a phrase: *the love that consists in this: that two solitudes protect and border and greet each other*. I thought of how my own solitude was a coat I kept hidden and refused to wear, even in inclement weather. I'd meet men at the gym, the supermarket, bars. Time and again, I went outside to search for love. I didn't think I would find it anywhere else.

The wait for my test results was excruciating. I had grown accustomed to a whirligig existence of long workdays, night classes, dinners with friends, dates, sometimes dancing on weekends. Removed from the relentless buzz of my work and social life, I felt alone. It was as if my life was a tape I had been listening to, and it was suddenly playing back at an agonizingly slow speed. During this time, I had a recurring thought: I wanted my mother to take care of me. I imagined myself back home, feeling safe and loved, believing that no harm could possibly ever come to me.

"Well," I said to my mother when I finally spoke with her on the phone, "the doctors aren't sure what it is, but they think it might just be a strong flu."

"Huh." My mother, who usually does not allow for a moment's silence, grew uncharacteristically quiet. "Are you sure you're okay?" she finally asked.

"Don't worry about me," I insisted. I knew that my mother's gravest concerns about my homosexuality were that I would have "a lonely life" and that I would get sick. I did not want to confirm these worries. While I spoke, I sensed that my mother was wondering if one of these chief fears was coming true. I felt a strong urge to fill myself. I wanted to eat. I wanted to stuff myself with bread, with

Sleeping at the Feet of the Prince

meat, with sugar.

"You know I love you," she said simply. My mother says "I love you" a lot. It comes naturally to her, and there's not an apologetic ring to it. It's not the dusty "I love you" of someone who rarely voices the sentiment. It feels true the way that an ocean is true.

"I love you," I replied. I thought of all of the times that I had not voiced those words back to her and felt ashamed. I wondered how much love my mother had felt from me all of those years. Was it enough? I envisioned my own feelings as colors, as shades of red. I thought, *You taught me love. I feel this because you taught it to me.*

"I think about you," she said. *I think about you, too,* I thought, but didn't say. There was a plaintive quality to my mother's voice, as if she were speaking about a son she did not expect to see for quite some time. And then there was a silence. "I hope that you're eating all right," she said flatly. "And I hope that you're wearing socks."

After saying good-bye to my mother, I turned off all of the lights and drew the curtains until my bedroom was completely black. I lay in bed as my fears pulled me toward them and entangled me. I wasn't afraid of the dark, but I was afraid of what could be in it.

While I was ill, my friend Jacob visited me regularly. He'd bring bananas, medicine, and videos. He attempted to make me laugh by telling me about amusing things that happened to him during the week. I found myself eagerly anticipating his visits.

"I went to the bar with a friend last night, and this guy kept hitting on me," Jacob began. His voice was quiet and gently conspiratorial, as if he were sharing information that he shouldn't. "He was fairly attractive, middle aged, but had this really *intense* eye contact. As soon as I'd look back at him, he'd turn away. When he made toward the exit he stopped by me. He said, 'I would like to draw you sometime.' And then he handed me a business card." Jacob's smile widened, and his hands shot up excitedly, as if he were flipping an enormous gob of pizza dough. "I was kind of stunned. I looked at the card later, and it said *Dr. Candypants* where the name usually goes, and it had a phone number attached." He began to chuckle.

This was the most promising thing I had heard all week. "You need to call him!" I insisted. "You've always wanted to be a doctor's wife. You can be Mrs. Candypants."

"We could live on Lollipop Lane," he said. "You'd have to visit."

"Could you imagine if he actually *was* a real doctor, with an office and everything?" I adopted a smooth operator's voice. "*Hello, Mr. Wagner, Dr. Candypants is ready to see you now.*" Jacob and I looked at each other, smiling, then laughing. It was a relief to experience an emotion that couldn't be filled in with a charcoal pencil.

"I'm scared of doctors now," I admitted. "I think of doctors, I think of bad news."

Jacob hugged me. "You're going to be all right," he said. We stayed like this until I felt strong enough to pretend that I was feeling better.

Once Jacob left, my mood quickly soured. I lay down and stared at the ceiling. I thought, *If I can make myself feel what I think the worst would feel like, then maybe it won't hurt so much if it happens.* I closed my eyes and tried to fall asleep. I imagined that I was lying at the bottom of a well, with the sun beating down on me. I imagined oppressive heat and not wanting to move. I thought of things I'd like to feel—water, lips on my lips, fingers on my skin. As I thought of them, I almost felt as if I were experiencing them, these sensual things that I would miss.

In this moment, I felt a lovesickness so intense that it took on a life of its own. A slideshow of images of men I had cared about, that I still cared about, flashed through my mind. Every heartbreak, every false start looked the same. I considered reasons why I felt undeserving of love. I imagined a future without love. I thought of another passage from *Letters to a Young Poet* that had resonated with me and given some hope: *Why do you want to shut out of your life any uneasiness, any misery, any depression, since after all you don't know what work these conditions are doing inside you?* I wanted to let my sadness be with me. Let it teach me something about myself that I would not otherwise see. I wanted to open the door to this possibility but, at that moment, I could not. I sat up and rocked myself back and forth.

I eventually turned on the TV. A movie was showing. "We need to get back to this business of our lives," a sharply dressed man said

Sleeping at the Feet of the Prince

to a woman. A little girl, who I assumed was supposed to be his daughter, tugged at his shirtsleeve. "I want to go to the playground," she interrupted. "I want to swing on the swings, and I want to stay *all day*." I thought of what it would be like to be her father. I saw myself kneeling down so that my eyes would meet hers. I would rest my arm on her shoulder. I would say, "You can go, but you can't stay."

In the mail were bank statements and a catalog from International Male. The man on the cover had a brick-shaped face and wore a poet's shirt and gold parachute pants. He looked like Liberace as thrown up by MC Hammer. As I picked up the catalog, an envelope fell out. The return address was California Pacific Medical Center. There were my test results.

I wanted to rip the Band-Aid off quickly. I wanted to know. No deliberation. No last-minute reflections. An answer. I wanted to fucking know.

My whole life might change, was my only thought. I wanted to be brave. I tore the envelope open, but I could not look at it yet. My hands were trembling. I glanced at it quickly and then averted my eyes. I only saw the words *California Pacific Medical Center*. I was failing myself. I tried again. This time, I only saw my own address. This strategy was clearly not working. Finally, I looked at the letter as one might look at the sun during an eclipse, curious but expecting to go blind.

Negative. Eight letters. I looked at it again. Was I reading it correctly? Negative. An adjective and a noun. A small word. There were also lab results indicating that I did not have any of the hepatitises that I was tested for. I pressed the letter against my chest. Negative. I wanted to tattoo it there.

That night, I went out with Jacob for dinner. Even though I could not eat much, I wished to mark the occasion. I wanted to be in the world. We were to meet a friend of his there, Lee. When I saw Jacob, I was speechless for some time. I smiled. He smiled back. "Thank you," I finally said.

When Lee arrived, I thought he looked like a sun-kissed surf deity, all blond hair, tan skin, sensual lips, big teeth, big grin. He was probably in his early thirties. He appeared to be over six feet tall, and he carried himself like someone who still wasn't entirely certain of how to make use of all of the space that nature had decided he would occupy. His presence was disarming. He sat down across from me and folded his hands, lacing his fingers together like he was hiding a secret behind them.

"Gosh!" Lee exclaimed. "This has been a *great* day." He unclasped his hands, and I expected a small bird to fly out.

Lee explained that he was starting a new job in Boston, as a math professor. He had just managed to negotiate a higher salary than he was expecting. He had also learned that his sister was pregnant, and he was excited about moving back to his hometown.

"I miss seasons," he said. "I like there to be something to mark off points in the year." I told him I was born in Rhode Island and that my sister lives in Boston. We exchanged notes on the area for about half an hour. His conversation was as sweet and fizzy as champagne. Half an hour in, I felt a hand on my thigh.

Lee asked what I did. I told him about the clinical psychology program.

"That's amazing," he said. "Good for you."

That hand was still there, and now it actually seemed to be *rubbing* my thigh. I was confused. While I was relieved by my good news, I did not think that I resembled anything approaching "attractive" at the moment. I was gaunt, pale, and weak. I considered alternate explanations. Had someone snuck under our table and placed a prosthetic hand on my lap? No, I decided. I concluded that it had to be Lee's hand. My legs started shaking.

"To changes," he said. He raised a martini glass. I joined in with a glass of water.

"To changes," I said. "And making the most of them."

Two weeks later I was eating chicken sandwiches and salads. I ordered a slice of cheesecake drizzled with raspberry sauce at Sweet Inspirations. I had a newfound appreciation for food. I had been

Sleeping at the Feet of the Prince

fantasizing about grilled steaks, creamy vegetable soups, pastas slathered in rich sauce, anything chocolate. I felt reinvigorated. How did this happen? I was preparing for an evening with Lee. He called me a week after the dinner with Jacob and asked me out.

The afternoon before the date, I received a message from my mother.

"I'm glad you're feeling better," she said. "I know a lot is going on with you. Mothers just *know* these things. Call me when you get a chance."

I returned her message. "Hi Mom," I said. "Your sixth sense is right. A lot *is* going on with me, but it's mostly all good. I'll talk to you soon. I love you."

While preparing for my date, I looked at myself in the mirror. I could see some color in my cheeks again. I had gained a few pounds back. I wondered, for a moment, what would have happened if the letter had said *positive*. Eight letters. An adjective and a noun. A small word, but one that seemed to contain a universe of loneliness. I did not want my gratitude to fade, although I knew that, in the face of impending papers and examinations, I'd be bustling again, eating on the go, talking about how I want things to *slow down*. Nonsense, I thought. I wanted to savor all that was before me. I buttoned my shirt and walked out the door.

Lee lived not too far from me, in a flat in the Lower Haight. I found his apartment and rang his bell. When the door opened, a yellow Labrador leapt toward me and dug his snout into my crotch.

Lee smiled. "He gets that from me." He kissed my cheek and held on to my waist for much longer than a friendly hug would require.

"I wanted to take you on a ride," he said. He disappeared inside and came back out with two helmets. He pointed to a motorcycle parked near the sidewalk. I was dumbfounded. I stared at it as if it were an army tank.

"I'm a safe ride," he said, somewhat teasingly. "Nothing to worry, nothing to fear. I'll take very good care of you."

Clutching on to Lee from behind, I felt the kind of rush of excitement I'd been missing. The city looks completely different when you're zipping around it on a badass motorcycle. Every cell of me felt alive. I clung to him and wanted to dig my hands into his pants. This Harley-riding math professor seemed incredibly masculine and sexy to me. I pressed myself as close to him as I could. I imagined him doing proofs on a blackboard while wearing just a jockstrap. I was giddy. It almost seemed perverse to me that my body could feel this way after the way it felt just a few weeks prior. *Enjoy this*, I said to myself. There were times when it felt like the bike wasn't even touching the pavement, as if we were hovering over the streets. I thought of the motorcycle crashing and felt a pang of regret. Was I doing something foolish and risky? I thought of how danger sometimes makes us appreciate life more. I want this. I don't want this. No. Yes. Yes.

He drove us through different neighborhoods in San Francisco—the Marina, Fisherman's Wharf, Russian Hill, North Beach—and then back to his place. I began to wonder if this was just another closing door that I'd end up running toward. My body tensed. When we stepped off of the bike, I felt as woozy as I would exiting an amusement park ride. "Thank you for taking me," I said a bit breathlessly. "Thank you for showing me this." He remained silent.

As we walked up the stairs, into Lee's apartment, and on toward his kitchen, I looked at my handsome date and thought *There's an expiration date on this milk.* I peeked inside the rooms we passed and noticed books squeezed into every nook and cranny. The hallway was also filled with books. Most of the spines were worn, and Post-its protruded out of the tops of several of them. A dog-eared copy of Samuel Richardson's *Pamela: Or, Virtue Rewarded* rested on his kitchen table.

"I read that in college," I announced. "I know it's a classic and all, but holy shit what a stink bomb that book was!" I laughed crazily. My personal brand of nervous laughter sounds like it should be echoing off the walls of an inpatient psychiatric ward. Lee looked startled, but grinned. I had a difficult time meeting his gaze. Why? It held heat and sweetness and longing.

I wanted him to see that I felt it back, but I was afraid of what my face might show. I looked around his kitchen. It was small and a bit of a mess. Random objects crowded a shelf above the sink: a flashlight, a

Sleeping at the Feet of the Prince

bottle of detergent, a beer pitcher, a placard advertising beauty lotion from the '40s. I propped myself up on the counter. *I will look at these things*, I decided. *Time will stand still for a moment if I look at these things.* Lee moved toward me, slowly. He put his hands around my waist. I stared at my lap. He kissed me on the forehead with a tenderness that almost made my eyes well up with tears.

I pulled him in further with my legs. I ran my hands through his hair, tilted his head back, and met his lips with mine. He held on to me. His hands were warm. While we kissed, he scooped me up, walked us to his bed, and lowered me onto it. He opened his mouth to nibble my chin. He traced my jaw with kisses. He removed my shirt, my pants, everything but my underwear. I did the same to him. I felt protected with his lithe, athletic body on top of mine. He seemed powerful to me, in a generous way—I felt powerful, too. Emboldened, I climbed on top of him.

Out of the corner of my eye, I saw a giant poster of Oscar Wilde hanging on his wall and a stuffed bear with a beret on a shelf. Slowly, I began to notice more of what was around me. Photograph albums. A chest that looked like it belonged on a pirate ship. A nightstand with a pile of books on top of it. Stacks of CDs. I knew Lee was touching me, but suddenly I could not feel it. *I cannot have this*, I thought. *I cannot feel this.*

"Are you okay?" Lee asked. I remained silent. "Hello," he said. "Are you there?" he waved his fingers in front of my eyes as if performing a DUI test. I finally looked at him. I could see him seeing me.

"Jacob told me some of what you've been through lately," he said. "It's all right. I really like you. We don't have to do anything."

I exhaled loudly. "I like you, too," I said. I placed my hand over my heart. I could feel it beating. I knew where I was. "I can't stay forever, you know, but I don't want to leave just yet." There was a long pause. "I'm sorry," I said. "Everything seems to be coming out funny.

Lee scratched my chin with his thumb affectionately. "You know what?" he asked. "We can read. Let's read something." He clapped his hands together and appeared satisfied with this idea. He leaned over toward the books stacked on his nightstand and picked out *The*

Complete Fairy Tales of Oscar Wilde. He handed it to me.

"Do you want me to read out loud?" I asked, perplexed. The idea seemed bizarre to me and I felt embarrassed. Lee wanted sex, and all I could give him was storytime.

Lee folded his arms across his chest. "I would *love* to hear you read," he said. "Read any one that you want." We sank back onto his pillows together. He put his arm around me. I turned to the first story, "The Happy Prince." I began reading, at first hesitantly. I quickly became engrossed in the story.

The story was about a statue of a prince, the Happy Prince. When the Happy Prince was alive, he was spoiled and knew only pleasure. The statue of the prince gazes upon the city and sees the ugliness and pain he had been sheltered from when he was alive. He sees how the world can sting and bruise. He sees how people get stung and bruised, and how they continue. The prince starts to give up pieces of himself—the ruby from his sword-hilt, the sapphires that are his eyes. He gives up one eye, and then the other.

A sparrow assists the prince in everything, and the bird loves him with a love that is both tender and melancholy. .

'You are blind now,' [the sparrow] said, 'so I will stay with you always.'

'No, little Swallow,' said the poor Prince, 'you must go away to Egypt.'

'I will stay with you always,' said the Swallow, and he slept at the Prince's feet.

As I read these words, tears started down my face. I read about the prince giving up his coat of gold: *'I am covered with fine gold' said the Prince, 'you must take it off, leaf by leaf, and give it to my poor; the living always think that gold can make them happy.* I thought about how love rendered the prince and the sparrow bigger and smaller at the same time, sadder and more beautiful. And how love, or at least the love I had experienced up until that point, was always a little bit sad for me. I wondered if it would continue to be like that. There are so many tiny ways in which we cross paths and yet miss each other. As I read to Lee, our bodies felt closer together, even though we had not moved much. It was as if we shared limbs and a secret code was pulsating between us.

When we kissed it was like catching a firefly in a jar and then letting it go.

The Road to Rehoboth
Stephen Greco

When I arrived at Cornell in 1968, a small-town kid from a modest family, I wasn't exactly literate. I knew more about music and art than I did about books, and had signed up to study architecture, which at that school and at that time did not require one to read very much literature. There was no time for reading, anyway. There were lectures on Rome to attend and statues of Hercules to sketch. And during the hours and hours of studio time that were required of architecture students, there were concepts to diagram, site conditions to discuss, and even buildings to draw—not to mention all the other college town diversions that an undergraduate, on his own for the first time ever, wanted to pursue. Then there were the revolutionary sentiments that were combusting all over campus that year, which wound up shutting down the university after militant black students seized the student union, armed with guns. The result was all-day sessions of a hastily contrived student-faculty congress in Barton Hall, the cavernous field house, during which the value of knowledge itself was debated with much electronically amplified shouting, while outside, in the main quad, members of a local natural foods collective sold plates of carrot stew for whatever people could afford.

"The faculty voted that this thing they called a principle was worth more to them than a black life—that's no surprise to us," intoned black student leader Tom Jones, in a rousing speech heard by thousands. It was that kind of time. Righteous words carried real power and changed lives. I felt instantly radicalized. And that was when I fell for an adorable New York City boy with longish hair and

The Road to Rehoboth

a breathy voice, named Barry.

The first time I saw him he was dancing—hopping around to some *paidushko* or *chope* with appealing masculine grace, dressed in the era's regulation cotton flannel shirt, probably vintage. The shirt, I believe, was open. I had been taken to the university's semiweekly folk dance that afternoon by my friend Ellie, the first girl I ever knew who wore peasant skirts, made her own earrings, and added her own raisins, nuts, and honey to plain yogurt. Ellie and Barry were friends; she told me he was a liberal arts student who was pursuing an independent major because he'd been such a star in high school. Among the things I learned from Barry that day, as we walked back to Ellie's house for dinner, was that he knew lots about Old English and something of *new* English, too—the glamorous-sounding world of ideas represented by a publication he pulled out of his bag, that I'd never heard of, called the *New York Review of Books*.

"Gore Vidal is such a genius," said Barry, showing me a piece on Nixon or maybe on pornography, or maybe both. I hadn't realized Vidal was a writer. He had run, a few years earlier, for a congressional seat in the district where I grew up, in upstate New York.

Barry seemed so much smarter than the smarty-pants architects I knew, so much worldlier and thus, of course, sexier. He and I walked hand in hand that afternoon, not because we were gay, but because this was the late '6os and times were changing and men could do that if they wanted. That night we slept side by side, fully clothed, on Ellie's floor. I remember feeling close to something extraordinary.

In fact, Barry was not gay, not yet. At the time, he had a girl-friend—a large girl I remember as Lorraine Bracco-ish—while I, on the other hand, was as out as could be and had known for years what I was and was happy about it, though at first I didn't know the word for it. A reproduction of Pollaiuolo's *Battle of the Nudes* in the family ency-clopedia had set me, as a child, on a course of secret research that led to unauthorized visits to the adult section of our little town library, which turned up plenty of words for what I was, though most of them, I knew even then, belonged to a system that needed rethinking. By the time I met Barry I was finding plenty of sex in campus men's rooms and enjoying it immensely, though I despaired of ever finding love among the guys I was meeting there or even among Cornell's newly formed Student Homophile League, where nerdy fellows co-ran spirited meetings and formulated illuminating critiques, but didn't impress me as candidates for happily-ever-after prince.

Barry, on the other hand, *was* my prince—I knew it the minute we met. And patiently, as we got to know each other, he introduced me to his version of literacy. He couldn't believe that I pontificated easily on subjects like the architectural superiority of Boromini over Bernini, yet knew nothing of *Bleak House, Emma,* and *Vanity Fair,* nothing of *Madame Bovary, Crime and Punishment, Death in Venice.* He lent me copies of all these works, but I didn't read them. There didn't seem to be time—what with all the political demonstrations and social reform planning sessions that occupied a large part of our dating.

Barry only asked that we proceed slowly with whatever it was we were doing together. The first physical moves took place in his room in the Prospect of Whitby, the solid old sorority house where he lived, which had been transformed into a sort of commune where the coed residents shared the responsibility, if not always the actual tasks, of cooking and cleaning. His room was on the third floor and boasted, if I recall correctly, a wall hanging in the form of a black-and-red Mexican bedspread decorated with Mayan motifs. The bed—a single, of course—was tucked into a narrow slot beneath a dormer window. As daylight flooded over us, we lay there kissing and talking one spring afternoon, the day after he'd returned from a month in Turkey—sharing stories and sharing breath, and, really, making each other breathless.

"Mmm," he said.

"Mmm," I said.

"Like that?"

"Mm-hmm."

I remember thinking that we were talking more during kissing than I had done with other men—a good sign. Then there was a special glow about him that day—enhanced by a beamy smile, the luxuriant

The Road to Rehoboth

hair that had been lightened by the Anatolian sun (he'd later go bald and look magnificent that way), and that tight, tanned chest beneath a clingy shirt of white gauze he'd bought in Izmir.

Lorraine Bracco's arrival in the front hall was announced by the barking of Whitby's dogs. Then someone shouted that she was on her way up. By the time Lorraine reached the third floor, Barry and I had composed ourselves and were sitting on the edge of the bed.

"Hi," said Lorraine, cheerfully. She dressed somewhat less counterculturally than the rest of us, I noticed.

"Hi," I said, rising to my feet.

"What'cha doin'?" she asked Barry.

"Talking about Turkey," he said, slipping his arm around her waist. Somehow I knew I needn't bother being jealous. The taste of the man's tongue was still in my mouth.

Over the next week or so, Barry and I progressed from kissing, to lying-and-napping-together-in-underpants-with-no-touching-down-there, to touching down there, and then to sex. The latter first took place while Lorraine was away visiting family. I don't think Barry and I had planned anything specific. We drove up to Cayuga Lake in my beat-up Dodge Dart for dinner at a vegan restaurant, then went back to my place. At the time I had an apartment, farther off campus in Cayuga Heights, in a glamorous but slightly ram-shackle house that dated from the 'teens, when *The Perils of Pauline* was filmed in Ithaca and the Heights burgeoned as a rustic sort of Hollywood. Again Barry was wearing a plaid flannel shirt, but this time, as I showed him to my bedroom, I was allowed to put my hand inside it. His chest was hard and the hair light, as I suspected. His nipples were small and flat, a type I'd never fancied but suddenly found heavenly. Soon, clothes were off and cocks were in mouths.

"Let's get a little sixty-nine going," said Barry, after we'd fooled around for a little while. I was charmed, again, that he made the sug-gestion verbally.

I climbed around and we went at it for a few minutes, until I threw up—all over Barry's cock and belly: sautéed vegetables, brown rice, apple strudel, local chardonnay. Laughing, we showered and

84

gargled, then went back to bed, where we made love and slept in blissful patches until morning.

The kitchen in that apartment was like something out of a movie—a sprawling layout, a wood-beamed ceiling, lots of nooks and crannies meant to add warmth to family life. And because architecture students prided themselves on recontextualizing their living spaces, even the lowliest dorm room, I'd upholstered the cushion of the window seat with an old drab-brown blanket, for a modern, neutral look, and installed a four-foot-high sculpture of crumpled, chrome car fenders on a pedestal next to the breakfast nook, which featured quaint diamond-paned windows. The sculpture was some fine arts student's discard, I told Barry, over slices of brown bread with apple butter.

"A discard?" he said. "You didn't steal it?"

"No!"

"But the pedestal?" It was a massive wooden thing, complete with plinth and capital, that I'd painted white.

"Well, that I may have borrowed from Franklin Hall."

"Borrowed."

"Stuart, the blond guy you met the other day, stole a six-foot color field painting from Franklin last fall and cut it into pieces for his roommates."

"Is that the gay guy?"

I didn't know how to respond. Stuart was another architecture student—not only gay but rich and flamboyant. Before I could say anything, Barry continued.

"Sorry, that came out wrong. I'm gay too, aren't I?"

"Are you?" I said it casually, but felt my whole life was hanging in the balance.

"Gay," he mused. The word seemed to sound new to him.

"You okay with that?"

"Absolutely. It's the coolest thing that ever happened to me."

And Barry proceeded to go about being gay in a totally gung ho way. Overnight, he became a coming out machine. We may all have been a bit like that then, and our friends couldn't accept him and

The Road to Rehoboth

me as a couple enthusiastically enough. Though we had different sets of friends, and were, in fact, from two distinct campus cultures—the scholars of the liberal arts school and the princes of architecture school, many of whom I saw now as "differently literate"—Barry and I had the habit of communication between us, as part of the joy of getting to know a first lover. Campus was ablaze that spring with the energy of communication—people sharing discoveries about themselves with each other. The relationship Barry and I had then often felt like a negotiation—and maybe our willingness to negotiate would have been enough for us to succeed as a couple. God knows, relationships have been built on less. Yet soon we would be blessed with much more.

A month later, we decided to join our friends Sarah and Philip on a road trip to Rehoboth Beach in Delaware. The trip would mean several hours in Philip's ancient and rattly (but now, as I think of it, completely mythic) customized Volkswagen van—a vehicle whose pillow-and-blanket-strewn rear salon, which Barry and I occupied, felt limitless with spots to sit and stow things and kiss in the sunlight, when, as during fair weather, we would roll back the retractable roof. For the trip Barry brought along plenty of reading material, which happened to include a book about literary translation, entitled *Proteus: His Lies, His Truth*, by Robert M. Adams. Though I knew little of James Joyce, whose novel *Ulysses* was the focus of Adams's book, I did know something of John Milton, whom the author also discussed, and that got me hooked.

Paradise Lost had always been a kind of symbol of adulthood to me, since the time when, as a child of maybe ten, I had found a battered copy in my grandmother's garage, along with decommissioned appliances, demoted crockery, and a can of still-liquid gold paint I was told a deceased uncle of mine had mixed years before, as a boy. The book was as seductively mysterious as the paint. *Cool,* I thought. *A vast poem with a sort of science fiction-y title. I'll bet nobody in Mrs. Hannan's class knows about that.* When I asked my grandmother if I could have the book, she said yes—proud, I suppose, that her grandson might be interested in such stuff. But then the book sat on my shelf for years.

Milton was hard to read! I tried again and again. Even the first few lines confused me, a fact that continued to surprise and, really, insult me, as I grew older, but also gave me a kind of challenge. I was certain I'd be able to understand the poem someday, when I became an adult.

And then I took the book to college, where it continued to sit on a shelf. I just couldn't make sense of the language.

> Of Man's First Disobedience, and the Fruit
> Of that Forbidden Tree, whose mortal taste
> Brought Death into the World, and all our woe,
> With loss of Eden, till one greater Man
> Restore us, and regain the blissful Seat,
> Sing Heav'nly Muse, that on the secret top
> Of Oreb, or of Sinai, didst inspire
> That Shepherd, who first taught the chosen Seed,
> In the Beginning how the Heav'ns and Earth
> Rose out of Chaos: Or if Sion Hill
> Delight thee more, and Siloa's Brook that flow'd
> Fast by the Oracle of God; I thence
> Invoke thy aid to my advent'rous Song,
> That with no middle flight intends to soar
> Above th' Aonian Mount, while it pursues
> Things unattempted yet in Prose or Rhyme....

Forget "Oreb" and "Siloa." How to parse the first few lines? "Of Man's First Disobedience...." Did they comprise a statement? A question? I seem to remember forcing myself, as a teenager, to scan, if not actually read, the first few books of the poem, and that way, perhaps, I acquired some rudimentary, abstract sense of its content—the way a dog might watch TV and somehow grasp that the anchor of a news show was a human being. But I understood little more of *Paradise Lost* until that day on the road to Rehoboth, in the back of the van, when I picked up the Adams, with Barry asleep next to me, and began reading about the challenges of translating Milton—a task, said

The Road to Rehoboth

the author, that required an understanding of how the poet's intention and chosen structure worked together.

He described sprung syntax, for example. I thought, *Hmm, now that sounds interesting.*

Of Man's First Disobedience... Sing Heav'nly Muse...

Oh—"sing" is a predicate! "Disobedience" is the object; "heavenly muse," the subject. The scale of the expression helps express the magnitude of the idea. This I could understand. The poem was about exactly what I had hoped it was about: Satan's vengeful mischief, the fall of Adam and Eve, the prospect of human redemption. But there was more to it than plot. Suddenly Milton felt lucid. Now, not only syntax, but other aspects of the poem and poetry itself felt available to me.

I read for hours, while Barry slept. It was too noisy to converse with Philip and Sarah, up front. Eagerly I consumed the rest of Adams's book and when Barry woke up I engaged him with a bundle of questions about Milton, whom I knew he'd studied.

"I had no idea you were interested in that kind of stuff," he said.

"I had no idea that words could provide this kind of pleasure," I said.

"Well, hello."

"Seriously. No one told me that there was the least thrill involved. Reading in high school was always a matter of learning the so-called 'meaning' and deriving some kind of lesson."

"Consider us even," said Barry. "You gave me something pretty terrific, too." His smile was always sly and seductive.

I think it was this connection between us around Milton, on that trip, as much as the exciting bouts of on-the-road sex—the greedy pleasure of licking nipples and rubbing cocks together, under a ratty blanket in the back of the van, while Philip or Sarah drove—that started us thinking seriously about a long-term relationship.

The moment we returned from Rehoboth I took *Paradise Lost* down from my bookshelf and started reading it—perhaps for the first time really reading anything. I think it took me a month to get through the thing, and I'm sure I stole time away from drawing buildings in order to do so. At the same time, I embarked on a crash course in the rest of world literature, asking everyone I knew, friends and professors alike, for top-ten lists, which I started ticking off with robotic diligence. I picked up *Bleak House* and wept at the death of Jo. I picked up *Crime and Punishment* and trembled in fear of justice with Raskolnikov. And periodically I shuddered at my own naiveté and the ludicrous thought that I had reached that far in my life having acquired bits of knowledge about Baroque churches and Bartok quartets, but nothing about Becky Sharp.

For me, it was great that the university collapsed when it did. It gave me time to fall in love and let love educate me. Afterward, the idea of designing a presidential complex for an emerging African nation seemed far less urgent than figuring out and being who I really was, which naturally involved making lots of love with my boyfriend and reading everything I could get my hands on—all of which led to my giving up architecture and beginning to write poetry. Which led, a few years later, once my stuff started getting published, to moving with Barry to New York, where we both became editors of the program magazine for Lincoln Center and Carnegie Hall, and eventually met James Baldwin, Allen Ginsberg, Richard Howard, Ned Rorem, and a host of others who became our models for the gay man of letters.

So began a period in my life that was a kind of paradise found. And though Barry died thirteen years after that, the paradise endures. His spirit is with me whenever I am reading or writing. I feel it almost physically. It is with me even now, as I write these words—the young folk dancer reading over my shoulder, breathing down my neck....

Telling Stories
Steve Nugent

When my third novel flamed out I tripled the martinis for a few weeks and then called on my editor John Stay.

"It's to be expected," he said. "I was surprised that the firm took it on at all. There's no-go on print porno right now."

"It wasn't all porno. There was some good stuff about relationships in it."

"Same difference."

He took another gulp of bottled water, carefully replacing the cap and storing it in his top drawer.

I didn't want to argue. I was in his hands. He was my only chance for the next try. "So what do you think I should do now, John?"

"A change from what you were doing."

"I know that, but what else is possible? You know the score. I don't want to hear again that what I do is flooding the market, or is done better online."

"Tell you what Mike—I'll give it some thought mixed with a little contact with a few people who are in the know about the next wave 'n' rave. I'll call you in a week or so."

I hung around doing little until John called me.

"I heard about a writer called Jorge Calvo. Do you know him?"

"No."

"He's one of these eccentric type guys, lives in Toronto but seldom leaves his apartment. He's written only one book, a kind of memoir about his family that a few of the critics loved, but it fell out of the sellers quickly. It's called *The Time of One's Life*. Know it?"

"Never heard of it."

Telling Stories

"Read it, and get back to me. We might be onto something."

I read it and got back to him.

"It's about this family in Buenos Aires with a ranch on the pampas. It's an Argentinean cliché. He's the wealthy only son, English-type schooling, incredibly handsome, girls of good families for marriage, sluts for sex. He lays on the Spanish atmosphere, writes with a lot of intensity, sifting through the family interaction. I didn't think it was that interesting. But then it's not quite my genre, as you would say."

John ignored me and rushed into his proposition.

"Since people are all hyped up by true stories these days, why don't you ferret this guy out and find out what makes him tick?"

"And write a novel about him?"

"No. A bio."

"But hasn't he done that already if he's written a memoir?"

"He evaded the press like the plague after the book came out so I reckon he has some things to hide. Check it out with him."

His number was unlisted but it wasn't too difficult to find his address after making a few inquiries with his publisher—or rather with somebody I knew who worked there and owed me.

He lived in a tired-looking, chipped-paint rental apartment block on the west side of town. I buzzed the number on the plate.

"Yes?"

"I'm Michael Dunbar, a writer, and I'm interested in meeting you."

I expected him to shut me out but he said, "Why do you want to see me?"

"I can explain more if I can talk to you."

He hesitated long enough for me to think he had walked away.

"Okay. Come on up. Sixteen-oh-six."

I could feel he was watching me through the peephole before he opened the door. I put myself squarely in his vision. A moment later the door swung open.

His face was carved from mahogany, his arm in a sling. He waved it in my direction.

"Sorry to greet you like this but I had a little accident."

The accent was Hispanic, deep toned, lathered in sensual slur, and delivered with a heavily lidded gaze. I took another look at his body and saw that what showed through the polo shirt resulted from some heavy gym work. When he turned to close the door his butt took a global shape. *Another hot-looking Mediterranean guy in my life,* I thought, *that's all I don't need.*

"What is it that you want from me?"

"I'm interested in your story and would like to write more about you in a short biography."

"You are, of course, joking," he said, his chestnut-brown eyes widening.

"No, I'm truly in earnest."

"I have written my memoirs. They tell all there is to tell."

"My editor suspects that you didn't tell all and that an independent piece would be revealing."

"Your editor is quite wrong. All that I wrote in my book is true. I think that it is wrong for you to come here and accuse me of not being truthful. This is the first such accusation that has been made against my book."

"What is there may be true, but what is not there?"

He looked puzzled, then gestured for me to sit down in a large overstuffed, multicushioned couch. I subsided into it while he sat opposite me. He ran his eyes over me for a while, and then began to speak.

"My father was a member of Isabel Perón's government. He was one of the *desaparecidos* who vanished during the dirty war when I was only six years old. It was a terrible time for my mother. I married my childhood sweetheart, joined the Argentinean army school and graduated as an officer."

"I don't recall reading this in your memoir," I interrupted. He smiled patronizingly and continued.

"I revealed the continuity of my life after the army as a businessman who made a lot of money in the ups and downs of the Argentinean economy."

I looked around his apartment.

"Perhaps you didn't include all of the downs?" He flinched, and

Telling Stories

quickly stood up.

"I don't think this is getting us too far, Mr. Dunbar. Perhaps you should go."

He was opening the door as I struggled out of the cushions. "Thank you for coming."

I dropped my card on the coffee table. I hadn't gotten a chance to ask about the arm sling. I called John's office and left a voice mail telling him that it wasn't the season for hunting recluse. A few days later I thought the mild voice on the phone was a solicitor.

"Mr. Dunbar? If you are still interested in seeing me I am available."

This time the sling was gone. He looked a lot more relaxed—like he might have had a toke. I was in the couch again and he sat at the other end of it, turned toward me. His voice was huskier.

"I'm sorry for my behavior when you were here last. When my past is challenged I get tense and it shows itself in anger. I suppose it is my hot blood."

I wanted to keep him in a good mood. "I understand fully, Jorge."

"Thank you. It is Michael, is it not?"

"Yes, it is."

"My true name is Pablo. I assumed the name Jorge after I left the ranch and came to live in Ricoleta, which is a part of Buenos Aires. Have you ever been there?"

"Sorry to say—no."

"It is a city of many diversions and personalities, which suited my purpose at the time."

"And what was your purpose, Pablo?"

"I wanted to escape."

"From?"

"The owner of the ranch."

"Your father?"

"No."

"In your book you claim that your family owned the ranch."

"That was not true. Escobar Gardel was the owner. I was sixteen then."

I didn't want to ask any more questions, though they were jumping at me. He seemed to be on the edge of something. I waited, gazing at him. He glanced at me, twisting his fingers, his face craggy and tired.

"I have said enough. I would like you to leave."

I wanted more. He might be playing with me, but this story could really pay off; I couldn't afford to lose out by being too pushy. At the door he said softly that he would like to see me again. His body inclined toward me. I could smell his spicy skin. I backed away, uncertain of his intent.

"Okay. I'll leave it up to you to call me when you feel ready."

He seemed pleased by that. Grasping my shoulder, he held it for a moment, then quickly turned and opened the door. On the pavement I realized that his body was becoming as interesting to me as his story.

By the time I got home he had left a message. Could he see me again, perhaps the next day? I felt I was on a merry-go-round but couldn't get off it.

I wasn't prepared for all-out seduction; men who looked like Pablo usually didn't have to work too hard to get me. As soon as I arrived the dance was on: his cinnamon-colored shirt gaped open to show edges of smooth defined pecs; there was a suspicion of a bulge in the white linen pants.

Sunk in the couch while Pablo moved sexily up and down the room, his ass moving rhythmically, I tried to divert my mind from what could happen between us.

"So what did you do on the ranch?"

"I looked after the horses. I was a gaucho, the illegitimate son of a former owner and his maid. She worked in the house until I was fourteen and she left without telling me. Then my relationship with Escobar Gardel started—against my wishes. I was a proud and honest boy but he harassed me perpetually until I surrendered to him. I had to endure many years of sex with him. He took me as he pleased,

Telling Stories

until I, like my mother, fled to the city."

"Why are you telling me all this now?"

"Because I trust you."

"I don't understand. You're telling the truth to someone who may expose the lies in your memoir. You will be seen not as that romantic macho man you painted in your book, but as a phony gay adventurer."

He winced at "gay adventurer," then stood looking out the window.

"You can do what you will with my story. I want to be honest with you," he said without turning. "I am telling you all this because I find you very attractive."

I knew what was coming and welcomed it, so when he turned to see what effect his words had had, I was already on my feet and moving to him.

"So you would tell me all this to get my sexual attention?"

"More than that. I need your love."

"It wouldn't be difficult to fall in love with you," I whispered, already sensing the words that he wanted to hear, that would arouse him even more. I moved closer to him; my hands roamed beneath his shirt feeling his warm moist skin, my mouth pressed into his neck; his scent was like a halo around him. I undid his fly and my hands moved down to his crack, parting his asscheeks and fingering his soft oozing cunt. He moaned my name, kicked off his pants, and pulled me to the floor on top of him, clinging to me, kissing me wildly until he turned over, spread his legs, and slid my cock into his crack. I fucked him hard and fast while he urged me on, pushing his body up to me and grasping my cock in his pulsing ass muscles until he came, bucking, draining me at the same time.

After all that he kissed me gently.

"That was so beautiful for me," he said in his breathy tone. "I hope that you found it the same." I'd have said anything then. I wanted more of him.

"Yes, it was amazing. This is just the beginning," I whispered.

John was impressed. I knew he'd pant for more information but I teased him without giving him all the details.

"You'll be on a winner if you can really pull this off, Mike. You know how people love an exposé. Just get the full story from him—we're talking the full treatment, nothing less. It's a book, not a news item."

I met Pablo at his apartment twice after that. He'd give me some new details—how he had eluded Escobar Gardel and the thugs who were sent to kidnap him after he left the ranch; how he had been befriended by an older woman whom he had escorted to Europe—then we'd have sex. The third time I returned, there was no reply. I repeatedly buzzed. I phoned. Nothing. After a few days I went to the super, who told me he couldn't give information about the tenants. I told him that my mother had a rare medical condition and that Pablo, an old family friend, might be able to help her as they shared the same rare blood type. If I was looking for Esteban Marques in 1606, the super told me, shaking his head, he had left a week ago, his lease expired.

John was pissed. "Fuck ! You don't have nearly enough for a book. Get another angle."

I nixed the possibility of doing more P.I. work to find Jorge/Pablo/Esteban, and decided to try writing a gay romance set in a resort in Cabo San Lucas with the usual cast of characters fucking and falling in love at first sight. By chapter five I knew I had once again come to a dead end, unable to create anything fresh. I decided what I needed was a break. I headed for New York to see a former lover, Tom, who had settled down with a new partner, Joshua, a feature writer at one of the New York dailies. They had an apartment on West Twenty-third, and on the first night, being relaxed and happy after some booze and tokes, we went out to an uptown bar. As we walked in Joshua looked around, turned to Tom, and grinned.

"Hey! This is where I met that weird guy from Argentina last summer."

"What guy?" Tom quickly asked.

"It was just before I met you," Joshua assured him. "I don't remember his name: he was probably in his forties, great face, hot body. He came on to me and told me that he found me very attractive and wanted to get to know me better. He was cute, so I went with it. When he heard that I worked for one of the dailies he said he had written some book about his life on a ranch—in Argentina, I think. The book had hit the bestseller lists, he told me, but most of it was fake—he was actually a mestizo born in Paraguay who became a well-known porno actor until he was threatened with death by a religious group. I remember that he said he had later married a beautiful girl who died when giving birth to their first child. It all sounded very dramatic. Things got kinda weird quickly. By our second date he said that he was in love with me, that was why he had told me that the book was a scam; if I reported what he'd told me it would be a great scoop for me. It sounded like there might be a story and I got very, very interested, but he never quite told me enough to write about. Strange guy." Joshua rolled his eyes. "But he was real sweet—and I tell ya, very energetic."

"Where did he live?" I asked.

"In the Village—on Bleecker. Over a store. Just a room. When I went there for our third date, I found out he'd moved out the day before."

"SNAP!" I said.

Several months later John called me. "That guy—Pablo, or whatever his real name is—phoned here. He wanted to know if you were around. He wants to see you again. Said he'd call back." I didn't really want to see him but still my dick twitched at the thought of him, and I also wanted to know what his game was.

He was in a rented furnished apartment in the Annex, and he looked just great.

"So what's this all about?"

"I want to tell you the full truth."

"Which truth?"

"The real truth."

I laughed. "Why choose me?"

"I like you."

"You used to love me. Okay, shoot!"

"Nothing that I tell you when we first met was true. I am not from Argentina. I am Mexican, my name is Francisco. My parents were separated and I never knew my father. My mother, a woman left with nothing but determination to make a life for me, moved from Guadalajara to Cincinnati when I was fifteen years old to make some money so that she could bring me there to live with her. I didn't hear from her for over a year so I jumped the border. I was beaten and raped on a rail car by drifters, but I finally found my mother and stayed with her until she died. I got a job as a security officer and spent most of my time writing that story to impress people."

"Which it did. You were almost famous."

He hesitated. Nothing seemed easy for him at that moment. He put his hand on my knee and looked into my eyes. "I swear to God that what I am saying now is true, though you may find it strange. I know I have an interesting story to tell, and a good body. I trade them off for love with people like you. I know what your kind likes and I hold the power to make it happen or to deny it to you. And that excites me. Sex with you was thrilling; I thought you might be different from the others when you sought me out. I told you that I wanted your love—but I never felt it. You faked it and lied to me, hoping to get what you wanted. I did the same."

He leaned toward me. "I realize this search for love is a kind of addiction. I look at my arms and expect to see needle marks." He began to cry.

"I do love you," I lied. I wanted him in his vulnerability, and something about his strange motivation heated me up. I moved my fingers to his face and played them on his lips. He kissed, then sucked them and moved his tongue to my palm. I shifted his hand to my cock and he unzipped me. His tongue tip teased me, his mouth surrounded my cockhead as my hard-on uncoiled; his hand grasped my shaft. He lost no time, fiercely manipulating his tough lean body onto me as if it would never be used again.

I left him sprawled naked, his wet, swollen cock a memory of lust. I was pretty sure I would never see him again. I thought sadly of his fruitless search for love, and of how the many stories of his lives never lived would be related again and again from a repertoire that would never run dry.

Itching to Go
Jim Coughenour

At ten J was easy prey for the filthy minded. Sly sixth-grade allusions to "the birds and the bees" or "the facts of life" slipped past him with the ease of a softball at recess. When the class clown teased him with the question, what starts with *f* and ends with *uck?* J naturally answered, *fuck?*

No, the clown said, *fire truck!*

J's classmates regarded him with the accusing glare of a corral of castrated cattle. He'd been tricked again.

The injustice was that ever since first grade he'd been in the "advanced" class—thanks to his grandmother who'd started him reading storybooks at four. By the second grade he'd discarded the *ménage à trois* of Dick, Jane and Sally for the menagerie of Doctor Doolittle. By the seventh, he'd skipped to the top of the SRA chart and read whatever he wanted. He segued from Steinbeck to Sherlock Holmes, from Lewis Carroll to Camus, with a facility that delighted his English teacher to the same degree that it disgusted the australopithecine who coached phys ed.

J treated all books as entertainment: either they engaged his imagination or they didn't. At the Christian college his parents sent him to, he was surprised to hear himself described as an "intellectual" because he enjoyed Francis Schaeffer, the evangelical author of *The God Who Is There* and *Escape from Reason*. J didn't mention that he'd first read these books under the impression that they were written by a woman with the name of a fountain pen.

Schaeffer was a '70s Savonarola, herding atheist artists and fallen philosophers into his *autos-da-fé*-Picasso, Kierkegaard, Dylan

Itching to Go

Thomas—luminous references that sent J scurrying for the card catalog. Sadly, the library was inadequate to his enthusiasm. The manager of the college bookstore, a starched spinster who perhaps detected in J something of her younger self, came to his rescue, instructing him in the intricacies of *Books in Print*. Soon J was placing orders with the abandon of an addict, and was forced to take a job as a dishwasher to finance his habit. Two or three times a week the spinster would drop a little note in his mailbox. He'd hurry over to her office and pick up his contraband, exchanging with her the smile of those whose sins shimmer with the soft gloss of virtue.

After college J got a job as a hotel desk clerk, giving no more thought to his career than he had to his education. Any job that allowed him to read was good enough. Yet, through a series of abstruse accidents, he ended up in Boston getting a master of arts. Just before graduation, he came out—an announcement that surprised no one but himself.

Of course for J being gay mainly meant reading books about being gay. He scoured the biographies at Glad Day Bookstore in mute rapture, rejoicing in the company of these misfits who'd been as queer and confused as he was. He spent the summer of 1980 loafing in the grass of the quadrangle, intoning Hart Crane, slumming with Christopher and his kind and solving murder mysteries with Dave Brandstetter.

Actual sex was another matter, *cruising* being the concept that eluded him. He had to start somewhere: at the end of June he took the T down to Buddies, an underground disco on Boylston, where he met a fuzzy-haired Jewish guy who, in turn, took him back to his flat on Kenmore Square. The guy couldn't stop laughing when he realized J had never tricked before. J wanted to make out, but the guy had a kiss like a jackhammer and only wanted to snorkel his dick.

Okay, J reasoned, so maybe this wasn't about kissing.

A couple of weeks later at Paradise Café in Cambridge, he met a lanky blond lad who invited him back to his mother's beach house in Gloucester—which sounded romantic enough—but in fact required J to follow the blond in his car thirty miles up the coast. As soon as they'd clambered into bed and exchanged some sloppy kisses, the blond passed out. In the moonlight his mouth hung open, his snore competing with the surf, his white genitals stranded on his thigh like a dead jellyfish. At dawn J drove back across the Mystic River Bridge, resolving never again to trick so far from home.

This is how you learn, he told himself. *This is how you turn yourself into a tragic statistic.*

At the end of the summer J met another guy at Chaps, a tawny athlete who led him back to his loft in the South End. After some preliminary frottage, the guy shoved an amber vial under his nose.

J jumped back. "What the hell is that?"

"Poppers?" the guy said, as if J were brain damaged.

"No thanks," J said. The guy shrugged and settled back to orchestrate his orgasm. J was instructed to shove two fingers up the jock's hard ass while he stroked, inhaled, arched his back, shouted and, finally, spasmed. Transfixed as he was by the ritual, J couldn't help wondering what particulate was lodging itself beneath his fingernails. Clearly he had, once again, misread the moment. J was not a good gay.

By the time J made up his mind to start a PhD at the University of Chicago, it was too late for the fall semester. He'd have to begin in January. In December J toured the frozen precincts of Hyde Park, almost instantly deciding he'd slit his wrists if he had to live down there. The aunt he was staying with in Park Ridge recommended Lakeview, "the area where *all* the artists live." The next day J drove into the neighborhood and looked around. Indeed, the sidewalks flocked with artists—mostly young and male and possessed of a certain ambulatory insouciance. *This is where I'll live,* J decided. *I'm an artist too.*

J spent Christmas week with his parents in Indianapolis, now living alone in their six-bedroom suburban ranch house. The first night after dinner J excused himself by saying he wanted to drive downtown to see the lights. After making the obligatory circuit around the 300-foot-tall "tree" strung from the top of the Soldiers

Itching to Go

and Sailors Monument, he headed over to Hunt & Chase, a three-story gay disco he'd never dared to visit in college. A couple Buds later he was chatting with a sandy-haired nurse slamming down shots. As he'd hoped, the nurse invited him back to his apartment.

At least I'm getting the hang of the "pickup" part, J thought.

J knew he'd made a mistake when the nurse put on Devo and started to strip. "Whip it!" the nurse raved, tearing off his shirt. His thin chest was thick with hair. Off came the pants. J hid his horror behind a smile as the nurse pranced across the room in a pair of black bikini briefs. "Off with them!" the nurse cried, waving his hands at J's corduroys. J undressed as quickly as he could. "Oh look, you're as hairy as I am!" The nurse scrabbled across J like a monkey, grinding against him with the beat. J fell back on the futon, rummaging for a fantasy, anything to make him come and get him out of there.

Twenty minutes later he sped back to the suburbs in his mother's Olds 98, the heat on high, the windows wide open, his chest hair matted with nurse cum.

"Nasty!" he shouted into the night. "Nasty! Nasty!"

With a climate comparable to Siberia, artistic Lakeview soon revealed its seamier side. The area's much-heralded homosexual gentrification had not reached J's block. One afternoon, huddling with his book next to his apartment's archaic gas heater, J heard a bang. He stared dimly out the front window, then returned to *Paradise Lost*. A few minutes later the street outside was crowded with cops. J stood dumbly by his desk as a body got carried to an ambulance from the three-flat across the street. So much for the urban experience.

J's classes were concentrated in the Divinity School, a Gothic monstrosity surrounded by a patch of tundra and denuded trees. The eighty-block journey down to the university was arduous and ugly, whether by train or by bus. The first week he missed his stop and slogged a mile against the freezing wind. He caught the flu. His dry skin itched insanely, despite its daily laminate of Jergens. His inadequate student loan had turned him into a pauper. At night he trod past prostitutes and graffiti to the grocery, where he was depressed by cuts of meat he'd never seen before—tongue, heart, tripe—and even more depressed by the cheap provisions he carried home.

His only solace was in the bags of books he carted home from the Seminary Co-op: textbooks, floppy Penguins, Norton critical editions, anthologies elucidating French structuralism and German hermeneutics. He gorged on them, astonished by everything he didn't know, carefully underlining and annotating. At the end of the day he was dizzy, a dervish in a whirl of *libido sciendi*.

Lust coexisted with his native sense of wonder. As a child, J had envisioned Jesus as a master magician who could turn water into wine or an eyelash into a pony. As J grew older, he'd redefined the terms, moving from magic through myth to "the symbol that gives rise to thought," but his low-grade mysticism persisted. Now he was fascinated with the religious idea itself—the way human imagination constructs "God" and so creates the very thing it worships. In time, of course, he would contract the virus of skepticism, but that devolution lay years ahead.

That first winter in Chicago, as the wind sliced through the mortar of the brick walls and froze the water in his humidifier, J was intoxicated by the *numinous*, the illumination of the world from within. His fundamental axis of perception could shift, he felt, due to the rustle of words in a line of poetry or a few plangent chords, or the slant of sun across the ice. These haphazard epiphanies added the base note to his taste for life, the secret pulse of everything hoped for and everything excused.

J's first visit to the bars of Boystown was a random act of reconnaissance. One evening on his way up Broadway he noticed Victoria's, its name scrawled in girlish neon across a strip of aluminum. He stepped inside and felt every face turn toward him, eyebrows arching, lips assuming the standard moue—receiving an overwhelming impression of queens with high hair and high voices. Whatever he wanted, this wasn't it. He fled.

He sought advice from the bright young homos of the Divinity

Itching to Go

School—a coterie of bespectacled, overeducated boys who saw them-selves as characters in *Brideshead Revisited*. "Dahling," said the Anthony Blanche impersonator, "Bushes is the bar you want. It's hot."

The next weekend J shut his books, put on his Christmas sweater and followed the bar map in *Gay Chicago*. East on Belmont, left at Halsted, past the hooker on Aldine, and there it was—Christmas lights still twinkling in the window, the drum of disco within. He stepped in past the cigarette machine: it was wall to wall with men in sweaters, mustaches and muscles. Everyone looked like each other's cousin.

J bought the first of the two beers he could afford, then made his way to the window at the back of the bar. Outside was a patio with a snow-crested barbecue, all aglitter in fairy lights. J turned back to the room. No one had noticed him.

At least the boys in Bushes were more his type: sturdy Midwestern guys, outgoing and open-faced, handsome in a confident corn-fed way. He could only envy their ease. His sense of isolation mounted by the moment—but he wouldn't run this time. He bought his second beer and settled back by the pinball machine. J hadn't really expected anything to happen, so this was fine. Pointless...but fine.

He focused on two guys leaning together at the end of the bar. The shorter one had a rough angular look—military haircut, stub-ble, square jaw—his dark eyes scanning the room. He was providing a commentary to his companion who looked a bit younger, late twenties maybe, with air-brushed features, lustrous hair, a mouth made for kissing. *It figures,* J thought, *there are only two guys in here who attract me and they're together.*

It took J a minute to register that they were actually looking back at him.

The dark one sported a wicked grin. He crooked his index fin-ger, the way you'd beckon a child, and J responded accordingly, stumbling through the crowd as if he were learning to walk.

"Hi," said the dark one. "I'm Finn. This is my lover, Eric."

"Hey." J introduced himself. "You guys look like you're hav-ing fun."

Why was he talking so loud? *Relax.*

"We are," Finn said. Apparently he did the talking for both of them. "Tonight is our anniversary."

"Oh. Happy anniversary," J mumbled, lifting his Miller High Life.

"We met a year ago tonight in this bar," Finn continued. "It's been a great year. We're still in love, and we are ready to celebrate."

J's brain had turned into a leaking honeycomb—no sooner had he felt flattered that they'd called him over than he felt excluded by their intimacy. He had nothing to offer, he was just some nerd out here on his own... "I'm sorry, what?" Finn had asked him a question.

"I said, who are you? We haven't seen you before and I think we would remember."

"I just moved here a couple weeks ago. This is my first time here."

"What do you do?" Eric's voice was toasty, slightly bored.

"Um, I'm a student. I just started a program at University of Chicago." A *program*? Now he sounded like an alcoholic.

Finn brightened. "I graduated from U of C. I got a degree in anthropology. Are you getting a PhD?"

"That's the idea," J said. He chattered with desperate charm, but what did he want to say? Finn seemed friendly, Eric was openly appraising him.

"The truth is," Finn interrupted, "we came out tonight to give ourselves a present. And we want *you* to be our present."

"Me."

"Yeah," said Eric. "You want to be our anniversary present?"

"Uh, yeah...sure."

Finn set his Heineken on the counter. "Come on. We'll grab a cab."

The cab dropped them off on Beldon Avenue in Lincoln Park. Finn unlocked the front door and gestured them in with a flourish. Low lights in the front room, low expensive furniture, bright paintings everywhere. Eric took the coats and disappeared.

"Make yourself comfy," Finn said. J heard a pop from the far end of the apartment. "Champagne?"

Finn pulled an album from a paper sleeve and set it on the

Itching to Go

turntable. "Coltrane," he said. "*A Love Supreme.*"

J nodded back. He had no idea what Finn was talking about. "I like your art."

"All original," Finn said. "Eric and I have been collecting for about a year."

"I just like the colors," Eric said, coming in with three flutes fizzing on a tray. "Finn's into the theory. And the artists."

J lifted one of the flutes, trying not to spill. These guys were out of his league.

Finn nestled down into the chocolate sofa next to Eric and picked up his champagne. "Hip hip, chin chin," he said.

"Uh...to you guys," J said. "Happy anniversary!" The bubbles effervesced into his brain. He coughed. Hopeless. Finn leaned over Eric for a long wet kiss, then smiled back at J as if to say, *See what I'm sharing with you?*

"Gawd," Eric pushed Finn back, "put something else on. This music is depressing."

J was spread out on a butcher block in the center of the kitchen, his sweater bunched around his nipples, his jeans, socks and boxers in a heap on the floor. Eric stroked and slurped his penis while Finn darted his tongue between his toes.

"*Niiice* feet!" Finn said. "Look, he's even got hair on his toes."

Eric's mouth pulled back, making a pop. A sparkling string of saliva spun from his lips to the head of J's cock. "Mmmm. This is nice too," he said, lowering his head.

J's mind raced like a panicked deer through the woods, breaking branches, crashing through the snow. The moment was hallucinogenic enough without someone sucking his toes.

Eric was lightly stroking the shaft and running his tongue along the base of J's balls. The realization that he'd been stripped and stretched while they remained fully clothed sent a shiver down J's loins.

"Oh Jesus," he said. "I'm gonna come!"

"Come on, soldier," Eric said. "We're just getting started."

An arc of semen landed near the set of knives. Then another.
"Yes!" said Finn. "Now it's my turn."

Around four in the morning they were wrapping up the third
round. The rules of attraction had been established: Finn was into
J, J preferred Eric, and Eric just wanted to go to sleep.

His first three-way was turning into a lot of work. His knees hurt
from crouching over Finn's burnished chest, where he'd been
ordered to shoot. Gazing at Eric's recumbent form (half-asleep
against his overcharged lover), J fantasized flipping him over, violat-
ing him from behind. That worked. A few short spurts, a shudder,
a low shout from Finn—and J was finished. He rolled over Eric to the
far side of the bed, unclenching his knees like an arthritic, his vas
deferens like strings unstrung from a harp. With a little clap Finn
hopped up and scampered off to the bathroom.

"Good night, soldier," Eric said, leaning over him for a kiss.
"Again."

J sensed himself slipping back into shadows of consciousness,
hearing a faint chorus of congratulation humming at the back of his
mind. This had been fun, except—he felt so sticky.

"I could use a shower," he joked.

"We could *all* use a shower," Finn said, marching back into the
bedroom. "Someone's got crabs."

At first J couldn't process what was happening. Eric had leaped out
of bed, Finn was laughing. *Crabs?* Wasn't that something straight guys
got from prostitutes? His mind skittered sideways into another association—a phrase he'd come across in a medieval account of the
murder of Thomas à Becket. When the monks removed the bloody
robe from the martyred archbishop, they discovered his hair shirt,
which was (in the words of the chronicler) *alive with vermin.*

"Crabs?" J croaked. Some part of him had already gotten up,
stumbled across the room and hanged itself.

"Crab lice," Finn confirmed. "They look like tiny crustaceans. I
just picked one off my cock."

Itching to Go

"But…"

"They're so small you don't normally see them. They fix their nits in your pubis, feeding off your blood."

"*Nits?*"

"Eggs. Haven't you been itching?"

"I thought it was dry skin," J said weakly. "I've been using lotion." He flashed on a frantic image of himself at his desk, digging at his crotch in an ecstasy of scratching. In the background he could hear Eric shouting in the shower.

"You need a different lotion," Finn said. "They're a bitch to kill. You'll need a prescription."

J tugged his boxers on, then his T-shirt, trying to cover himself. Eric reappeared, his face a mask of horror in the flickering candle-light.

"I caught them once before from a *very* cute boy on a field trip to Jamaica." Finn laughed. "Eric's never had them. It'll be a good experience for him."

Eric stared at the rug.

"It's no big deal. We'll get some Kwell in the morning. Let's go back to bed, there's no escaping them now." Finn blew out the candles.

A wounded caterpillar, J contracted to the corner of the bed, aching to disappear into the dark. In the chancel at the back of his mind the choir chanted a single word: *Unclean. Unclean.*

That fucking nurse. It had to be the cretin in bikini briefs. Until tonight, that was the only sex J had had for three months. He remembered the disappointing dick—a nasty nubbin in an infested bush.

Both Finn and Eric seemed to be asleep at the far side of the bed. A ghost of winter light etched itself at the edge of the designer blinds.

When he woke again, the bed was empty. Low voices filtered from the kitchen. As he scrambled into his jeans, Finn appeared with a piece of paper. "Here's the number for our doctor. He's gay. Call him, tell him you got the number from me—he'll fix you up."

J jammed the paper into his pocket. "Thanks."

"You'll need to wash your sheets, your towels, everything that's been in contact with your skin." Finn ran his finger up and down J's tummy under his T-shirt. "*So* much hair! You must have a whole zoo nesting in there."

Flay me now, J thought. *Strip the scabrous skin from my flesh.* It was kind— it was *incredible* that Finn treated all this as a joke, but J knew his crime could not be pardoned.

In the kitchen Eric came over and gave him a wee kiss. "Morning," he said. "Coffee?"

"No, thanks." J waved his hands. He'd turned into an untouchable, someone to be shrieked and pointed at.

"I gave you our number too," Finn said. "Give us a ring, okay?"

Ten minutes later J stood on the platform of the Fullerton el, watching the train emerge from its foul tunnel into the weak winter sun. The air was icy but the wind had dropped. Dry bits of snow swirled under the heat lamps. Again he shuddered at the thought of their tongues exploring him, at the idiocy of his hooting laughter. The train rattled to a halt, the doors wheezed open. He stepped inside.

Sweet Nothings
Danny Gruber

I met Tim at a gay men's meeting at the community center near the university campus. I was in my freshman year and he was a grad student, majoring in English Lit. He had been invited to give a lecture and demonstration on massage—sensual massage. There were thirty of us gay guys packed into the tiny room at the Canyon Center. We met every Thursday night, one of us picking a subject to "lecture" on or inviting someone we knew from the gay community to enlighten us in his field of expertise. While Tim was not exactly an expert on massage, he was ghostwriting a book on massage therapy for one of the Phys Ed instructors on campus, which made him fair game for that week's open spot as a guest speaker.

He introduced himself while setting up a portable massage table and selected a volunteer from the audience. All of us were more than willing to get a free massage from this tall, rawboned man with Harry Potter glasses, but he picked a small nelly guy named Dennis to be his guinea pig. Dennis grinned widely at being chosen for the rubdown and quickly stripped off his jeans and tight green T-shirt and climbed up on the table. We collectively drew in our breath as the completely naked Dennis sat facing the audience.

Although when he was clothed you'd never have guessed it, this queeny little guy was one hundred and thirty pounds of muscle and seventy pounds of that was in his nuts. They were large and hung suspended in a big, loose free-swinging bag. I am not a size queen, but I will tell you that I can be impressed. We all were impressed.

Dennis lay prone on the table while Tim poured a thin stream of oil from a plastic squeeze bottle across his chest and down his legs.

Sweet Nothings

We watched as Dennis's flaccid cock slowly started filling up and edged up toward his belly button. There were a few nervous giggles and someone whistled seductively.

"One of the things that can happen during a massage is this," Tim said in an astonishingly deep voice while he grasped Dennis's penis in his fist. "If it's your boyfriend, it's no big deal. If it's a guy that you might not want to have sex with, however, you can use a folded towel as a makeshift covering and simply make the problem go away."

He looked down and gave Dennis's dick a single quick stroke. "Do you require a towel to cover yourself?"

Dennis grinned and shook his head and Tim set the small folded towel aside.

For the next half hour Tim showed us how to work each of the muscle groups and explained how massage can be used for drugless therapy as well as sexual enjoyment. To illustrate his point, he gripped Dennis in his hand again and stroked his shaft slowly, rhythmically. Dennis closed his eyes and let out a low sigh. Even from where I was sitting I could see his balls draw up closer to his body, churning in their silky sack. We sat transfixed as Tim's large hand worked up and down the stiff, oil-slickened dick. Several guys in the group shifted in their seats because of the stiffness in their own crotches. I myself had a dime-sized wet spot in my lap that was spreading across the front of my trousers.

I held my breath and watched, oblivious to the guys around me, as Dennis groaned, thrust his hips into the air once, and jetted several spurts of cum across his belly and chest.

Everybody clapped like we do every week after a presentation, but this week the applause lasted a little longer than usual. It was certainly both more, and at the same time less, meaty than our usual fare.

Two weeks later, Tim became my first official boyfriend. I hounded everyone I knew that knew him until I was satisfied that word of my interest would get back to him. When we first hooked up I knew he was a writer, because he was ghostwriting the massage book, but one thing I didn't know was that he was also a writer in his own right. A romance writer, no less! Yes, those kinds of romance novels with the purple and red covers that you might see in the checkout line at the supermarket.

His real name was Tim but he wrote romance novels for women under the name Karen. I'm not going to mention Tim's real last name or the last name he used when writing as Karen because I still see his books on the shelf when I go into Barnes and Noble. Not that I look for them, mind you, but I do happen to spot his name and a book title now and again. I even pulled one off the shelf once and opened it to a random page and read a few paragraphs. I will tell you his latest title—*Sweet Nothings*—because that pretty much sums up the relationship we had.

Damn shame about him, too. Not that he wrote romances, although that certainly garnered more than one snicker out of my buddies; it was a shame that it didn't last between us, because Harry Potter specs and all, he was still one fine lookin' man.

And he was hung, too. Mule hung. Again, I am not a size queen, but I can be impressed. Unfortunately, he was also a big ol' bottom. The bottom bit might have been okay with me, too, except he wasn't a very good bottom. I'll tell you about our first—and only—attempt at sex and you can decide for yourself.

He had invited me over on a Friday night, which I remember as the beginning of a three-day weekend. I knew when he called that this was going to be the time when we would have sex. We had been out on three or four dates where we went to a movie or had dinner or both, but we'd never slept together. It wasn't that I didn't want to, mind you. For the most part I've usually had sex on all of my first dates, mostly just some oral stuff and a smattering of JO and a lot of kissing. I use the word *date* loosely. Really they were one-night stands, even if we never went all the way. Sure, I could reach into a guy's fly, pull out every inch that made him a man, and proceed to lick him like candy, but that was not sex in my mind.

This time, though, I kept thinking about that massage Tim had performed on Dennis, and I was prepared for a fuck that would rival any ride at Disneyland. To me a fuck would be the ultimate act, the ultimate surrender, and I wanted my first time to be with a guy who had an IQ higher than that of a zipper. I took an extra shower, paying close attention to my butt and dick, cleaning under my loose-hanging

Sweet Nothings

foreskin and plucking the stray hairs off my nuts. I even wore clean underwear. I needn't have bothered!

We had dinner at his place, a basement apartment near the university. I was a little surprised to see a platter with sliced red onions on it when we walked into the small kitchen. I instantly grew paranoid about my breath, but then I figured he would be having onions as well, so maybe the two negatives would cancel each other out.

"What are we having?" I asked.

"Bagels with lox, red onion, avocado and cream cheese. How does that sound?"

To tell the truth, I would never have dreamed of serving a potential boyfriend anything so "cafeteria," although I didn't say that. At least it wasn't a TV dinner in a foil tray. We ate the bagels at a leisurely pace while gossiping about people from the gay community that we both knew. Then we switched to the topic of writing romance novels.

"So you write these books for women?" I asked.

"Yep." He took a large bite of bagel.

"How do you write the love scenes? Have you ever been with a woman? I mean, I don't think I could even begin to describe, uh, how women's bodies are sexually. And you did it so well! Okay, I admit, I went out and bought one of your novels."

I paused for Tim's reaction. He just smiled and nodded in encouragement.

"I think the title was *The Hour of None* and your heroine, Paige, sure was smoldering. I guess I never thought of a gem cutter that way. And when she talked Lincoln into taking a dildo up his ass, and then he rewarded her with a dual orgasm, I felt *myself* getting wet! I think that's the term you used, wasn't it?"

Without waiting for him to respond I quoted: "*She felt the dampness spread across her lap as Lincoln groaned and took another inch of the dildo.* How the heck do you know anything about a woman's body parts—and how her vagina opened like a flower?"

"It's called research," he said, tapping his left temple with a finger. "I write the story I want to tell except for the love scenes, then, after I've done some research, I get drunk and fill in the sex parts."

"You're kidding, right?"

He wasn't.

"I want to get sexual with you. Is that okay?" He leaned across the little table and cupped my face in his two big hands, peering at me through those glasses. I stifled a giggle, trying to picture his heroine, Paige Parsons, responding to this seduction, but I nodded without saying anything. I wanted whatever my author-boyfriend was going to offer.

He led me over to the floor in front of the TV. I was surprised when he popped in a porn video called *Fort Dicks* and then stripped off his shorts and polo shirt and peeled off his underwear. His cock, already stiff and leaking, smacked against his belly, dotting his treasure trail with shiny droplets of pre-cum. He pulled off my shirt, shorts, and underwear and placed his hand on my dick.

In spite of my being disappointed at our not having sex in a real bed, my cock responded to the attention. It's true that a hard dick has no conscience. While I was thinking that the heroines in his novels probably didn't have boyfriends that fucked them in front of the television to a porno called *Fort Dicks,* it appeared that I did. He coated my cock liberally and reached around and applied a generous scoop to his brown hole, working it in for a good minute.

As we crawled into position on the floor he turned and picked up a little brown bottle that had an aroma to it that would melt glass. I later learned from a friend this was called "poppers." He took a couple of deep pulls of the aroma and then stuck his ass in my face and commanded: "Fuck me."

I slowly positioned the head of my cock against his puckered hole and popped it in. Never having actually fucked anyone before, I wasn't sure how it was supposed to feel, but it kind of felt like the head of my dick was numbed. I pushed the rest of it in with a quick motion.

"Jesus Christ!" Tim leaned forward quickly, gripping the sides of his head.

I slowly started to pull out.

"Don't!" he shrieked. "Just give me a fuckin' minute."

I could feel the blush creeping across my cheeks. I waited a minute

Sweet Nothings

and then slowly pulled my cock almost all the way out of Tim's ass, then, just as slowly, pushed it back in. I could feel his body relax beneath me. That was about all I was able to feel. My dick may have been buried in Tim's ass, but my mind was wondering why I was doing this and how he could possibly think it was going to get enjoyable.

Evidently he didn't think so, because he pulled himself from my lap and spun around, pulling the rubber off my cock with a snap. He dropped the condom on the floor next to us and the smell of shit wafted upward. I felt my stomach churn a bit. What would Paige have done?

"Let me show you how you fuck a guy," he said. He leaned over to the television and turned up the volume. The current scene depicted a prison warden being hammered from behind by a prisoner with a very, very big schlong. The warden's butt was bouncing against the thighs of the felon; at the same time he was grabbing his own dick and pounding it furiously.

I sat mesmerized by the scene. I had seen a little porn, sure, but nothing that would have prepared me for the anal scene being played out before me. The warden was crying out from the pain and the prisoner was showing no mercy.

"And THAT is how you fuck another guy."

Tim may have hoped that this was going to be as big an educational success as his massage workshop had been, but it actually had the opposite effect on me. I sat there and stared at the images on the screen without any of it really registering. My dick, meanwhile, drained itself of blood, leaving me feeling very naked, and it, soft and shriveled.

I got up, pulled on my shorts and T-shirt, and located my Birkenstocks under the coffee table. Tim sat and watched me in silence, his own sizable piece of meat having gone soft as well. I gave one final glance at the TV and left without saying another word, and I never talked to him again. Thankfully, I never saw him at the Thursday night men's group again, either.

On the way back to the dorms I replayed the scene with Tim. I knew this would probably be one of those things I would be able to laugh about in a couple of years. In fact, not long after this I had a boyfriend named Brent who made *my* "vagina open like a flower" and it was under his tutelage that I learned the art of being a great bottom as well as what it takes to be a great top.

My tutor was not a writer or even a reader, unless you count newspapers or stroke magazines, but he did make a damn fine lover, which really made the whole Tim affair even stranger than fiction. After all, what could be funnier than a barber who needs a haircut, a dentist with dentures, or a doctor whose kids were always sick?

Or a romance writer who has no clue what it means to be sexy, sensual, or a compassionate lover. Though he did know how to give a decent massage.

Something about Wittgenstein
Van Scott

N.

When I passed him on the street he was speaking in that appealing way of his, waving his hands in front of his face, yellow hair streaming out from his head. I imagined he was talking about something utterly quotidian, something along the lines of finding food and lodging, or which train to take to Bergen and how to escape harassment by the authorities. Imagine my surprise when I heard the name of a certain noted thinker temporarily filling the air. He was speaking with another like himself. This other looked far worse than he; he also seemed lost in his own poetic reverie, his hair too was matted with bits of material sticking out of it. His face seemed blackened as if with coal, probably from not having been washed for weeks. Both inspired a touch of envy in me, particularly as I was on my way to work; I was going to catch the train to my office. Wittgenstein, I think I heard him say as I passed him on the street, which seemed inconceivable coming from the mouth of a blond urchin who seemed barely past the age of eighteen. What struck me most was the look on his face: it was a face inhabited by ideas. An expression of thorough contemplation and whimsy sat there, as if he got the joke about discussing the products of cultured minds while being in the gutter. I very badly wanted to talk to him, to invite him out for a cup of coffee, to make an inquiry into his life and thoughts. He lived on the street, scrounging crumbs from trash bins; I once caught sight of him emptying the soiled contents of a bakery bag into his fresh mouth. Heroin chic was in that year, and he fitted the mold perfectly. Although he was filthy, one couldn't mistake his beauty, with

Something about Wittgenstein

days' growth of stubble giving his face a rough-hewn quality, accentu-
ating the planar rise of his cheekbones. Admittedly, I'd passed him
several times on the street, with the most intense interest and the most
careful observations. I formerly thought he might be a bit of an imbe-
cile, because he was barefoot when I first laid eyes on him. This struck
me as definitely out of place in the city. He'd gazed back at me then.

Chance had it that I found him standing on line in a patisserie,
looking unshaven and bereft. He apparently took pride in being able
to buy a cup of coffee for himself. Because I was ahead of him in line
I had to think of something so I spilled some loose change all over
the floor. As coins rolled in all directions I found myself scrambling
needlessly at his feet. Can you lift your foot? I asked politely. He
looked down and lifted his foot; for all his worries he seemed indifferent to my gratuitous groveling. I noted the red lace that bound his
boot together; a very worn boot it was, with frayed tongues of
leather. I could smell the unmistakable odor of his body too,
unadulterated by perfumes or soap or even the application of a
washcloth. I quickly ordered a latte and lingered while it was prepared. When his turn came, he ordered a coffee, black with no
sugar. At the last second, when his blackened fingers were placing his
few coins on the counter, I slid a bill across the surface. For a split
second I thought I saw something indiscreet come into his eyes. He
thanked me with a shy nod, averting his eyes quickly. God forbid I
should think I could actually buy a part of him.

I sat beside him on a stool at the counter. He was obviously hungry, making do with the coffee. His bare kneecap jutted from a not
unfashionable rip in the leg of his jeans, which gaped widely, allowing the viewer a glimpse of still-tanned thigh. I told him I'd seen
him before, on the street in fact, talking with "a fellow traveler." You
mean a bum, he said. Before he could say anything further I said I
couldn't help but notice you were speaking about Wittgenstein.
Wittgenstein? he asked. Yes, I said, burning my mouth on the latte.
You were talking with your carefree friend about matters of philosophy it would seem... Wittgenstein? he asked. The man, I said. The
thinker. Almost saying out loud—the homosexual—but thinking bet-

ter of it. He sat silently over his coffee. *The Blue Book,* I said. Have you read it? He remained grimly silent. No private languages, I said. The world is a word game. The set of its rules is...

The gloomy look in his eyes made my heart sink. It was evident that what lay in my wallet would far better serve his needs. Would you like something to eat? I asked. He glanced at his dirty fingers, holding the handle of the cup tentatively outward, the little pinkie separated from the rest. His eyes cast about for the menu that hung on the back wall of the café. Not this place, I replied. I have something better in mind.

I asked for nothing in return, though I am by nature thrifty, conservative, and a bit of a cheapskate.

The brunette behind the counter catalogued our departure, judging by the vulgar expression on her face as she watched us leave. As for myself, my eyes were on his ass moving stealthily beneath filthy denim. Score one for the gentleman in the velvet coat, I mentally noted. He carried a small satchel against his right shoulder and wore a battered leather jacket whose original color was left to the imagination. He appeared more vulnerable out on the street as he awaited further instruction. It was clear he was in need of simple fare. I queried as to the cuisine he preferred but his only response was a word that sounded to my ear like *pits* but was actually *pizza.* As it was too early for that kind of food I suggested a small café that served Italian. We found the place and sat down at a small table, where we carried our conversation further. Perhaps you could tell me a little bit about yourself, I said. Do you go to school? I read books, he said, looking about him. But you've quit school. Something like that, he said. And you've read Wittgenstein? I asked. He wrinkled his nose in disgust, whether at the mention of Wittgenstein I wasn't certain. He seemed to be eagerly awaiting the food and kept turning his head in the direction of the waiter. When it came finally, he shoved as much of it in his mouth as he could, saying I don't give a fig's ass about Wittgenstein. Then: it seemed he didn't like people very much. Yes, I said, placing a glass of red wine to my lips. He was some kind of inventor, I think. A designer of airplane wings, I volunteered. And

Something about Wittgenstein

Derrida? I asked. Have you read him? Derrida? he asked, wrinkling his nose again. I prefer Lacan. But then you haven't read Derrida? I asked. He grunted, in between attempts at plying his mouth with yet more food. It took me a while before I got around to asking him if he'd like to come over to my place. "To get cleaned up," I suggested.

G.

I met this guy on the street today. The first thing I thought was, He wants to screw me.

I'd seen him before. You couldn't mistake the velvet jacket and the awful sunglasses. What he wanted with my ass I had no idea. Of course it all boils down to that in the end. The meat-rack. He pretended he wanted to talk about Wittgenstein, and to get my attention he dumped a handful of coins at my feet. I knew I had it coming when he practically licked my boot while he was crawling around on the floor. Then he bought me a cup of coffee. Before I knew it he was buying me lunch, and I stuffed myself on whatever I could get my hands on. All the while he kept on about Wittgenstein, even asking me about the other philosophers, you know, the French ones (the only interesting ones as far as I'm concerned). I wasn't really in the mood to wax philosophical and I said so. His hard-on was obviously making him desperate; he kept looking at my kneecap, then checked out my ass, even while I was sitting. I knew I had to placate him, so I told him some boring story about being remotely related to Wittgenstein—you know, a nephew's nephew. Idiot that he was, he'd never heard of Thomas Bernhard, so he didn't get the joke, but I bet he'd heard of Steve Forbes (or was it Malcolm Forbes?). He drank a lot of wine and started to make passes at me from across the table. At one point he broke off a piece of bread and shoved it in my mouth. I don't know what his thing was. With all the money he had, and he positively stank of it, he must have been pretty secure. Having a guy suck my prick isn't exactly my bag, but these days if such a thing should happen, I might just look the other way. When he babbled on about Wittgenstein, talking about private language, even intimating that the guy had been queer (first I heard of it), I jumped on the bandwagon and said up front: So you're looking for sex. It was more of a question. Dessert had arrived. His mouth dropped open, and his eyes lit up. He let his fork fall into his Napoleon, and for a moment he just stared. He was going to come out with a proposition, I was waiting. He apologized, as if he had to cover for my indiscretion. What makes you think I want to do that? he asked, carefully avoiding the word *screw*. He didn't say anything after that, just paid the check, then invited me to his place, "to get cleaned up."

When we passed the doorman on the way in, he put a pile of books in my hands (did I mention that he was carrying books?), as if I were his flunky. He was an editor of one of those pretentious magazines, fashion, pop culture, it's all the same to me. My eyes almost fell out when I got a load of his flat; he had paintings hanging off his walls by de Kooning, Leger, Beckman, real vintage stuff. In the bathroom there was an obscene photo of a dick, cock ring and all. I supposed that he masturbated to it after he finished pissing. It was a real tearoom. My first intention was to take him for all he was worth. It's embarrassing to admit, but it's the only idea that motivates me these days. I took a shower.

He was really into me and obviously couldn't come to terms with his homosexuality because he persisted in intellectual discussion, despite the obvious bulge in his pants. I don't know much about Derrida, except that be suffers from logorrhea, I told him. Bookstores have entire shelves of his books; there must have been at least thirty books by him the last time I looked.... He (his name began with an *N*) said that I seemed like a smart lad and that I could probably make something of my life. So I can be like you, I said, and pick up homeless kids....

At this point things took a queer turn. He was playing this antiquated jazz music; I thought I was going to keel over. I told him I'm not into this crap, it's techno I'm into. He asked me where I bought my clothes. I told him everything I wore was donated. Then he bent down to read the label on my jeans, and once he reached dick level I knew he wouldn't come up for air. I was looking out of the window into the courtyard below, where an old woman was trying to place a

Something about Wittgenstein

bag of empty bottles into a large bin.

While on his knees, he asked, Who donated their Armani jeans to you? A friend, I said. A generous friend, he replied. The best kind, I said. He was down there, poking around, uncertain whether to unzip or not. He pretended to be embarrassed. I moved away toward the bookcase. There were only philosophy books there.

He wasn't joking about Wittgenstein, there were at least five by him alone, as well as some French titles.

He'd been drinking a beer, and it really loosened him up. Look, he said when I turned around to face him, you must have the most beautiful ass... I moved backward until my hands met the bookcase. He unzipped my fly.

What bothered me most was that I could still see the old lady by the bins through the window. She was scrambling inside them now, looking for deposit returns, I suppose. It bothers me to look at such things, especially when I'm trying to get it on with someone. By the time I shot my wad, some of the books had fallen off the shelf. He wiped his mouth and picked them up and pressed them to his chest. His eyes glistened gratefully and glowed with a peculiar glint that seemed to approximate desire...or love....

Now that you've practically fucked Wittgenstein, I said, how about contributing to my education?

I put my prick back from whence it came. He ran into the kitchen to get a glass and poured me some wine from a refrigerated bottle. Strenuous, he said. Yeah, I laughed, like a marathon. He leaned over and put his tongue in my mouth, but I didn't like that so I bit it. I'm not a fag, I said. Neither am I, he replied.

I looked at him real hard and thought, Man, this guy hasn't been paying attention to his Lacan. Shit, I said.

What? he asked. Man, you are repressed, I said.

While I sat eating biscuits, he said I'd like to buy you a pair of shoes. He took his wallet out and laid two twenty dollar bills on the table in front of me. Instead of saying for the blow job, he said for new shoes. I thanked him, of course. And finished off his tin of biscuits. You are one square dude, I said. Who needs shoes? You need them, my dear boy, he replied. As well as a desk to sit at, food in your stomach, a bed to sleep in... Sure, I said....

—and strong arms around you, he said. Yours? I asked. I prefer chicks, I continued, in case you're interested. A faux pas. He recoiled, as if struck. Girls? he asked. Yes, I said. The species. Chicks. Babes. Dolls. Molls. Women. Whatever. With a nice pair of jugs too, I said, holding my hands in front of my chest. I retreated to the far end of the table. It's too bad you're not a girl, I said. This is a nice setup. You'll get used to it, he said. I didn't say anything.

Shouldn't you have said, I asked finally, that I could get used to it? That's what I meant, he said, but he was full of shit. I led him further into the trap. Get used to what, I asked? A man's affection, he said tentatively.

By now I'd been fed, relieved of sexual tension and compensated. I really don't equate the preceding with love in the remotest sense, I replied.

Well, that's the most philosophical thing I've heard out of you all day, he replied.

Philosophical as opposed to amorous? I asked. It takes a while, I told him.

Then I added: You know, it's difficult to philosophize on an empty stomach.

Philosophy bakes no bread, he said.

But advertising does, I said. Or whatever shit it is you do.

The shit I do, he replied, emphatically, takes care of the little things....

I imagined my sperm in his stomach, a pod of live creatures driven deep into his guts, doomed to extinction.

He had a little dried cum at the corners of his mouth.

And the not so little things, I said, as I was dying to mention his amateur art collection, which I hadn't been able to take my eyes off since I walked in the door. I envied the bastard and felt a vague desire to bludgeon him to death. There's always that risk; either he could do me in, or vice versa. If he kept this up, he might find himself in a compromising situation someday. As for myself, my position was

Something about Wittgenstein

already compromised. That is to say, there was no way it could actually get worse.

Well of course it could.

But, like my semen, I was swimming in a pretty rich sea.

N.

Logorrhea, now that was a big word. Never mind what it meant, the question was where had he learned it? All my gentle inquiries were met with cold stares of incomprehension as if I had asked him the secret code to his phone card. But he owned neither a phone card nor underwear, nor that brand of self-esteem that lets everyone know that he is not to be trifled with. I let everything he said pass through me like a knife into ether. I paused when asking him pressing questions. (Do you do drugs? What kind of sex are you into?) It turned out that he was kind of square—conservative—in the hetero sense. He hadn't yet been dragged down to the extreme level of those willing to pay for satisfying their greatest desires. Anything was possible; the way his white teeth sat in his mouth, set in a shark's grin, but also easily reminding me of a pearly shore I'd like to wash my tongue against. You'd think he'd only just graduated from washing behind his ears and playing with his rubber ducky in the tub.

G.

How many do you bring in here? I asked. He was washing the glass I'd drunk from. How many guys have you brought up here—you know—to fuck?

He winced again. He smiled. Not many, actually...

I wasn't happy with the forty bucks. It seemed I was worth more than that. Yes, I wanted more. It would have been nice to walk away with a small lithograph, the one in black and red ink, for example, a Miró perhaps? I was certain I was worth the price of a small artwork. Of course on the street a Miró would make a poor pillow, and it would be worth crap with my connections.

He could tell I was thinking about flying the coop. You could stay here, he suggested.

I laughed. With a key to his flat I could walk away with everything. This guy was a pansy through and through.

I just looked at him. He wasn't bad looking, really. The first thing you notice when you get down to these well-bred types is how clean they are. His skin was like a baby's after it was scrubbed. His hands were soft, womanly, and smelled of soap. It was obvious that he'd never done a stitch of hard work in his life. His body, though a little too bulky on the bottom, was well-formed and not too hairy on top. He had removed his tie and unbuttoned his shirt, so I could see halfway down his shirt when he was blowing me. He also kept his eyes fixed on me the whole time. I hate that, when someone's watching you when you're about to get off.

He left the room and returned with a pile of books. Wittgenstein and Lacan, of course. For you, he said, placing them on the table in front of me. As if the first thing I'd do was open them and start reading them. To tell you the truth, I'd probably hock them first chance.

I opened the cover of one of them and looked at its table of contents. Groovy, I said. He disappeared into his closet to look for a pair of shoes that might fit me, "in place of those useless boots."

A cock ring might fit me too. He had a La-Z-Boy chair, one of those numbers you can fall asleep in. I wanted to see how far I could push him. No homicidal impulses rose in my throat this time. He came back into the room while I was setting myself up in the chair. As I leaned back in the chair he stared unabashedly at my crotch. He held the shoes before him.

Some of them just want to get you in a back alley. This one was thinking about love. Boy was he going to get screwed.

He held the shoes in his hand as if they were brand new. They were those corduroy jobs, dark green, square in the front. I tried them on, and they fit. But there was no telling how long they'd stay clear of piss and filth.

You're welcome to stay here, he told me, as I stretched out in the chair. Then I actually fell asleep. When I woke up a note on the table told me he'd be back by eight. He'd written his work number, as if I'd need him. His handwriting had that pathetic spindly quality that little

Something about Wittgenstein

boys' writing has. Splayed out and unsure, the letters barely held themselves together. It amazed me that this guy could function at all.

Feeling strangely discreet, I decided not to poke around. I just went through his refrigerator to see if he was one of those well-stocked types. All he had was cheese and some grapes. And a bottle of wine. A real gastronome.

N.

One of the first things I noticed was that his dialogue was peppered with the most vile language, mostly slang from the street, but utter filth nonetheless. One ought to wash his mouth out with soap, I thought, and realized that the idea gave me a certain pleasure. His language, which suited neither his features nor his angelic mannerisms, surprised me at first, but like every thing concerning him I quickly got used to it.

I fetched him home, making him carry a parcel of books on the way in. We skipped the elevator and took the stairs. It was only two flights, but he appeared fairly winded judging by his labored breathing. When we got to the flat, I told him to go in first. He looked about with surprise; it was impossible to tell whether he'd expected a minor castle or a major dump. Put the books there, I said, and he dumped them onto the couch as if he hadn't heard me. I winced perceptibly, but he was too busy sticking his hands into the back pockets of his jeans and examining the walls, where several of my collected artworks hung.

Though I love filthy but beautiful bodies I bade him wash up, at least in the sink or whatever. He suggested a shower, much to my delight. I could hear him lathering up and singing lustily in jock fashion while I set about straightening up the place. The place suddenly seemed to me dry, fusty, with too many porn magazines lying about. When he came out of the bathroom he caught me sticking a pile of *Gerbils* under the cushion of the easy chair. He walked in a sprawling way with his legs turning outward, as if he weren't certain which direction they were taking him. He darted in and out of the rooms wearing only a towel and disappeared only to reemerge wearing jeans and an undershirt.

Van Scott

It was only a matter of time before I had him cornered against the bookcase while I unfolded his lovely cock out of the confines of his Armani jeans (donated, he informed me, by friends). At first he protested, saying that he didn't screw boys. My groping intentions were then met with a blithe indifference as he looked away, toward the window. As he charmingly put it, he let it slide when someone was willing to compensate him for the "gift of unloading." I kept an eye peeled to his face as I took his cock in my mouth, running my tongue up and down his shaft. I tried my best to accommodate him, more for my pleasure than his. I could have prostrated myself before his feet, sucked his toes, and considered myself happy.

It didn't make me feel valiant or dignified in the least to have this young urchin pressed against the bookcase, while almost imperceptible moans escaped his lips and I gobbled his prick. I didn't care what it made me look like, I cared only for the feeling. His eyebrows were dark in contrast to the rest of his hair, and his lips stayed open in a gentle O. He threw his head back in the brief spasm that overtook him while coming; I couldn't quite get enough of his taut blond thighs as I stroked them. Just as he peaked, his lips parted and some smut flowed out: "Oh, you fucking scumbag" is what I caught; it was a literal sigh.

When it was over he folded his prick back into his pants like a wilted flower and guiltily looked down at the floor where several of my books had dislodged themselves.

I plied him with juice and an old pair of shoes. I left two twenties on the table in front of him. He examined everything with a rough-and-ready expression, as if, having exposed his prick to a stranger, he was now open to the most unexpected of assaults or situations. I noticed the haughty expression on his face when I offered him the money, as if he wasn't certain he was going to accept it, but I offered it with the whitewash of using it to buy new shoes.

He smoked extensively and asked me about my work. Then he went through my cupboard in search of sweets. It was late afternoon, and I had not returned to work yet, having gone out originally for an early lunch.

I told him he could stay of course and make himself at home.

Something about Wittgenstein

Which he did with a somewhat indignant air.

We talked very little about Wittgenstein, because he was tired and nodded out in the easy chair. I left him there, asleep. I was almost incapable of keeping my eyes off his crotch as he lolled there, completely unaware of my presence, that rip in the pants leg intriguing me with its implications... I wasn't certain whether it was his sweet face I craved or the lovely tumescence of his crotch. I hastily scribbled a note and fled to the office, uncertain whether I'd still find him there when I got back.

I found him curled up in a ball on the floor when I got home, naked except for a pair of my underwear. My place is covered in wall-to-wall carpet, so I suppose it made a nice resting place. Oddly, he was right next to the bed, facing it in a pseudo-fetal position. This disturbed me a little. Evidently our student had a tendency to revert to the wild when left on his own. I'd have to rectify that. I stood staring at him for a long time, watching his milk-white skin aglow from a distance, his spine bent in a sublime curve as he slept; the golden array of his curls lying flat on the surface of the floor startled me with its beauty.

I thought how nice it would be to keep him in a cage, this leonine youth, whose energy I could share, whose body I could have as my own. I felt a certain need to trap him; I couldn't just let him wander in and out at will.

I went into the kitchen. The books I'd given him were still piled on the kitchen table, apparently unread. There was a plate beside them with the remains of grapes and a few dried pieces of Swiss cheese. I looked in the garbage and saw an empty box of Camels.

What a specimen he was. I didn't know whether I should step over him to get into bed or wait until he awoke. I suspected that if I woke him he'd want to go out. A creature such as he probably came alive only at night. The idea that I'd get into bed and he'd knife me in my sleep—something weird like that—occurred to me. So why should I trust him? I had a shower, prepared my clothes for tomorrow. It was past twelve, and he'd barely moved. I cautiously stepped over him and he grabbed my ankle suddenly in a kind of reflex. It's me, I said. His startled eyes peered out from beneath his wild locks, but his face was suddenly blocked by my erection, which filled a good deal of the space above him. Come into bed with me, I said. You can't be too comfortable down there.

He uttered some curses, words that I didn't catch this time, but minutes later he had his back to me and was in the bed with me. I placed a hand on his slender waist, but he appeared a little uptight about it so I removed it, only saying good night, my angel.

G.

So what's your story? I asked. Mine? he said. Yeah, what's your story? You've got to have a story. Everyone does. Immediately his hands started to flutter to his lips; it made me want to hit him.

He saw the malice come into my eyes and swallowed rapidly. He was probably getting a hard-on. It's complicated, he said, for now.

Oh, I replied, a real fairy tale gone awry, right? Well, not exactly, he said. He appeared uncomfortable for a moment. Then he folded his hands in his lap, in an attempt to placate some kind of innate tendency. I went to school, he began, at a very distinguished institution. He'd studied, of all things, architecture. This ornate travelogue concerning the milestones in his life proved so uninteresting that I preferred him naked with a paper bag over his head. But to get what I wanted I decided to play the game—not to speak out of turn and to reward his arduous foray into his past with a boyish smile or something I thought was innocent.

It must be difficult living alone, I said, with the heavy responsibility of being executive editor of some sloshy fashion mag. It was known as the "cake," this slick packet of pages whose icing was advertising. Well, whatever, I said. Then we got down to the business of skin on skin again, that is, to the blowing of my cock.

It seemed he wanted it shoved down his throat at all hours of the day. And I was always a little drunk when the time came around. He started to talk garbage after only two beers. For a man who liked boys, *cunt* seemed to be his favorite word. Besides Wittgenstein and those ridiculous word games he kept mentioning.

A word game is...the use of language is... even between mouthfuls

Something about Wittgenstein

of prick, mind you. As if I needed a lesson in the use of a phrase to gather its meaning. The man was a zealot in the worst way. Bordering on pathology. I got sick of it pretty fast.

I think I fascinated him because I was exotic to him; he was interested in me precisely because I was of the street; plus I was young, fair-skinned, while he was dark, overweight, and stuck in some middle-aged rut. For these reasons I tried to look on the good side of my predicament. The less fixed I was anywhere, the more attractive I became to the fixed types. I would win, he would win, but who would come out on top? I wondered. I didn't have the right to an attitude but I did have the right to something. I needed so much, and I knew nothing would ever satisfy me. I was suffering from some kind of deprivation—who knew what it was? But paired with this guy who was hard up, I realized we had this complementary thing going, his hard dick for my hard ass, my hard heart for that soft thing fluttering in his chest, his softness and kindness bringing out the worst in me. It was a jigsaw puzzle I fell into. Soon it got to be that I was fucking him, and I developed a taste for things I'd never done before.

He was all over me as usual, praising me from here to hell and back, smoking like a fucking chimney. We were smoking together. He let on like I was his soon-to-be husband and that I was going to marry him.

Are you kidding? I asked. I told him I'd think about it.

Here we were shacking up, and the time frame was barely two and a half weeks. Some people know how to go for broke in the shortest time imaginable.

Sometimes I wished he'd shut the fuck up. If you want to be charming, it's better to keep your mouth closed. I thought this as I watched his boring face go on interminably about intellectual matters. As the words flowed ceaselessly and I saw the grimaces he made along with the bemused expression that tangled up his face, I literally wanted to ball up my underwear and stuff it in his mouth. It made me sick that he was really talking to himself and not to me at all. I noticed how he didn't make eye contact; he went on moving his hands in tight circles, talking to someone who obviously knew as much or more than he did, which wasn't me. I was trying to keep from drawing conclusions that inevitably featured his body in ultimate states of torture—just for fun, of course, not to make any sense of what things could happen inside my head—but it didn't matter, because he kept talking anyway, until I reached out a hand and held it to his lips. Whatever matters to you, I said, but what about me?

It was that fucking Wittgenstein again.

When he felt my finger on his lips, he said What is it, my dove?

I had to ask him to stop calling me those stupid names. They were driving me crazy. Sweethearts okay, I said, but I'm not your golden studkin or your sex kitten or baby doll. First of all, those are for girls, and I'm not a girl. I know; you're my man, he said. Okay, I said, I'm your man. Just call me by my name and stop degrading me.

It seemed to hit him like a sack of potatoes in the head. I guess it was the word *degrading*. Who's degrading you? I'm not degrading you, he said. If anything... (The silence made me complete the thought. I'm degrading him.) Yeah, love can be degrading. Just keep it to yourself, I said. I guess I looked like I wanted to smash him in the mouth, because he looked hurt.

I started pretty early on calling him pretty much anything that came to mind. I let myself run the gamut with every filthy word I could think of. Of course I couldn't help but capitalize on the word *fag*. Your mother's a fag hag, I told him, which happened to be true. She called him practically every day. I sat there listening to her stupid voice, the volume on the answering machine turned up (he was hard of hearing). She wanted to know how junior was getting on. Did she know that junior had a liking for the uncut cocks of street boys? I didn't think so.

I wouldn't discuss HIV. It's one topic I hate to discuss. You been tested? Ever suck on a guy? Take it in the ass without a rubber? Man, what the fuck do I look like? I said, when he started getting on my nerves about the disease. I could be, you know. I've never been tested. Actually I'm afraid that I might have it, and I just don't want to know.

That look on his face was like he had just fallen off a horse. I could see him counting in his mind how many times he had sucked me off.

Something about Wittgenstein

Did he have enough fingers? Well, it wasn't that bad, considering.

Since I had never *really* fucked guys before, I guess he thought he was safe on that account.

It's just that when the words came out of his mouth—those silly, dittylike things—Tarzan, little goat (my wild goat, I liked that one)... Hey, I was taking it in the ass but I wasn't a fag. He was a fag, because he couldn't get it up for a woman. He was a fag, because deep in his little heart of hearts the words *love* and *lust* were so mixed up with filth that had to put himself on the floor and let the desired love object piss all over him.

I didn't object, of course. To pissing on him when the time came. And he didn't object to my harping on the word *fag*. Just as he couldn't help but call me "his beautiful cunt" when he was at the end of something; I called him "the fucking fag" whenever I referred to him in my head. Wittgenstein be damned.

N.

I walked in on him going through my drawers. In search of what, I don't know. Can I help you with something? I asked. He was pretty suave about it, sliding the drawer shut neatly so that just the tips of his fingers were inside it. I was looking for matches, he said. I don't keep matches in my underwear drawer, I said. He stood stiffly for a moment, as if I had pointed a gun at his head. Next time, I said softly, just ask. Oh, yeah, he said absentmindedly. Then, Thanks, man, when I handed him a pack from my jacket pocket.

I'd just come home from work, and as usual he had lounged about in my flat the whole day, apparently not lifting a finger to do anything, not to wash the dishes, not to clear the breakfast plates off the table, nothing. I could only imagine what he'd spent his day doing.

I walked into the living room and couldn't believe my eyes; my porn collection (an indiscreet stack of videocassettes containing juvenile porn) had obviously been riffled through; the stack was just a little off center and tilted at a slight angle. The VCR was on, channel 03 staring me straight in the face. I looked at the easy chair and imagined him sitting there—in my underwear—with his legs spread, jerking off, or watching the action with a rapt expression.

I went through my head imagining what other private things of mine he'd tampered with: there was the safe in the back of my closet... He must know about that by now. He probably knew how to break into it too. But he wasn't going to let me know that he knew about it.

So, why was I doing this, housing this hoodlum? Because his face was angelic, haven't I said that already? I kept telling myself, After all, it's been so long since I've had someone who mattered in my life.

He was stretched out on the bed, naked as usual, casual as a young lion, smoking, his nicotine-stained fingers held the butt delicately, as a small frown on his face showed how grave the situation was. What's the matter? I asked. My dad... he said.

What? I asked. I said I thought there was something wrong with my dad, he said. Your dad? I asked. Yeah, my old man who was not my old man, he said. Because, you know, my mom remarried when I was still playing with Tonka trucks. He must have been off or something.

Mmm... I said. You want to talk about it?

A beautiful sneer appeared on his face, as if he were going to spit on me. Tell you what? he asked, defensively. What it felt like to have some old prick's tongue in my ass when I was nine? He looked as if he were about to fall apart—or smash his fist into my face. I was anxious to hear every detail. But once he got an eyeful of my concentrated expression he became intractable.

Get the fuck off me, he said, jumping off the bed. His penis hung down between his thighs like an oversized dead snail; the golden triangle of his pubic hair seemed so perfect I could have fallen to my knees and worshipped it. I tried to tease the details out of him. They were essential to my interests, you see. I had to imagine that I was the first one who'd had entry into his body. He would always have entry into mine. And I would never get a chance with another like him.

I was ashamed and embarrassed at myself, further corrupting a youth who'd obviously been manhandled far too early in life.

Where is this bastard? I asked. Who the fuck knows? he said. I don't know where my family is...and I don't care, either. Any sisters

Something about Wittgenstein

or brothers? I asked.

Again that mistrustful look came into his eyes, as he squinted at me through golden hair. Yeah, a sister and a brother, he said. Okay, I said. You'll tell me about them when you want to.

He seemed to become more hostile and indifferent toward me after that. And we never got around to discussing things of a philosophical nature at all, though I continued with my usual studies, whether in his presence or not. After all, I couldn't spend every minute sucking his beautiful cock or caressing his testicles—he wouldn't have let me, anyway. He said that I made it sore, keeping it in my mouth for that length of time. I wasn't certain whether I felt kinship or antipathy toward the man who'd taken advantage of him. Still, I couldn't contain my excitement when he finally spared me a few facts. I catalogued them in my head like vignettes from a porn film.

So I had him, all five feet eleven inches of him, sprawled on my bed, asscheeks resting against my sheets, head on my pillow, spilling his urine into my toilet bowl and pressing his lips against my drinking glasses. It was too good to be true.

I wanted him to make use of my body in any way he saw fit with the language of the gutter flowing from his lips and I said so. If you could just understand that being in his presence alone was enough to satisfy me: to have his fingers trace the marks where they'd left their sharp indent, to see his features tighten while I sucked his cock and let his cum flow down my throat.

It was getting a bit out of control though, that is, our manner of congress was rapidly leaping into hard-core domain. He insisted that I *pay* him for the privilege of allowing him to come in my mouth. Then he insisted that I pay double for the privilege of my coming in his presence. He demanded that I "keep that vile shit directed somewhere else" when I inevitably shot my load, and I could sympathize with that request, as one must develop a taste for the fluid, at least these days. He didn't want to admit it, but he had the makings of a real hustler, and he seemed very relaxed in the role, as if he would always fall into the right kind of situation, intuitively finding that special someone who would open up his life to my angel in a way that could only prove beneficial to him. And whether his eyes were closed, whether his hands were tied, whether he was floating on his back in the middle of a bed, staring at the ceiling, one could sense that he would always rise to the top, in any situation.

G.

I took one last look around his apartment going over in my head the things I'd like to take. He had this splendid painting of a bunch of flowers in a vase that were like zinnias or something. I got such a good feeling from that painting. He said it was French, seventeenth century. There's no way I could ever take that thing with me—it was too big.

Then there were the lithographs… I smoked a cigarette, took a beer out of the fridge.

Cool pad; I was going to miss it.

Trouble was that I'd had an offer I couldn't refuse. One of those situations where the geezers are coming out of the woodwork. This friend was going away with one of them for the weekend—the island getaway. He needed a second, a go-go boy who could shake his ass. That would be me. I realized N. was strangling me with his gaga love shit. I'll fly the coop, but I can always come back. Sitting stationary, it's not a good thing. They start thinking you haven't got wings. They start thinking you're getting a little domestic. Buck naked with an apron tied around your waist, standing over the stove, acting like you love the whole thing. My friend and the old dude, it was promising something else. Like switching horses in midstride. A breath of fresh air and a change of scenery. That was my scene. Not this stultifying atmosphere of the morgue on its way to becoming a mausoleum. I went through his drawers—found some nice clothes for the weekend and a money clip as well. And—ah—guess what I took from the walls? That's right. Old N. would have a shit fit. Fag had no choice.

N.

It surprised me, the way he disappeared. It was so sudden. I thought we were a team and that we made a handsome couple. You can't question these things too closely. He came and went as he pleased. I

Something about Wittgenstein

gave him what he needed, that composed look on his face hadn't remained indefinitely. Our highbrow lad was in fact a person of mixed proportions. Part street, part Rimbaud, one-quarter angel, the rest unmentionable. He'd worn no clothes the whole time except my brand-new underwear, which he didn't change unless I told him to. He stayed in my flat a total of three weeks before disappearing mysteriously on the third Thursday. I was out at the time. Running some fool's errand. The only things missing were a Miró lithograph, whose value I'm sure he didn't appreciate, and a money clip containing several hundred-dollar bills. Admittedly I'd left the money in a bedroom drawer to test him. It would stand him in good stead. Perhaps it would give him the opportunity to start over on the right foot. Perhaps he'd return to me, after his venture failed.

All I knew was that he'd run off with a pair of my best slacks, the shoes I'd given him, and a linen jacket as well. I couldn't help but express a sob when I spotted a few golden hairs on my pillow, as I prepared for bed later that night. He didn't leave a note or anything. But the unflushed urine in the toilet said "I'll be back."

You'd think I'd learn my lesson. On the bedroom dresser was a Polaroid of him. Taken in the late afternoon when he'd finally roused himself from bed. Leaning against the wall in the kitchen hallway, with a smile lost among all those curls. I swallowed hard when I looked at that photo. I knew what it all meant.

I thought about the first time I'd seen him. It was right in front of the Gap store on Aspen Place; I saw him lying stretched out in public view, practically in the way of the passersby, dirty but wearing designer jeans, his bare feet poking up in the air as he lay on his back. Just then a train went by underneath him, and hot air from the station came rushing through the grate on which he was lying. His clothes fluttered in its breeze, and he smiled at me, and I realized that it was rather chilly and that the subway grating was probably the best place to be.

Provocative Kitch
Simon Sheppard

Yeah, so I'm a pornographic writer. And maybe it's because I'm a dinosaur from the Last Gasp of the Age of Literacy, but I guess I figured—at least to begin with—that it might have gotten me a little more dick.

I made it to puberty long, long ago—before Stonewall, after the invention of movable type. Back then, horny in high school, I'd smuggle home copies of physique magazines like *Young Demigods* and *Tomorrow's Man;* these days, the posing-strap-and-overdone-décor nature of those esteemed publications have lent them a kitschy cachet. But back then, those oiled-up hunks dressed up as gladiators and cowboys were transcendently desirable—at least to me, as I approached the in-the-rear precincts of a Trenton newsstand with a slightly sick feeling in my stomach, and a greatly anticipatory feeling further down in my groin.

But I was literate, too. And geekily precocious. By the time I was a high school senior, I'd bought *Howl* and hung a poster of Allen Ginsberg in my room. Gore Vidal's *The City and the Pillar?* Yep, read it. Isherwood's *A Single Man?* Uh-huh. James Baldwin, too. Proust? Shit, still haven't gotten around to that.

I wish I could say I romped through the racks of pulp porn novels—Greenleaf Classics and the like—that were just beginning to flood the shelves of the less reputable bookstores. Didn't though—I was just too damn sophisticated for *Homos in Heat.*

Tonier fag stuff? By college, I suppose I'd read James Barr's *Quatrefoil.* I know for sure I read Sanford Friedman's *Totempole,* a novel of queerness in the Korean War. I even now recall devouring

Provocative Kitch

Totempole while tucked up in bed, eating Bing cherries in syrup directly from the jar after a day at my very first job, doing tech at the McCarter Theater of Princeton University. Okay, at this remove I really don't remember the details of the book, but I seem to recall it had something to do with prisoners of war and fucking. Especially fucking. As in "anal sex is the ultimate expression of male/male love." As in: the climax of the book (at least as I now remember it) came when one fellow surrendered his cherry to another guy.

Totempole was, to the best of my knowledge, the first time I learned just precisely what one might do to one of those Young Demigods, should he put down his spear, drop his posing pouch, and throw his legs in the air.

This bit of literary education was to have fairly real consequences once I fell in love. I'd already had sex with a couple of men, but nothing beyond a bit of frottage and sucking. And then came Jim. Amidst the Sturm, Drang, and LSD of a 1960s first love, the Friedman Buttfuck Motif gained special resonance. If Jim and I really loved each other—and we did, we did—we'd have anal sex. Just like in the book.

Unfortunately, *Totempole* was no *Joy of Gay Sex,* and was therefore woefully short on how-to details. So—and isn't it amazing how this memory, inaccurate as it may be, is still more vivid than whatever happened last week?—I momentously tried sitting on Jim's dick. And of course it hurt. And it was, um, scary to my boyfriend's raised-good-Catholic sensibilities. The attempt collapsed in tears and awkwardness, probably to a soundtrack of The Velvet Underground. Within a year, Jim went on—perhaps inspired by our mutually adored bible, Leonard Cohen's *Beautiful Losers*—to explore his bisexuality and eventually, get married. Who knows, maybe if it hadn't been for the traumatic *Totempole* fuck, we'd still be together.

No, just kidding.

Later, in my twenties, I found a tattered first edition of Larry Townsend's seminal *The Leatherman's Handbook* on sale for a quarter at the Salvation Army. Really I did; why would I make that up? Having only read one leathersex story in my life, a really scary one I found in an old *Drummer* magazine that I'd run across somewhere, I was amazed and excited by Townsend's tome. So *that's* what those guys in chaps at the Folsom Street bars were up to! Even if I was later to discover that some of what Townsend wrote was less authoritative than opinionated, the secondhand paperback did open up new vistas of perversion for me.

So when I began writing porn, I already owed a certain debt to tawdry texts. And when my erotica first saw print in a book, it was as part of an anthology edited by the legendary porn star Scott O'Hara, a man whose reputation was as big as his dick, and whose heart turned out to be equally well hung. Suddenly I'd gone from being just another wanker to a full-fledged purveyor of smut. And rather prestigious smut, at that.

There's sort of an erotica-writers' circuit out there. And when I elbowed my way in, I found that, as in any workplace situation, things could get complex. Despite our being unrecognized and underpaid—or maybe because of it—us porn writers' camaraderie had its limits. For instance, two editors I was selling my early work to were having a major feud. I, idealist that I am, decided to stay clear of personality clashes and just go off in a corner and write dirty stuff. If this were in short order to prove easier to say than do, if I myself were to wind up on thoroughly bad terms with one of the feuders, and to resent and/or envy a small-but-distinct clutch of my fellow pornographers, well, that's life, ain't it?

I have had sex with a few other erotic writers: one's dick was huge, another's damn near huge, the third's merely limp. In one of the three cases—okay, unsurprisingly, the third—it turned out to be a fairly significant mistake, one I strongly suspect may have led to my not being included in several anthologies. Repeat after me, class: "Work and sex don't mix." Even if that work is writing about sex.

Scott O'Hara always said he couldn't write erotica unless his dick was hard. I rapidly discovered that in my case the opposite stood true; that an erection was a distraction from the task at hand. But it turned out that I was nearly as adept at putting sex into words as I was at pulling my pud, albeit it at different times. Even now, the cum

Provocative Kitch

stains on my keyboard result from recreation, not my occupation.

People sometimes ask if I write out of personal experience. Well, Jesus, I've published around two hundred stories. I'd have to be really sluttish—and lucky—to have ended up with that many tricks who were interesting enough to actually write about. But I do write about real guys, sometimes. Every once in a great while, a piece of mine is merely regurgitated real life, but more often I take bits and pieces of men and experiences and do my damnedest to transform the mess into First-Rate Erotic Literature. Speedfreak in diapers? Masochist dancer-boy? Teenage-trick-turned-hustler? Sure thing! Right this way. Hop into my prose...

Not to sound maudlin, but...hey, I'm not getting any younger. Chronicling the dicks I've known and—at least for a minute—loved is a way to make things stickily immortal.

More: writing about guys gives me a certain added measure of control, be it ever so illusory. It's as though I were a dom top directing a group scene, exerting the power that dominant tops...oh, wait, that's largely illusory, too. Well, even so, being able to rewrite my sexual history has certainly been bracing on occasion.

What writing smut hasn't been, though, is sex bait. Churning out porn has been a better way to get paid (usually badly) than laid.

When I was in college, and still pretty deep in the closet, I nourished a crush on a fellow student, Michael, a crush so abiding that I can still remember his smile, the sound of his laugh, his curly blond hair. And he was a professed bisexual. (Since he professed that to me in private, it was at least moderately likely an invitation—an invitation I was too stupid to recognize, much less accept, but never mind. The snows of yesteryear and all that.) Michael claimed to have had sex with Allen Ginsberg, which lent him a certain cachet in our circles. But I'm betting if he'd just said, "Hey, I had sex with a paunchy, balding, hairy Jew," it wouldn't have been nearly as provocative a boast. Face it, if Ginsberg got boys like Michael in bed—and I'm sure hoping he did—then it was because he was *Allen Ginsberg,* dammit. Not even because he was a terrific writer (when he wasn't setting down self-indulgent run-on twaddle, that is) but because he was a celebrity, the Madonna of gay Beat poetry.

But, sadly, though I myself am now a balding, hairy, and only slightly paunchy Jew, I ain't famous. I *have* met guys at readings I've given and ended up in bed with them. In one memorable case, the guy in question was an impossibly lovely boy in his twenties, a skinny lad who simply loved to be spanked. I think he appreciated my spanking talents more than my way with words, though, and after he left town, I discovered pictures of him, ass bright red, on a corporal-punishment website. Later, I found out he'd moved back to a small town in Alabama or Georgia or somewhere and was managing a pizza parlor. Which just goes to show you. Though what, I'm not sure.

Sad but true: when the boys I snag via Craigslist are wiping off their dicks and pulling up their baggy shorts (or shredded jeans or whatever is currently in fashion), the sentence "I'm a writer" is more often than not met with utter disinterest. Sure, many of these boys actually think that *you* is spelled *u,* but even so...I'm an award-winning writer, for Christ's sake. I can put you in a *story.*

Come to think of it, that tack is probably the wrong one to take.

Mostly, the real-life guys who do make their way, more or less fictionalized, into my work are one-off...well, let's call them tricks, shall we? They're unlikely, therefore, to have any notion of their iconic status. I'm betting that that tweaker in diapers has no notion of how widely known his proclivities have become. Nor the male model who threw my ass out of his hotel room with a fuck-off line so jaw-droppingly improbable that I had no choice but to use it verbatim. (For the record: "You may not believe this, but pretty people are the loneliest people in the world.")

Yes, maybe I tend to think too much while I'm having sex. But there are times when I find myself in a sexual situation so weird that I think *Jesus, this is just like a Simon Sheppard story!* And who am I to deny the beneficent bounty of the universe?

I did put a couple of my long-term play buddies into prose, with their full knowledge and consent; in neither case did things end particularly well. One, the cutest little pain pig, got transmuted, details somewhat changed, into the bottom boy in a piece of mine that made it into *Best Gay Erotica*. Which didn't stop him from standing me up multiple times, until we both got sick of the whole thing.

The other was a more complex case, a college boy who met me when he'd only had sex with a couple of men, and had never been fucked. Actually, he originally shaded the truth enough to convince me he'd been a virgin, which inspired me to write a story about him that made it into *My First Time 4*. But he truly never had been fucked before—though he turned out to be a natural, eager fuckee—and I wrote about that in a piece that was published in the presciently titled *Everything You Know About Sex Is Wrong*. On top of all that, I tracked our adventures in a column I wrote for Gay.com before it was unceremoniously killed in a cost-cutting move. Like a slaughtered hog, nothing about him went to waste.

Unfortunately, some of what I thought about Daniel (he told me I could use his real first name in print, and I see no particular reason to stop now) was not quite on target. I wanted him to be a sweet, honest, innocent, slightly goofy kid, and undoubtedly part of him was. But after we'd been seeing each other on and off for over a year, he broke the news that he'd been hustling. My former slots on his schedule were now to be filled by cash customers...unless I wanted to pony up a couple of hundred bucks, a figure equivalent to selling four or five stories to some of the spectacularly underpaying publishers I deal with. At this point, I'm ungenerously sorry I gave him copies of the books he was in. I should have charged him the cover price, so my career would be indirectly underwritten by the middle-aged businessmen who paid to use the asshole I trained so well. Not that I'm bitter.

Even as I sit here typing away, I'm waiting for a callback from an extraordinarily handsome college student I met online, one who actually *was* moderately impressed when we discussed our respective careers—he's a *barrista* for Starbuck's. Which hasn't, apparently, prevented him from standing me up. And though, yes, that's given me more time to write, I'd rather get laid than wallow in self-pity, thank you very much.

Simon Sheppard

I recently put together an anthology, *Homosex,* that surveys six decades' worth of male/male porn. In my research, I ran across a lot of fascinating stuff, some of it ferociously well written, some of it garden-variety stroke-fuel...though still interesting in an it's-all-grist-for-the-postmodern-mill way. I didn't do the book, though, in an effort to make gay erotica more respectable, more worthy of critical notice. Porn needs no justification—like springtime or ring-around-the-collar, it just *is.*

There's just so much to say about queer sex. So many ways to say it. And I've tried to do my part. In print, when possible. I do hope that, even in this Internet-sex-saturated age, some young guy some-where comes across one of my stories and finds it both stimulating and enlightening. I write gay porn because I honestly love gay men, especially when they're naked and tumescent.

I'll never be as famous as Allen Ginsberg. My books, even the one that won a rather prestigious award, have been met with semi-deafen-ing silence by the mainstream media, both gay and straight. The high-circulation gay glossy *Out* did mention me once, though: it called a story about Liberace I'd been asked to write "provocative kitsch."

Provocative kitsch.

MacArthur Genius Grant, here I come!

Hmm. Well, well. The *barrista* just phoned a couple of sentences ago. Really he did. He'll be here in ten minutes. I'd better go get ready.

I can always finish this piece later.

Sex with Librarians
Ron Gutierrez

I'd rented a small one-bedroom apartment near the beach town of
Marina Del Rey that summer. I wasn't so interested in being close to
the beach as I was in being close to my job. I was working three days
a week in a data services company on Lincoln Avenue and I wanted
to avoid as much wear on my old Pontiac as possible. I needed some-
place I could bike to work from in twenty minutes or drive to in ten.
I was part of a team of workers that rotated shifts together as a unit:
three months of days, followed by three months of nights. I was on
nights that summer and I made an effort to keep to the same sleep
hours during my off days. That, of course, made for a lot of late
nights at the Eagle, the Spike, and Rafters—all convenient walking
distance from each other. I'd nurse three or four beers, make polite
conversation, then drive home. Those were my nights off.

I was twenty-four and knew I hadn't found my true calling yet but
that didn't really weigh on me. My brother made piñatas for a small
company in Pico Rivera. He had mild Down syndrome so he was the
one everyone was proud of. My six-year-old sister had been in a couple of Band-Aid and Bactine commercials because she cried real good
and looked even better when she stopped. But apparently she didn't
have the right kind of cuteness in her voice to actually get lines, so
lately when I saw her on TV she was either spilling grape juice on a
white carpet or having a thermometer stuck in her mouth. So while I
did spend the requisite dark moment wondering what direction my
life would take, I didn't feel any immediate pressure to overachieve.

My one true obsession had always been books. I'd grown up in
an alcoholic household and reading was the only thing that managed

to soften the jagged edges of the world. It didn't matter what the book was about, just as long as it was told in an articulate voice and had a satisfying ending. That's all I asked. I devoted many a late night to a good book, my music of choice in the background and a strong cup of coffee at hand. I never read to discuss or argue the meaning of a thing afterward. I assumed people who did had a special gene that allowed them to conjure up those remembered windows to the human condition and painlessly find their applicability to their own lives. For me, the act of reading was more than enough.

But that summer of working nights and sleeping during the day, I couldn't keep my mind focused on a book for more than a few minutes. It seemed the shelves lining the one-bedroom, second-floor apartment were stacked with books I'd either already read or had every intention of reading but didn't feel like reading right then. Plus something inside me was restless. I needed something more physical.

"You could help your brother make piñatas one day. He'd like that," my mom offered during a phone conversation.

She meant well. But instead I decided to take up classical guitar, maybe find my soul that way. There was a music shop two blocks away where I bought a Spanish guitar and signed up for lessons. The abandoned literature on my shelves stood quietly by as I practiced Malagueña. I knew they were waiting patiently for me to fail in my new passion. Books can be very jealous. They weren't meant to be stacked away and made mute, their covers closed with not so much as a dog-ear to mark where they'd see the light of day again.

After several weeks of ignoring my books and imagining some-day I'd be playing classical guitar by the fireplace while my future lover was setting the table in our villa in Spain, I considered calling it quits. I clearly wasn't devoting enough hours to practicing, and my fingers had not developed the necessary calluses to play for more than a few minutes without hurting.

"The process of developing calluses is painful, but once you have them you can play beautifully and for all day long," my instructor told me, clearly displeased with my progress.

Sometimes late at night when I was sitting at Rafters, I would press my fingers hard against my beer bottle, trying to make the hurting stop and thinking this was God's way of punishing me for not helping my brother make piñatas.

"You don't have to hold it so tight. No one's going to take it from you."

I turned to see the guy sitting next to me squinting as he lit a cigarette, inhaled, then looked at me like he'd asked an important question. I'm right-handed but the soreness was in my left fingers, so I had both hands on my bottle.

I took him in. He had a lanky body, a two-day beard, and shoulder-length dirty-blond hair. I pegged him as either a mechanic or unemployed. I found the blue-collar boys more down to earth, easier to talk to, and more aggressive in bed. I extended my hand and introduced myself. "Tony," I said, then added, "My fingers hurt. I practiced guitar too much today."

"Well, my eyes hurt," he replied. "I read too much today." Then he put down his cigarette and shook my hand. "Bruce."

I'm sure if you looked up the name *Bruce* you'd find it had regal and sexy beginnings like Brice or Emmet. But to me Bruce had always been a really gay name, not unlike Brice or Emmet. But this guy sitting next to me was nothing like his name. He was unkempt, windswept, and, I would soon learn, had an obscenely well-read background in an array of disciplines that gave him a skuzzy intellectual kind of swagger. Not one you could see from a distance, because it wasn't in his gait so much as in his countenance and premature crow's-feet when you said something he found particularly intriguing.

He worked in the UCLA library, the reserve section. Days before any student got his or her hands on the books, articles, and journals that their professor had set aside as required reading, Bruce had been there first, read every word, and come to his own conclusions as to their merit. I envied him his job perk.

"Go put your name up," he said, nodding toward the chalkboard.

I declined but told him I'd go watch him when they called his

Sex with Librarians

name. He liked pool a lot and was good enough to get himself into the gay pool league a couple years ago, but now, he said, he just played for fun. When his turn came we both got up and went to the back of the bar. I watched him choose his cue stick then case the table, looking for his move. His ass, when he bent over to make a shot, then another, then try for the third but not make it, studying the table like just that moment the geometry had presented itself to him, was the sexiest thing I'd ever seen. Then he'd come over and give me a self-admonishing growl and he'd flash deep Einstein eyes at me like I was his equal.

We had sex that night in my car in a parking structure near Santa Monica Beach after walking along the shore for a while. We'd driven there because he said no one ever took him there. No one ever took me there either. We trekked through the sand toward the water till the waves got louder than our voices. The salt in the air and the lapping foam running up to our shoes made me want him, made me need everything about this young pool-playing librarian. He told me that he'd just broken up with someone, and I thought maybe he wanted to make sure the world was still out there somewhere. If it was, I wanted him to find it for us both.

On the way back to the car, we both peed on a trash can and I made a comment about how this was now sacred ground and I raised my hands in a Catholic blessing and it made him laugh. It makes me wince to think of it now, but hell, maybe it was true—the sacred part. Maybe wincing is the greater sacrilege.

Once we got back in the car we talked some more. I could tell he was letting me make the first move, mainly, I think now, because he was studying me, wanting to see how I worked. For me it was like jumping off a building—so much is at stake and you can't do it unless you're really sure. I think I actually liked prolonging that moment, the wavering and second-guessing, that mysterious mating dance of self-inflicted torture that you get only once per partner. When I finally put my hand through his long hair and touched his warm neck, suddenly this dream I'd been talking to all night, christening the beach with, had now became flesh and bone, the musk of his body making him real in a way he almost hadn't been before.

Although I didn't make car sex a habit, there is one thing I can say for it. It forces you into lewd contortions you couldn't possibly achieve otherwise. Undressing like you're half paralyzed, snaking into the backseat like you're tunneling your way out of Alcatraz. One moment his balls are in your face, the next, they're woefully unattainable; you manage a necessary twist of the torso so he can pull off your T-shirt but then sucking his cock becomes impossible; still, here was his nipple for now, and not too far away his armpit was waiting for my pleasure later. Then more shifting and grunting and we were back to square one, devouring, planning anew, tumbling and climbing over each other. The windows were covered with a thick fog so it was impossible to tell or even remember where we were anymore, and when we came it was like two bulls hatching out of an egg. I had to open up a window to breathe.

"So, that's sex with librarians in cars," I panted, looking at his sweat-covered body, both of us dehydrated and gratified into near stupor. I realized I'd never been completely naked in a car before.

"Little did you know," he said between heavy breaths, like I'd been foolishly misinformed all my life. His foot was resting on my chest and I cupped my hand on his sticky dick, hoping I hadn't seen the last of it. The smell of semen mingled with wet vinyl and his taste was still in my mouth.

"Well, now I know," I said.

"Use the information wisely," he added. Then his smoker's cough started and he fished around for his jeans and dug out his cigarettes.

He started coming over twice a week with an overnight bag, and I liked having two coffee cups to clean, an ashtray to empty and a bed that smelled of him. My apartment finally felt like I lived there. When he knocked on my door it made my heart quicken like we were having an affair, like I was stealing him. Sometimes I opened the door to find him standing there holding a half-empty beer bottle. Bruce didn't have a problem with drinking. He had a problem with

Sex with Librarians

rules. He also thought I followed too many of them.

I never knew why he fell for me. My brown skin, black hair, and timid life experiences must have surely paled next to his blond-haired, been everywhere, done everything counterculture life. I could almost see him making an agenda to bring me up to speed. He wanted me to be more reckless and I wondered if he had something specific in mind or if he was just teasing me.

I had an oversized vinyl couch against the wall opposite the book-shelf and after sex we'd lie on it naked, drinks in hand, dry cum on us we hadn't managed to find with the towel earlier, and he'd become for the next couple of hours the wise sage that very few who knew him could understand. He talked incessantly, intensely turning over the nuances of any subject, his mind unfolding in a fascinating array before my eyes, as his hands would occasionally stroke my leg or my stomach. Authors, books, world religions, drugs, men, women, the bizarre sexual needs of people, bands he'd partied with, and on and on. He talked for both of us. My part was to understand—him, me, us, the world, whatever. I tried not to judge. He came from a rich family in Kentucky and had turned his back on their world. That stunned me. I had no idea there were rich people in Kentucky. Or that they produced offspring as captivating as this guy.

He found my book collecting eccentric when any library had everything I could ever want and didn't cost anything. He ignored my best sellers while not holding them against me, approved of my Marx-Engels while knowing it was required reading from a prior life and that I was unlikely to ever open it again. He tossed around names like Nathaniel Branden and Ayn Rand and talked about objectivist epistemology while he'd ask me to hold his cigarette, go pee, and come back, positioning his naked body between my legs as I simply reclined there, fascinated he could do all that without miss-ing a beat in his talking. I could follow him perfectly, his logic seemed just right, but wherever he took me, I could never remem-ber how we got there.

He was usually blunt and decisive but once in a while it took him a long time to ask certain things about me, like he was respecting my privacy or couldn't imagine there'd be a satisfying answer.

"I've been meaning to ask you," he said once. "Why do you have a piñata hanging in your kitchen?"

I thought about that for a moment. Why *did* I have it hanging there?

"I guess it reminds me of what we're capable of," I replied.

He looked at me for a minute then laughed like I'd just told him the meaning of life and it was really stupid. Then he got quiet. "Thank you," he said and I could see his eyes were the slightest bit red. He grabbed my cock and balls with one hand and took a few more drags with the other before putting out the cigarette. "School day tomorrow," he said.

He liked that I lived alone—it helped me become an individual. He liked that I was Latino—it gave me a nonmainstream soul. He liked that I had a working car—so many guys in the bars didn't. He spent a lot of time telling me who I was and mostly I hung on every word, even though he didn't approve of everything about me. I was too quiet, he said. But he found it ironic that I wasn't inhibited in bed. And it was true. I was rough, greedy and kept him guessing what would happen next. Plus I was stronger than him and oftentimes I'd overpower him and have my way, and sometimes when we finally came it was only because it was either that or die. And while sexually we were good together, outside of bed he mesmerized me even more, and I hardly saw the value of a sentence unless it came from him.

I took him to the very first Cirque du Soleil when it came to L.A. I was apprehensive for weeks that I had crossed the line and offered up a generic or mushy family event to him, something that wouldn't survive his disdain for mass-marketed entertainment. But I worried for nothing. Its glamor and French-Canadian sensibilities were just unique enough to pass muster with him, and when I looked at his face, there was a kind of smile on it I hadn't seen before. One that I'd earned and could take home with me in my pocket.

He always preferred coming to my place and I only went to his rented house once. It was on a dark street near the Magic Castle in Hollywood and once inside, I thought the place should have been

Sex with Librarians

condemned. The floors creaked and the bathroom and kitchen looked like they hadn't been cleaned since he moved in. I could sense that he didn't really want me there. We sat and watched Larry King, and when I got up to use the restroom, the light wouldn't work. I kept flipping it up and down and I heard him call out "Don't do that." I felt slighted because it was the first time he ever told me not to do something. He said doing that could make the circuits go out.

But I was glad I was finally able to be in his place, like I'd risen up a notch. He said he didn't like inviting guys over because they always wanted to clean and he considered that invasive, even pathological behavior. I made a mental note never to clean anything there. That night we slept at my place. It was what he wanted.

During one of his sage sessions he began enumerating my qualities that struck him as either pertinent or bizarre. Pertinent to *what* I didn't know—my survival, I assumed—and bizarre was just a favorite word of his. Finally he added, "...but you give yourself away." Then he smiled and took another drink of his beer. "You give yourself away," he repeated. He said it like I couldn't fool *him*. His hand caressed me strongly like he was glad I was his. I didn't understand what he meant. But I loved his hands and his smile. He got up and got us both another beer.

Sometimes the sex was aggressive, sometimes not. Once he was digging his two-day-old beard deep into the back of my shoulder as he pulled me close. He dug and scratched and didn't stop. I told him it hurt.

"That's the point," he said. "So you feel me. I thought you liked that."

I'd forgotten already. I did like that. I felt bad both for not remembering and for having changed.

By the end of the summer I was back on day shift and I had to go back to sleeping regular night hours. I continued to see Bruce, but I was showing up late to work a lot. Also, now that fall was here, Bruce's schedule at UCLA was more grueling and often he seemed tired and preoccupied.

"The professors, especially some of the women, act like they're hot shit and berate *me* when their course materials are not ready in time for their classes. That's their own fault for giving us the lists at the last minute. Sometimes they think *we* should make all the copies for them. I set them straight right away. I want to tell them that with the unsophisticated selections they're forcing down their students' throats—mostly because the professors themselves wrote them—it's just as well that they weren't available."

Meanwhile, my guitar playing stayed at the level it would for anyone who was down to only two hours a week of practice. I suppose it should have bothered me more than it did that I was letting myself stay mediocre. Sometime I'd turn on the stereo and listen to Andre Segovia or Julian Bream and think, wasn't this better and easier than wanting to learn to play myself? Wasn't it presumptuous or even selfish to aspire to greatness on that instrument when I had a so-called real life? But it was too hard to admit defeat. Every time I picked up that guitar I loved too much the way the wood felt in my arms, the way the strings responded to my amateur touch.

Eventually I began to sense that Bruce was distancing himself and even though I didn't know why, I half expected it. I suspected that as he was getting to know me, his curiosity was being satisfied and I was becoming less of a draw. I wouldn't hear from him for days, but then I'd call and he'd come over and it would be good again—except that it felt episodic, and I didn't have the language for asking him about it. I knew that sometimes when you talk you scare things away faster.

Bruce had wanted to get deeper inside of me, to take me apart and see how I worked. It made no sense to me since I wasn't the complicated one. As far as I was concerned there was nothing to see after dissecting me. He said two things that actually frightened me. He wanted to do drugs with me because he thought I should at least have that in my background. "I'd be there with you, you wouldn't be doing it alone," he reassured me. I froze but managed to act noncommittal. Even in college I'd only smoked pot. He also said, "I haven't met your friends," with an edge of can't-you-see-how-

Sex with Librarians

you're-leaving-me-out? in his voice. I felt my well was running dry
and he wanted either drugs or other people to offer clues to me.
Well, there was no way I was going to start taking drugs at this stage
of my life and I think he probably knew that. So that left my friends.
And I was embarrassed to tell him that I hadn't really made any.

I occasionally went biking with a local gay group but Bruce wasn't
an exercise kind of person. There was a small neighborhood pub
called the Annex near me and once, several weeks before, I had
walked in out of curiosity but then walked out immediately. It was
dark smelling and depressing. There were older flamers with pudgy
bodies and showy rings, lonely looking hoodlum types, a drag queen
or two—in short, an odd clique that seemed watertight and content
just the way they were.

But I decided I was going to go back and give it another chance.
I liked the idea of having a local group of bar buddies and I lived too
far away from West Hollywood for that to happen there. In time
maybe I could introduce Bruce to them. If he was beginning to get
bored at my place, this might make our evenings more fun.

I drove down La Brea, parked, walked into the Annex and sat
myself down at the bar. I noticed my hands were shaking. There was
no music playing. A jukebox was against the far wall but apparently
everyone was fine if it got quiet once in a while.

"What'll it be, handsome?"

"Miller Lite, please."

I was surprised the first step was that simple. At first I felt guilty
drinking in a bar without Bruce, and as I looked around at the var-
ious patrons, I didn't trust my chances of insinuating myself into
their clubhouse. But after a few weeks of hanging out, not only did
I become comfortable with the place, I made some friends and even
garnered a reputation for playing hard to get and talking about an
imaginary boyfriend. I used the word *boyfriend* with them even though
Bruce and I hadn't succumbed to the lingo of possession yet. I
learned how to read a pool table. Jim, an older black guy, used to wet
his finger and make a mark on the felt to show me exactly where to
aim the ball. Gloria, a straight Latina who was always inebriated,

used to wax philosophical on bar subjects ("Patti LaBelle had a lot of great songs, but give 'Over the Rainbow' to Sam Harris. It's only right."). There was also Dale, the flirty black bartender; Tom, a young recluse who I might have liked if I didn't have Bruce; Jamie, the talkative sweet one who could only handle three beers before walking funny, and a couple of others with their own stale brand of redeeming qualities. The more I went, the more I felt at home.

I asked Bruce to meet me there one night; I still don't know if it was my fault or his, but the evening was a disaster. When he walked in and saw me, he didn't give me the sexy smile I had been counting on, and even after I bought him a beer he never eased into the place. His guard was up and we couldn't seem to get a conversation going. When Jamie walked in and I nodded an acknowledgment, I didn't wave him over. I wanted to show off Bruce when he was his normal self, not when he was holding back like this. I tried acting like we were just our old selves and would go to my place afterward, but I began to doubt that was going to happen. And the more I realized that, the more it was all I cared about.

"Go put your name up on the board," I said, hoping he'd come back to life around the familiarity of the pool table's constantly changing array of solids and stripes, angle and decision, every break a new constellation to play out.

He looked at me for a long moment and I felt like an eight ball rolling too close to him.

"Come on," I said glancing around. I wanted Jim to come over and tell him what a great person I was, how Bruce was a lucky guy. I didn't like feeling I should be ashamed for liking this place, for having found some new people to hang out with. If I could just get Bruce to put his name on the board, maybe it would be a nice night.

Bruce slowly got up from the bar stool. "I'm gonna get going," he said. He told me he was tired and was going to go home and watch the late rebroadcast of *Larry King Live*.

I wanted to ask if I could come with him, but I didn't. Instead I sat there trying not to feel humiliated because I didn't believe him.

I thought about following him that night or at least driving by his

Sex with Librarians

house but I knew that was too obsessive. I didn't care if he wasn't going straight home, but I didn't want him to go to a bar. I decided to drive to the Eagle just to see if he was there. If he wasn't then maybe he really was tired and wasn't into a night out tonight, and I would just get back in my car and drive home.

I saw him playing pool. That hurt me, and yet I wasn't surprised. I was relieved. At least now I knew. It was me he didn't want to be with.

I stood there till he saw me, hoping my mere presence would speak for me. I hadn't learned the words to win over a man's heart. They'd sound corny and vulnerable. When I went up to him he was standoffish and when he peered at me, it wasn't like my sexy Einstein, more like he'd realized there was no formula for relativity to be found with me—we were just barking up the wrong tree. After some awkward questions, which he answered with a small "I don't know," I left and drove home.

When I called a week later, the last part of our conversation went something like this.

Him: "I don't like dating more than one person at a time."

Me: Silence. I didn't want to admit I'd heard that. And why did he say "dating" all of a sudden? We never called it that. It was food and beer and sex and then the sage. *We never said dating.*

"So what's the problem?" I asked. "Why don't you just come over for a while? You'll feel better." But I didn't get it. I refused to get it.

Him: "I don't know if I'm what you need. And like I said I don't LIKE to see more than one person at a time. I mean, I've done it before, but it's not what I like doing."

Me: Silence. I wished he would stop saying that. I couldn't offer anything against everything it implied. Denial was the only way I could hold my head up through this. This was unfair. He had told me dating was something he wasn't ready for. I thought what we had was better than the dating thing.

I heard a beep. My phone had call waiting and I asked Bruce to hold, grateful that I had some time to think of what to say next. It was my mom.

"I'm just calling to say your sister's new commercial is on in thirty minutes. The one where she gets run over. Well not *really* run over, but almost. It's for reflective outerwear. Channel Five."

"Okay, I'll watch it. I'm on the other line now."

"All right. You've been well? What have you been doing?"

"Having sex with librarians," I said in a voice I realized was angry. "I'm just kidding. Not really."

I clicked over. Bruce was still there. We used to watch my sister's commercials together, his arm around me as he'd tease me by saying mean things like "Spank her!" or "Give her a damn line to say, then maybe she won't be sick all the time!"

Now he wasn't saying anything. He wanted me to make the first move toward saying good-bye. So instead I said those awful things. The wince category of things. I told him I cared about him, that he was a diamond in the rough, that I wanted more time with him and I saw something special when I looked at him, beneath the self-destructive act, beneath the world-on-his-shoulders persona he dragged around with him all the time.

I never heard from him again.

I did however manage to keep my friends at the Annex. At first it was a small consolation, having friends but feeling all alone. The following month was my birthday and I celebrated it at the bar. They put my name and HAPPY BIRTHDAY on a long sheet of butcher paper. It looked nice. I'd taken the piñata from my kitchen and filled it with plastic minibar bottles of booze. It was a fun night but afterward I came home alone to an empty apartment.

The books on the shelves seemed equally abandoned. Bruce had spoken for them all summer, reminded me of their themes and importance, the authors' lives and loves; told me the ones I should throw away, the ones I should reread. Now I was all alone with them again. I could feel their authors staring at me from behind the impassive curtain of dust jackets and glossy vibrations of cover art. I'd always thought the day would come when he'd actually go through them and physically separate them into different stacks for me, or when he'd take me to his job and show me what sections to spend the

Sex with Librarians

day in, maybe even arrange for me to have a student library card.

Bruce had lent me a book, *Trout Fishing in America*. It was still sitting on the coffee table like he was going to be coming by for it any minute. It was a surreal novel from the hippie era. I think he felt that if I didn't have drugs in my background then I should at least read this book. Among its rules were that when you go to a junkyard you should take along a yardstick to measure off sections of a used trout stream stacked up for sale. Printed on the back cover, for no apparent reason, was simply the word *mayonnaise*. It was hardback and the only thing I had to remind me of him. It lay there like a house he used to live in but had now abandoned. Bruce liked the author's abstract social commentary, the way he redefined the limits of reality and put things in a displaced order, leaping recklessly from one disjointed scene to another. I guess that's the same way he talked to me when he was the sage. There was a line in the book that stayed with me, and on one of his visits I had told him about it. The main character thinks he sees a trout stream but it turns out to be just a woman walking down the road. He tells her, "Excuse me, I thought you were a trout stream."

Then Bruce repeated her indignant response, "I'm not," and we both laughed.

I remember thinking it was funny that someone would mistake a person for a trout stream. I remember thinking it was funny that the woman had to assure him she wasn't one.

But now I know you can mistake a person for anything, including a trout stream. Eventually I put his book on the shelf where it could stare at me along with the others. I stopped guitar altogether and went back to reading. It seems I never could develop my calluses. Out of habit I continued to press my fingers against the cold beer bottle, waiting for the hurting to stop. Sometimes I remember pressing so hard on those nylon strings, especially the thin ones for the high notes, wanting the music I made to be perfect, and I swear I can still feel the tender grooves it made in them.

Hard-Boiled
Landon Dixon

He fanned the pictures across my desk.

It was all there in black and white—me sucking "Big Deal" Rigoletti's cock, licking his balls, getting fucked deep in the ass, the expression on my rugged pan one of inescapable ecstasy. I had to hand it to the mug, he could really handle a Speed Graphic camera and a flashgun—hiding behind a two-way mirror.

But this was face-to-face. And I wasn't passing out any kudos.

"It's gonna cost you plenty, Mr. D.A.," Convey sneered, gathering up the smut pics, stuffing them back into a manila envelope. "The big, tough, manly crime crusader for the people gettin' all swishy with the state's number one gang boss. You'll be ruined."

I sat back and crossed my legs, a smile tugging up the corners of my Valentino-like kisser.

Time dragged, sweat spreading in trickles across Convey's clock. He tried a grin, but it didn't take. He pushed a shaking mitt through his short, white-blond hair, his blue eyes watering.

"I—I want money—lotsa dough!" he bleated.

Two-bit blackmailer.

I knew something about the guy, could read him like a cheap pulp magazine. "You don't want money," I stated.

His gob dropped open. "W-what? Either you make with the geetus—and plenty— or I cart these sex shots on over to the papers...or maybe the governor." He shook his envelope at me.

I rubbed the cigar I'd been toying with underneath my nose and repeated, "You don't want money."

His Adam's apple did a jig. "Huh!?"

I filed the fifty-cent stogie in the breast pocket of my two-hundred-dollar pinstripe, climbed to my feet. Then I strode around the wide expanse of desk toward Convey.

He backed away, eyes bugging, hands thrusting out the thick envelope like a shield.

Hard-Boiled

I swatted it aside. Pictures of two big-dicked, hard-bodied he-men fucking up a storm spilled out all over the carpet. I grabbed Convey by his bow tie and shook him like my prick after pissing.

"What're you gonna do!?" he screamed. "I'll scream!"

I jerked his sweaty expression close, knocking his fishy glims down with my blazing headlights. Then I planted one on him—square on the mug's moist, red lips.

His eyes just about popped out of his head.

"You don't want money," I snarled, breathing his hot breath. "You want me." I plugged his pucker again, holding the lip-lock longer and harder this time, really working the guy's soft, wet mouth. Until his body went limp as Sammy Wong's famous egg noodles.

"I saw it in your eyes—and groin. Those pictures turn you on. You got all hard and hot lensing me and Rigoletti. Didn't you, blackmailer?"

He nodded so hard his neck creaked.

I sent a hand sailing down to his crotch, grabbing on to the pole testing the seams of his checkered five-and-dime suit. He groaned, eyelids all aflutter. I kissed him again, shooting my tongue into his open mouth, exploring; my hand squeezing, rubbing his stiff, clothed cock.

"You want to suck my cock?" I growled.

His eyes burst open. He bubbled affirmatives.

"Then do it," I rasped, shoving him down to his knees.

He had me unbelted and unbuttoned in the time it took to spring a dirty crook with a pile of filthy lucre. He pulled my semi-hard out of my drawers and clung to it, like it was the stuff that wet dreams are made of. Then he started fisting my swelling dick with a damp paw, then two, really pulling. Getting me hard as the Law's supposed to be on mugs like him.

"It's b-beautiful," Convey marveled. "So—"

"So, do you have an answer for the class, Mr. Schiller?"

I blinked blur out of my eyes, mouthed, "Huh?"

The class laughed. Professor Convey didn't. "My question was: how did Raymond Chandler reshape and refine what Dashiell Hammett had done earlier in hard-boiled, turn it into true literature?"

I blinked again, the fog lifting slowly from my brain. I stared at Professor Convey; the man's tanned, rugged face; his shock of white-blond hair and piercing blue eyes; full lips; thick body immaculately clothed in a soft, brown turtleneck and tan, gabardine pants. "Hammett?" I stalled.

The class erupted with more laughter. Professor Convey snorted. "If you have any intention of passing Hard-Boiled American Literature of the Nineteen-Thirties, Mr. Schiller, I suggest you start paying attention in class."

He moved on to another student, one who was actually compos mentis. I crossed my legs, burying my achingly hard erection between my hot thighs.

Class over, I waited for Professor Convey in the hallway. Not to talk to the man—to tail him. I just had to know more about the thirtysomething literary hunk—where he lived, and with whom, his hobbies, his turn-offs, and, god yes, his turn-ons. Although I appreciated the hard-boiled scribblings of Horace McCoy and Edward Anderson and James M. Cain and Raymond Chandler, I appreciated the hard, boiled body and hot good looks of Professor Convey even more.

He finally exited the classroom and strode down the hall, smooth leather folio tucked under his left arm, as always. I loitered over the water fountain, spraying the side of my face, absorbed in the man's taut, round buttocks as they shuddered back and forth in his tight slacks.

"You gonna take a shower, too, bub?"

I jerked my head around, stared at the gum-smacking coed waiting for her turn at the tap. Then I fled down the hall after the professor. He was just exiting the Arts Building, striding out into the crisp fall day. I trailed after him.

His house was a couple of blocks off-campus—a modest, blue and white bungalow that smacked of singlehood. I rejoiced from behind a big, old oak tree in the tiny park across from the man's house. A light went on in the living room, and I settled in alongside the bark.

Three minutes later, my mind was wandering off on its own again. Back to a Depression-era scene playing out in a big-city

Hard-Boiled

D.A.'s office. There was a man on the floor, on his knees, the hard-boiled D.A.'s huge cock in his trembling hands...

"So big and hard and smooth," Convey breathed, stroking in awe.

The mug was really getting through to me, my cock throbbing, body seeping heat and balls tightening. Shivers of sensual delight prickled my skin, as the guy vigorously two-fisted my prick. But I didn't let on to Convey. I was the one doing him a favor.

"I told you to suck it," I gritted.

He looked up at me with his baby-blues, drool crowding the corners of his mouth. Then he bent my rod down with his humid mitts and gulped my shining hood.

I shook, a little.

The guy's warm, thick mouthflaps stretched over my mushroomed cockhead and he started sucking on my cap; wet, eager tongue swabbing the pulsing underside of my dick. He moved his head forward, taking rigid shaft into his hot, damp maw.

I stripped off my jacket and tie and shirt, draping them carefully over the back of a green leather chair, then letting the dirty blackmailer get a good gander at my gleaming-white, muscle-humped torso. He got an eyeful, all right, along with his mouthful, watching me pinch a pair of stiffened pink nipples even stiffer, as he shifted his head to and fro and slid his lips up and down my dong.

He grabbed my balls and squeezed. I bucked my hips, fingernails biting into my nipples. Convey's eyes lit up like a Wurlitzer. He excitedly pulled my gleaming rod out of his mouth and slammed it up against my washboard abdomen. He stuck out his tongue and lapped at my pinned prick, painting pipe with hot spit; dragging his beaded, red-velvet tongue over the length of my shaft, up from my hairy balls to my bloated cap, over and over.

Until my sacked sperm started heading for higher ground. "You're going to take it in the ass," I informed the ardent cock-lick, pushing him away in the nick of time.

He shucked his pants and drawers like it was bath-time at the flophouse. He spread out on his hands and knees. His ass was small and tight, the mounded half-moons dusted with white-blond hair. I got in behind and spread his crack, spat into his asshole.

"Fuck me, big man!" he squealed.

And I obliged.

I speared my slimy dickhead into his manhole, popping his rim, barging meat down his chute. He groaned, grabbing up his cock and tugging with hard, urgent strokes, as I sunk shaft inside him to the fur-line.

"You're not going to the papers with those pictures of me and Rigoletti, Convey—if you know what's good for you." I gripped the mug's narrow waist and pumped him, once,

slamming the statement home, making my case.

"Yes...I mean, no—I won't go to the papers!" he cried, feeling the full impact of what was good for him.

I started churning his chute, reaming him, setting his body to rocking and his cheeks to gyrating. I surged with the wicked sight, the wanton feel of my cock plunging that man's ass.

I slammed back and forth in Convey's hungry chute. His face was buried in the broadloom, hand desperately working his own cock. The crisp smack of my powerful thighs against his rippling buttcheeks filled the heated room, making a sweet mockery of my oath, and office.

Convey clutched at a chair leg for support. It knocked against the wall as I cocked him, knocking...

Someone was knocking on Professor Convey's front door.

My eyes came back into focus. I pulled my fingernails out of the oak.

A guy about my age was knuckling the professor's door. The door opened, and my hero appeared. The two men exchanged greetings, then quick glances up and down the quiet, leafy street, before the door closed on them.

I looked right, left, back at the three kids sitting on the swings staring at me. I raced across the street, and in behind Professor Convey's bungalow. His backyard was as small as his house, withered tomato plants filling most of it. A light burned in the partially open kitchen window, and I ducked down and latched on to the frame, peeking over and in.

"Five hundred dollars, Brady—give it or leave it," Professor Convey stated, holding up a manila envelope.

Brady was a buzz-cut blond, with the cinder-block head, lantern jaw, and brick-house body that spelled *football* in big, white letters on his university jacket. "That's a lotta green," he groused, rubbing the back of his sunburnt neck. "The test's only worth ten percent of my final mark."

"Ten out of ten's better than zero. And don't complain to me about money, Brady. I happen to know you're receiving more alumni support than the college's endowment fund."

I bit my lip, eyebrows skying. Professor Convey was selling exam answers! The guy was as crooked as Francois Sagat's dick.

I watched, wide-eyed, as the flat-top jock reluctantly forked over the cash, five C-notes. Professor Convey handed him the manila envelope for his efforts.

I studied the situation, the professor's rugged body and Daniel Craigesque face, wondering: what would hard-boiled P.I. Philip Marlowe do in this situation? The Continental Op? Any twenty-minute yegg from the pages of the hard-boiled literature the "good" professor taught?

And as I was pondering, a bird suddenly let loose a caw and took a swoop at my head. There must've been a nest or feeder nearby. Tweety taloned my hair and I slammed my face up against the kitchen window to get away—alerting the parties inside.

Brady tucked the answer envelope under his arm like it was made of pigskin. He barreled out of the kitchen, steaming for the front exit, while Professor Convey dashed out the back door and splayed me up against the wall like a cockroach.

"Mr. Schiller," he growled, shaking his head, before yanking me off the wall and marching me inside his house.

He slammed me down into a kitchen chair, towering and glowering over me. "Just what did you see, Schiller?"

I swallowed hard and looked up at—but no longer "to"—him. He wasn't a revered sexpot scholar anymore; he was just a man—a greedy, grubbing man like the rest of us, with five bills in his pocket and plenty more where that came from. And I was just a hard-up college kid—like any student outside of the athletic program and the blue-blood set—who could really use some extra dough. Tuition and text-books didn't come cheap, like academic integrity.

I stood up, standing tall, thrusting out what little chin I had to the point where it just about poked Convey in the chest. "I saw you selling test answers to the starting D-line, is what I saw. Grades for gelt." I squared my bony shoulders. "And now I want a piece of the action. And a boost in *my* grades."

Convey rubbed his dimpled chin with a big, brown mitt. Then slapped me across the face, sending my glasses and bravado flying.

"You pay attention here, but not in class, eh?" he mused. "Just why were you watching me, anyway?"

I hung my head like a bum in a breadline.

"I think I know why," Professor Convey continued. He reached out and lifted my chin, staring into my watery eyes. "Maybe we can make some sort of...arrangement."

I lit up like a Philco radio.

Professor Convey gripped my shoulders and shoved me down to my knees; his belt and zipper were undone before my brain had even stopped spinning. Then, like an astute educator, he observed, "I've noticed the looks you've given me in class...Melvin. I understand why your attention wanders."

I gulped, staring at the big bulge in the big man's blazingly white briefs. It was moving, growing, uncoiling, taking shape long and hard right in front of me, stretching the fabric and the edges of my endurance. Professor Convey dug his hand in and pulled his cock out, slapping my burning face with it.

"This is what you really want, isn't it, blackmailer?"

I answered by eagerly grabbing on to the man's monster erection, the both of us shuddering with the erotic impact. His huge snake pulsed in my hot little hand, both hands, as I took hold and tugged.

The professor's cock was beautiful—pink and smooth, clean-cut, purple hood thick and shining. I pumped and pumped his pulsating shaft with my sweaty hands, pulling so hard his balls flapped.

He stood firm, hips outthrust, thunder cock filling my worshipping hands and eyes. "You want to suck on my cock, don't you?" he said. "Well, do it."

I pulled his awesome tool down until his bloated hood was level with my mouth, slit staring me in the eyes. Then I opened wide and engulfed his cockhead.

"Yes!" he groaned, clutching my black curls.

His hood was soft and chewable. I pulled on it with my lips, scraped it with my teeth, tongue swabbing shaft. I felt the man's entire body vibrate through his cock.

He yanked my head forward, forcing more of his meat into my

Hard-Boiled

mouth. I happily consumed all I could before gagging, his cap bumping against the back of my throat. He grunted and pumped his hips, fucking my mouth.

I gripped Professor Convey's moving hips and went cross-eyed watching his gleaming pole glide back and forth between my stretched lips, pulsing shaft bulging my cheeks, hood tickling my tonsils. He tasted so very good, filled me up so very well.

He churned my mouth until snot bubbled out of my nose and spit hung down in spaghetti strings from the corners of my overfull kisser. Then I grabbed his hairy balls and squeezed, and he pumped even faster, fucking my face like it was his own personal glory hole.

I gained strength from the man's strength, from what he was doing to me and what I was doing to him. I jerked my head back, leaving him dangling and dripping. I gulped for air and courageously stated, "I'm going to fuck you."

"Like hell you are!" Professor Convey roared. "That's a man's job."

He shoved me backward, toppling me onto all fours. Then he pulled my pants and shorts down, digging in behind me with his now-latexed prick and a bottle of lube. I clawed at the tile as he greased my crack, brought the hard-boiled home by busting my butthole and cramming cock down my chute.

"Fuck me, big man!" I squealed.

And he obliged.

Professor Convey hung on to my hips and pounded his cock into my ass, stretching my chute like never before. I flooded with wicked, tingling heat; sliding back and forth on the linoleum, desperately pulling on my own numb-hard dong whenever I could.

"Now you're getting what you deserve!" the professor bellowed, spanking my cheeks with his heavy balls, blowing me wide open with his sledge of a cock.

I frantically jacked in rhythm to the man's pistoning prick, face mopping the floor, body and ass swollen with sexual electricity, brimming with sensual joy. The sharp, quick smack of the professor's powerful thighs against my rippling buttocks was erotic music to my ears, striking just above our ragged grunting and groaning.

"Here it comes, Melvin! The payoff!"

His rugged body jerked, his cock jumping in my butt. Hot cum spilled into his condom, deep within my ass, just as my own balls boiled over and I was jolted by ecstasy, spurting jizz all over the floor in rapid, fiery bursts.

We danced around like we were dodging bullets, coming and coming and coming, connected at the ass and cock. I full-body quivered with the ball-draining strength of my hand-cranked orgasm and the wicked rush of the big man emptying himself inside my raw, fucked-over anus.

My bank account and grades are as low as ever these days. But at least I'm getting all the hot, hard-boiled sex and literature I can handle. Professor Convey gives me what I want, if not always what I ask for.

When I Was a Poet
Kevin Bentley

The tables at Café Tremors were taken up by an assortment of odd-looking individuals frantically shuffling typescript pages of poetry; Laura, conferring importantly with several older women, was easy to spot, though I hadn't seen her since she'd left the bookstore we worked at twenty-five years before. Her hair was shorter—it used to flow over her shoulders, pale blonde—and now an ash-blonde that might have been gray; she wore some sort of limp rayon Madame Nu pants and smock printed with a jumble of colors and patterns, bringing to mind the Sunday paper comics section. Still the oversized glasses, still the dangling chandelier earrings. She saw Gina and me and waved a hand vaguely in that phony Eleanor Roosevelt manner of hers I remembered so well, and the long, tedious reading unfolded. I gulped two glasses of awful red wine and tried not to grimace. "If I make *this* face," I'd teased Gina outside, mugging and rolling my eyes like Pee-wee Herman, "that'll be the signal for *Let's get the hell out of here.*"

Laura's couple of poems were short and not bad, spare still-lifes set in the Arizona desert; most of the other readers wailed and postured and ranted with fake British accents and that annoying interrogative rise at each line break. Laura had e-mailed, *There's someone who knew Brad Huff coming who'll be reading a poem about him!* Laura had fixed me up with her friend Brad, now long dead, with whom I'd slept maybe a half dozen times in late '79. A woman at a table right in front of us had caught my eye; she seemed frantic and sad, an elderly bohemian with long, wild, thin gray hair; a pale, waxy face; little reading specs perched at the end of her sharp nose; and wearing a long velvet black skirt that fell awkwardly over a bulging midriff, with a poofy-sleeved

When I Was a Poet

gypsy blouse. She ignored the other readers, determinedly snapping open a three-ring binder (worn, splitting, labeled *Spinning Hippos and Other Poems*) and pulling out yellowed onionskin pages, squinting at a few lines, then putting them back and popping the rings shut again. This was probably her first chance to read in public in years—although, but for me and Gina, her audience seemed to be only the other contributors to the debut issue of *Va-Va-Voom* and the Asian guy behind the counter noisily bussing dishes. I felt sorry for her. Naturally she turned out to be the one who'd known Brad. The poem didn't tell me much, as it was a kind of impressionist moment, "Brad, Dancing": *Fingers/Snapping/Foot/Stamping!/Foot foot foot/Stamping stamping/Finger/Snap/Foot...!* "Must have been after I knew him," I told Gina, and made the face.

I used to be a poet. It was a highbrow coming out vehicle—the poems I published in the weekly college mag, *Headframe,* were laced with gay sex, which the other fresh-faced lit majors around the table in my Promethean Myth seminar assiduously ignored, but which led the dorky former sports editor from my high school newspaper, four years my senior, to write me a cryptic fan letter and then meet me for several fumbling but smutty daytime assignations in my parents' house.

I had a three-month relationship with a thirtysomething park ranger from my Seventeenth-Century Prose and Poetry class (actually he did the lights for a national park theater that staged regional extravaganzas like *Viva El Paso!,* but he looked great in the uniform) and he was the recipient of a number of sonnets in praise of his thighs, beard, and dick.

One night in the hectic July before my parents threw me out of the house, I hooked up with an Ivy League science major home for the summer, at the Time Machine. Aldo liked Plath, Hughes, Joni Mitchell, pharmaceutical speed—of which he had plenty—and amateur S/M sex that involved his being tied spread-eagled to bedposts, the legs of overturned couches, and weights equipment, and vigorously sodomized by me, surely not the usual effect *Ladies of the Canyon* has on listeners. (*Moon-eyed Aldo/in our wargame loveplay/snakes split eggshell wrist/and ankle in knots, slithered four ways, till,/taut, you quivered a spread-eagled swastika...)* These athletics, and the speed, fueled lots of poetry.

Still ego-inflated and sore from my DIY Daddy stint—and still popping the speed Aldo'd poured into my cupped hands—I picked up my second place award in the Rocky Mountain Collegiate Press Association poetry competition, but not a diploma, loaded up the VW with a box full of diaries and poetry volumes, and my mother's boxy green Samsonite suitcase that smelled of Taboo and face powder, and cleared out for San Francisco.

A couple of my new roommates in the city, also Texas refugees, toyed with writing as well, and I arrived with a sheaf of new poems to read—but after that first midnight at the Elephant Walk on Quaaludes, clone rush hour thronging the sidewalk beyond the windows, Baudelairian excess was my vocation.

I only ended up at the Mission poetry workshop because my friend Steve, fed up—briefly—with disco and drugs, brought a night school catalog to the bookstore where we worked and threw it on my desk in the shipping room. "We need to broaden our interests," he said, lighting a cigarette. Mrs. Eidenmueller forbade smoking at the register.

"By that you mean we should try meeting men somewhere besides in bars, right?" I said.

"Right," he said, with a little snicker. "No, I *mean* it, I'm taking this camera class. I'm pretty good with a camera, you know?" I knew we had recently taken arty naked snapshots of each other with his Instamatic. If Steve was going to take a class, I guessed I might as well; I scanned the catalog and found a listing for a poetry workshop that ran the same Thursday nights as his Introductory Photography.

Steve met a hot divorced Italian guy at his first class, went home with him at the break and dropped out. It was an intense affair and I saw less of my best pal for a while but by then I was swept away by the poetry workshop—the new friends I made there and the interest my talent aroused in the teacher.

The workshop had been going on for years with a different mix of newcomers and longtime veterans each semester. It met in a middle school classroom on Church Street; the echoing linoleum hallways

When I Was a Poet

had that sour smell of teenagers, textbooks, and Lysol. That first winter night—Thursday, February 2, 1978—I gawked at the teacher when he came rushing in late, spilled a pile of purple mimeographed handouts and paperback poetry volumes from his worn satchel onto the old blond wood teacher's desk, and sat on the edge, eyes darting around mischievously as he stretched out his long legs. "I see some old faces—haha, not *old* old, but familiar—and some interesting new ones, great!" he said, looking directly at me. Staring back at him, I saw a tall, bony, pale, thirtyish man with wiry ginger-colored hair, a little red goatee, and a big sexy Gérard Depardieu nose, wearing worn, tight cords that showed an obscene bulge at the crotch, a Mr. Natural T-shirt, and a dark blue jean jacket. I'd hoped to find some good-looking guys in the class but I hadn't expected the teacher to be one. Was he straight? Gay? The women all hung on his every word; he smiled broadly at me as he passed around copies of a poem for us to read and discuss.

"Looks like Barry Manilow's singing to you, honey."

I was milling around in the hall at break and turned to see a heavyset girl in purple leotards, black skirt and black sweatshirt, with long wild dark hair, freckles, and a pair of black kit-cat glasses, blowing a cloud of Marlboro smoke at me. She looked like a cross between Wednesday Addams and Little Lotta. "Jeez, can you believe some of these morons? I feel like I'm in Barbie's dream school. Here." She thrust a crumpled paper bag at me and I took a burning swig of Johnny Walker.

"Aaack!" I said, and she laughed a wheezy smoker's laugh.

"Put hair on your chest. The boys'll like that. I'm Kate."

Kate was a sarcastic punk who worked in a kite shop at Fisherman's Wharf; lived at a seedy women's hotel on California Street called The Elizabeth Inn; worshipped Anne Sexton, Debbie Harry, and Lou Reed, whom she called "Uncle Louie"; and referred to herself as The Wolfwoman of Polk Street. She knew all about the fey black guy who danced with his turban in the doorway of the Polk Gulch Saloon and had even put him in a poem. "Seriously, Mr. Julian can't seem to take his eyes off your boy-bod."

"Teacher's pet," I sang. "I wanna be teacher's pet..."

Among the mix of white English majors who came to the workshop were the Boronskys, a stylish, blond Marina couple who looked more like siblings than husband and wife, who read an arch poem comparing their marriage to a foofy three-layered cocktail of the day. ("Methinks the Borax Twins are looking for a three-way," Kate stage-whispered.) There was Daniel, a sexy troubled straight guy with a bum eye who wrote a poem about a lonely stoic prehistoric fish at the bottom of the sea; Ames Goodman, the requisite elderly man in a funny cap who wrote traditional verse decrying the insensitivity of youth and the loneliness of age; Rhonda, a rail-thin, tart-tongued thirtyish Jewish woman who wrote very good Plath-like poems about the heartlessness of men; several pre-Raphaelite princesses with flowing blonde hair and watery eyes who, judging by their poems, had been molested and thought a lot about their periods. There was a matronly Irish-American girl, Mary Conley, whose poems usually involved overhearing her two handsome gay roommates, one of them her college boyfriend, making love in the next room. And there was a diminutive, shy girl named Gina with the same last name as one of the younger beat poets, so I assumed she must be his wife or sister and was appropriately intimidated, who read so softly people yelled "We can't hear you!" and dragged their desks closer. But best of all was the flamboyant German, Ergemon von Dylt, who styled himself a poet of the Romantic era, wearing pirate shirts and capes, and writing and performing long, highfalutin rhyming cantos liberally salted with *thees, thines,* and *doths* that caused Kate and me—who dubbed him Eggnog von Overture, or simply Eggy—to sputter and choke and pinch ourselves till we bruised. Julian would look very stern trying to keep a straight face during one of Eggnog's readings, which always had to be cut off in mid-swoon.

But for me, too, poetry was a coded language for moments of heightened perception, a way of capturing peak experiences: love, sex, death. I didn't have any firsthand knowledge of the latter, so I'd taken a page from Sylvia Plath and Maura Stanton and written monologs based on macabre news clippings or historical literary figures: the

When I Was a Poet

overdose of Buffy from *Family Affair*, a man who killed and ate his abusive father, Bosie writing to Oscar. *That first day on the divan/at Tite Street.../you murmured/Rather and O my beautiful boy/with your hand in my pants...*

Write what you know, went the maxim. Go where the pain is. Blah-blah. Kate and I had signed up to read at the next session, and our chief aim was to shock. She planned to read her profane poem in the voice of the virgin Mary (*For God's sake, why all the fuss?*); I wrote the first of my attempts to make art out of a pivotal experience in my life, the period of childhood during which an older male relative had had sex with me.

> Baby, you were the first.
> It was a gothic romance,
> werewolf acts strewing the dark's motes,
> phantom hands on the organ...
> *Close the blinds. Strip.*
> *Get on your stomach.*
> You made me want that...

I had saved the incest for last. My other poems were met with a liberal smattering of those sighs, exclamations, and lip-pursings poetry fans make over particular lines they like at a reading, as if they'd just tasted something delicious; an older woman—an emergency ward nurse—actually gasped when she caught the drift of my finale. I'd missed the encouragement I'd received back in college (*Certainly you have the verbal talent and, I think, the deeper character to be a poet*, soft-spoken, Zen-like Dr. Burlingame had once written on one of my poems). Now, to have the handsome instructor murmuring "Ah," over certain lines as I read—as well as eyeing me with apparent desire—was awfully thrilling. When I finished there were several seconds of awkward silence, then lonely fish Daniel yelled "Bravo!" and everyone joined in the wild applause, even the couple of other straight guys who went on looking at the floor.

"Can I give you a lift?" Julian asked, walking up behind Kate and me in the hallway after class. Soon we were bumping along Market and up Van Ness in a book and paper-strewn compact, passing around a pencil-thin joint Julian had pulled from under the visor. "I think you gave Ames Goodman a coronary," he said, laughing and coughing at the same time.

"That's the first time I've seen him breathing," Kate said, taking a long toke. "Why don't you drop me off in front of Cala—I've got to pick up some Wonder Bread." She gave me a meaningful look and an elbow in the side as she climbed out of the backseat. "Write a son-net for me, Shakespeare," she said over her shoulder. Now my heart was pounding so ridiculously in my chest that Julian had to be able to hear it. He whizzed around corners and down a busy block with-out speaking again, and then we were sitting in a parking place in front of my building and the joint was out.

"Are you going to ask me in?" he said, and then I knew I wasn't deluded, and whether or not he shared a big Victorian in Noe Valley with his lover the doctor, he wanted me. We barely got the door to my dark little studio closed before we were frantically embracing and kissing; bumping heads, teeth; staggering across the dusty, warped parquet floor in a sort of Apache dance as we wrangled each other's shirts off and pants down and fell back on the rickety daybed. "This's all I could think about during class," he panted. He was still driving, it seemed to me: one minute he was gripping the stick shift in his Chevette; the next, my hard-on. I could feel his unusually long, slender boner jabbing my thigh. "Where did you come from, I love you, I can't think about anything but you..." His pale, wired, hard body jerked against me like a rebellious puppet; I could smell his Brut cologne, the sharp scent from his pits, coffee and pot on his breath. "I *love* you," he said again, between chattering teeth—we were both trembling violently, were we coming down with something?—and then we were making out again, our dicks rolling and bumping against each other till we came simultaneously and then lay panting, laughing, Julian blowing across my drenched brow and planting lit-tle kisses on my eyelids, his damp goatee tickling my face, a slippery sheet of semen marrying us at belly and chest. Twenty minutes later, cautious about accommodating his long penis, I was frantically

When I Was a Poet

pumping mine into his bony rear while he writhed beneath me and turned his head to meet my lips.

I started dripping three days later. I hadn't had the clap before, but I knew all about it from Steve, who was unsurprised at my news. "I could tell this was going to be intense. Don't you remember how I got it the first night with Sal?" I called Julian at work when I got back from the Fourth Street clinic. "Oh, Charles will take care of me, but *you*—the city clinic! You poor thing! I haven't been able to think of anything but seeing you again. Let's go out after class Thursday."

Kate met me at the Gulch later that evening, handing me a little gray chapbook of Patti Smith's "Ha! Ha! Houdini!" inscribed, *Something to do until the penicillin wears off.* "Even the angels are clapping," she said, clinking her Budweiser against my Calistoga.

"I went out with Larry for four months and he never came close to saying I love you," I said. "Isn't this weird?" Larry was an est convert whose addled conviction that "we're all assholes, but so what?" had kept us from growing as close as I might have liked.

"Welcome to the literary world, baby. Remember, 'Everything is only a metaphor...' God this music sucks." The DJ was playing "Disco Inferno."

The black guy in the doorway snapped one end of his unspooling turban at us like a bullwhip.

> At the bar we arranged our colors
> two characters in a lurid strip...
> At my place, the superman suit
> was up for grabs. I wanted to grapple diamond,
> he wanted to open under like
> a new leaf snapping with
> a rubber-gloved sound. As I fucked him
> we made words that pierced the floor.

The poem I brought for that week's critique raised eyebrows.

"There're some issues of accessibility here," Julian said, rubbing his hands together, "but, ah, I think we can assume this poem is describing two men having sex, yes?" Kate's coughing fit halted the discussion momentarily.

Victor, a cute straight Italian guy who hadn't shown up with a poem of his own so far, said, not looking at me, "I have to give you credit for being so willing to put your shit right out there."

"I get the feeling one of the men in the poem doesn't really trust the other one, but wishes he could." This was Mary Conley, the fag hag.

"Hmm, I'm not really seeing that," said Julian. "Where are you seeing that?"

Two hours later Julian and I stood facing each other in the back of the Gulch. I was wearing a red and tan plaid cowboy shirt with white pearl snaps I'd bought at Goodwill a few days before, hoping, with my longish hair and clipped beard, I looked like the Stud-frequenting gay hippie I wanted to be. "You look so adorable," Julian said. He was wearing his usual tight cords and a boyish striped T-shirt under his jean jacket. "You too," I said. We kissed and embraced; when he stepped back, my front pocket peeled away from my chest in slow motion and fell to the floor and we both laughed nervously. The trembling and tearing up were starting again. "I don't know how I'm going to keep my hands off you for two more days," he said, before we went around the corner to my studio and, following a blurred interlude of struggling with good intentions, clothing, and lubricant, he wedged an impressive portion of his long cock inside me with my legs pushed back to my chest and gently thrust till we both came and I shot in our faces.

"What am I going to do about you?" he said, leaning up on one elbow, eyes gleaming.

Gina, who'd slept with Julian's lover, told Kate and me as we passed the bottle one evening during the break that Charles had told her, "Julian has a rule about never sleeping with his students—until he

When I Was a Poet

has one he wants to sleep with."

"Isn't Charles bothered by this?" I asked Julian one night as we lay sweaty and catching our breath in my narrow bed. "Oh no, not at all. He'd love to have a three-way actually—but I want to keep you all to myself," he said, growling and pulling me close.

Although he had an ongoing gig teaching the workshop each semester, Julian had an administrative day job. Charles was by all accounts a level-headed fellow who calmly weathered Julian's extracurricular passions, dispensing wise and sometimes tart advice along the lines of Sada Thompson on the TV drama *Family*, and nursing him back to psychic health when the latest idyll ended.

How did I feel about Julian? I'd only ever been involved with older men; Julian was another. I had just turned twenty-two but I'd slept with plenty of "married" men and deep down I knew Julian's impassioned protestations didn't wash. On the other hand, what did I, an aimless party boy and ribbon clerk—and despite all pretensions otherwise, a bookstore job is no less retail than folding jeans and T-shirts at the Gap—have to offer Julian but youth, sexual vigor and variety, and a literary bent? How many men, I sometimes wonder, fled before coffee when morning exposed the cramped studio and the poems came out? *Pain can be trusted to stay the night/most come, then turn on the light/and find their socks.../Some cad rises with the mist/and I'm off for the blonde cendré/the month in the country/the plugged heart.*

Kate and I went out several times trawling the bars on Polk Street; since she also worked downtown I met Mary Conley for chatty lunches over which we dissected Julian and her drama-filled relationship with her gay ex-boyfriend, and laughed about Eggy, who, perhaps having recognized my shout-outs to Julian, had adopted Mary as his muse and solemnly intoned thinly veiled love poems dedicated to "Yram." There were evenings when most of the class, usually sans Julian, adjourned to a seedy hofbrau near the school for heavy drinking and literary conversation that quickly progressed to gossip. On one of these occasions, Daniel, trying to recall a particularly good line, mentioned a former workshop student named Tom Miles, and several people glanced at me. "*Last* semester's Kevin Bentley," Mary explained.

That first night on the cell block
cold cocks and steel bars
indistinguishable
love a honed table knife at the throat...

My weekly offerings, at first celebratory and boastful, acquired a
sinister tone. *Looking for Mr. Goodbar* had confirmed the gay murder
clippings my mother dutifully mailed me from back in Texas; that,
and a general foreboding, fed a fatalism out of keeping with the joy-
ously promiscuous pre-AIDS moment. Julian's quick ardor cooled
and the rides home grew sporadic. Like many a teenage lass, I had
always turned to poetry as exorcism or elegy for a lost boyfriend. My
friend John at the bookstore used to look up from counting his
drawer as I slunk in red-eyed after another bad breakup and say,
"Are we in for another poem, girl?" This time I took the role of
Fortunato: *In the bowel of your catacombs/we waded through natty shrouds/and
strewn bones for a wine I knew/wasn't the point.../each scuttling bug another sleek
word/from your mouth.../Your love, implacable as masonry/back turned to stop the
last/ gap. A caked-blood darkness/I admired. Amontillado.*

Then, a blank. I can't remember exactly how it stopped—but my not
remembering seems suspect. Once I fully grasped that despite the
intensely romantic soundtrack, Julian was entirely unavailable to
me, and after several subsequent gonorrhea scares, I probably
showed a more cynical face. It wasn't because, during one of our
later encounters, Julian had suggested an act for which there's a
coordinated colored handkerchief, although it didn't seem very
romantic. I'd like to think I cut him off, but more likely, as must
have happened to Tom Miles, he just didn't call me anymore when
the semester ended.

Kate came down with hepatitis and moved home to New Jersey,
Mary Conley decided all gay men were bastards and snubbed me.
Gina, with whom I'd only spoken a few times at the workshop, spotted me on Market Street one day a year or so later, pulled out a joint,
and invited me to lunch. I wouldn't find a lover for another seven

When I Was a Poet

years, but I'd stumbled across a best friend who'd stick by me to the present day.

My star turn at the workshop left me with a sadness that stopped my mouth for nearly a year in which I made few attempts to write poems and only several brief entries in my journal—before I reemerged and resumed diary keeping, still only twenty-three, still a retail drone, still ricocheting from man to man, but harder, less quick to say, or believe it when told, I love you; a tougher cookie who'd lost the knack of imagining my life was fit subject for a poem or that I could write it. Though I went on loving certain unassailable poets, after that, poetry, however free of cliché or kitsch, became associated in my mind with sentimentality and sophomoric posturing—the opposite of sophistication, disappointment, and reality, which of course it is.

The Monk in the Stacks
Mark Wildyr

I accepted the job without thinking twice. My love of books, the need for a little pocket money, and the offer of a position at the campus library perfectly melded into—if not a marriage, a ménage à trois. I had loved working at my high school library and I looked forward to a continuation of that rewarding experience. It should be a snap; they all used the same Dewey Decimal System.

On the evening of the second day of my freshman semester at Jemez International College, a small, exclusive school catering to brainiacs and foreign exchange students located high in the northern New Mexico mountains, I reported for duty on the night shift. The Woolshard Memorial Library occupied a three-story pile of red stone with rounded turrets known by all as the Castle.

I walked into the rambling and somewhat spooky building around five o'clock for an orientation session with the faculty librarian, a dour, middle-aged matron with gray-streaked hair pulled into a bun. I knew from yesterday's interview that she wasn't as forbidding as she appeared.

"Ah, Mr. Wells. It's Brodie, isn't it?" she asked as I stepped up to her desk. "Punctual, I see." She gave me no time to respond. "Punctuality is a virtue I treasure."

I took note of that fair warning. By six o'clock, I had the lay of the land, and by seven, I was handling things solo.

Quiet, introspective, and not terribly athletic, I had led a sheltered existence. My parents ran a small construction company where I'd labored alongside carpenters and masons and roofers for a good part of my life. Although the work had adequately developed my

The Monk in the Stacks

form, I didn't work at keeping in physical shape other than hitting the swimming pool more or less regularly. My interests ran almost exclusively to intellectual pursuits—more specifically to the magic of the printed word. My summertime delights were James Agee's *A Death in the Family*, Willa Cather's *My Antonia*, or Robert Cormier's *The Chocolate War* rather than football and baseball and basketball...although I had enjoyed many a game of horse at our driveway hoop with my best friend, Jim Hall.

Looking back, I realize it was the physical interplay with Jimbo that got me out there in sneakers and shorts and T-shirt—or sometimes *no* shirt. I had tingled in strange places whenever we brushed or bumped against each other to make a basket. It was exciting that a local star athlete who'd actually screwed a few girls chose to pal around with me. It was sort of sex by proxy.

Now I was experiencing my first extended period away from a closely supervised home environment, and it was liberating, although I missed Jimbo terribly, especially when lying in bed in my cell-like dorm room. The night before, I'd imagined him doing it to his current girlfriend and got so excited that I did something about it. Afterward, I wondered if lonely masturbation was destined to be my lot in life.

I quickly learned that fully half the student body was foreign exchange students from all over the world. The cultural potpourri was exciting, but the individuals themselves were positively fascinating. It was like living a novel. Within a week I'd mentally placed my new friend Amy Leung in the middle of Amy Tan's *The Joy Luck Club* and pictured Henri Arquette as Albert Camus's hapless *The Stranger*. Andreas Mellant, I cast as a character in Erich Maria Remarque's *All Quiet on the Western Front*.

Andreas intrigued me. Although I'd pictured him as the disillusioned World War I German soldier, I wasn't certain of his nationality. The accent, though slight, sounded Teutonic, but the name Andreas seemed middle European or possibly Greek. I had no idea of the national origin of his family name, Mellant. He reminded me of Jimbo—tall, dark haired, brown eyed, and full of unconscious grace—classically handsome. No, I take that back. "Classically handsome" conveys an ethereal quality; Andreas's physical impact was earthy, magnetic. It pleased me that he did a lot of his night studying at the Castle where I could surreptitiously watch him. A couple of times, I imagined that strong, lithe body mounting some nameless blonde beauty. Immediately afterward, I would sit and hope no one had caught me blushing. Such erotic thoughts were embarrassing.

As the first weekend on campus loomed, I drank coffee with Amy Leung and Henri Arquette in the corner of the cafeteria serving as our student union. Amy leveled her beautiful dark eyes at me and asked a question in an innocent voice.

"Have you heard them yet?"

"Heard what?"

"The noises," Henri Arquette pitched in. "Those ghostly noises that spook the late-night librarians."

"Well," Amy corrected, "not all of the librarians. Just some librarians."

Convinced I was the butt of a local joke, I grinned. "And how do they decide who gets to hear them—these mysterious noises of yours?"

"I'm serious," Henri said, his charming accent growing thicker. "Odd things happen in that old rock pile."

"I get a chill the moment I pass through the doorway," Amy assured me.

"Have you been through the building?" That was Henri again.

"Just the first two floors."

"And that's all you'll ever see. The third landing has been sealed up for years. How much do you know about the history of this place?"

I twitched my shoulders. "Not much. Just that it's owned by some rich oilmen. I heard it was originally a hotel, but who'd build a hotel on the road to nowhere?"

"It's true. It was originally a railroad hotel...a sort of spa. There are some hot springs up the canyon, and there's great trout fishing

The Monk in the Stacks

up there, too. Of course, it was the gambling room that was probably the best draw. That was back before Las Vegas became the gaming mecca."

"And after that, it was a monastery for a little while."

"For a very little while," Henri emphasized.

"Why?"

"Now we come back to the third floor of the Castle," Amy replied, "and the reason it is closed up tight as a drum—I believe is your expression. Because there's still a monk up there."

I glanced in the direction of the library. "A *monk* lives up there?"

"I didn't say lives up there."

"Come on, guys! You're trying to freak me out."

Henri gave a very Gallic shrug. "Ask around. Legend says he was walled up in there because he was a danger to the others."

Amy picked it up. "I imagine he took after the members of the order with a meat cleaver or something. Ask around." She read the skepticism on my face. "Ask Ms. Ordoñez."

"I will," I assured them as I got up to toss away my trash. "And I'll come back to see you guys when she tells me it's a load of bull."

But that would have to wait for Monday; Ms. Ordoñez did not work the weekend. As I relieved Helen Margoles at the desk, I was tempted to ask if she'd ever heard weird goings-on in the place, but she was anxious to go meet some friends. So I swallowed my questions and surveyed the big room. Only a few students were taking advantage of the wealth of literature stored in the old library. Andreas, I was pleased to note, was one of them.

Since he sat alone, I was tempted to go over and strike up a conversation, but for the life of me, I couldn't think of a good excuse for interrupting his study. It wasn't that Andreas was aloof—maybe sort of reserved—but I'm more at home with fictional friends unless a flesh and blood one makes the first move. I settled in at the counter and started clearing the check-in shelf that Mary had left for me. After fifteen minutes or so, I glanced up—and lost the ability to breathe.

Andreas leaned back in his chair, his right arm thrown across the back of the seat next to him as he frowned over the text on the table.

But the thing that paralyzed my thorax was the way his leg was thrown out at an angle, pulling the fabric of his trousers tight across his inner thighs. I swallowed hard at the bulge distorting his groin. At first, I thought he had reacted to some erotic reading, but as I stood blushing, I realized that was merely his normal—package, I think one book called it. No—basket. Swallowing hard, I tore my eyes away as I experienced the first purely homoerotic thought of my life. It had been different with Jimbo. Curiosity. Mild titillation. Nothing more. When I pictured Jim in that certain way, it was with a pretty girl. This quick, powerful reaction to Andreas was primal; I wanted no woman between us. It was an unexpected and undeniable craving.

Shocked and embarrassed, I quickly turned my back, startled to realize that my body had responded. Thank goodness the counter had been between us, even though he appeared oblivious to my scrutiny. Shaken, I returned to my desk and sat down. My god, what was going on? Wasn't I just a shy, backward guy? But someone merely socially retarded doesn't get a hard-on from looking at a handsome youth. Was I queer? If I was, why didn't I know it—or at least suspect it? But maybe I was overreacting. Had I ever responded to another human being as I had to Andreas Mellant? Girl...boy...man...woman? Anyone? I let out a gasp as the answer slammed me right in the head. No! Never!

"What's the matter, Wells? You look like you just walked over your own grave!"

Caught by surprise, I flinched. I knew that voice without looking. The *w*'s were virtually *v*'s; the vowels were broad; the consonants, harsh. Andreas stood at the counter studying me oddly.

"Are you all right?" he added in a disturbingly deep voice

Was everything about this guy erotic? "Yeah. Doing okay. Can I help you?"

"Ya. Need to borrow a pen if you have one. Mine ran dry."

"Sure. Got an extra one here," I said, rising to reach beneath the counter, bent over awkwardly at the waist to hide my erection.

Pressing against the counter to offer the pen, I casually lowered my eyes. His crotch was less evident, but still exciting. What would he do if he knew of my interest in his person—his manhood? I resisted the urge to lick my dry lips.

"You like working here?" he asked. Unfortunately, he leaned against the counter, cutting off my view. I raised my gaze and met his big, kelp-brown eyes. They were just as disconcerting.

"Love it!" I said, immediately regretting my choice of words. "Love it" sounded like a girl—or a fairy. A little shiver ran down my back. "Yeah, it's a great job. I lo...uh, like books. I can get lost in them. My folks used to throw me outside to get some exercise." Good lord, I was babbling.

"Yes, they can grab the imagination." The way his Adam's apple moved as he spoke fascinated me. I resisted an urge to touch it. "I read a lot, as well. Not as much now, of course. I'm carrying a rather heavy load."

Oh, man, are you! I recoiled, afraid for a moment that I had spoken the lewd thought aloud. "What are you, a senior?"

"No. A junior. I spent a year traveling Europe before crossing the pond. I am taking a major in civil engineering? You?"

"Literature." I laughed self-consciously. "What else?"

"Ya. What else for a bibliophile, eh? Do you lock the place down at night?"

"Down? Oh, you mean do I lock up at closing? Yeah. That's part of my job."

"If you do not mind, I will remain here until that time comes. Let me know when you close up. Okay?"

"Yeah, sure."

I watched as he strolled back to his table, enjoying the graceful swagger of his gait. I found the view from the rear as exciting as the front.

By ten o'clock, closing time, we were the only two left in the big building. As soon as I stood, he glanced up and stretched. Languidly, he rose and gathered his things.

"Time to go back to the cells we call rooms." I tried making casual conversation, but my throat was too tight. In my imagination, he strode to the door, threw the lock, and came back to vault the counter and—

And what? What did I want to happen? *Anything he wanted!* The enormity of that answer hit me hard. An alpha male like Andreas would not be satisfied with just fooling around.

My dream faded as he paused at the big double doors to wave good-bye before leaving. Disappointed, I went about the lock-up procedure. After turning out most of the lights, I realized I had not checked the small door at the rear of the ground floor. It was seldom unlocked, but still, it was part of my duties to make sure.

I glanced into the darkness and was strangely reluctant to step into it. Nonetheless, I started back without bothering to flip the light switches. I had taken no more than a dozen steps into the shadowy racks of books before something halted me in my tracks. A stirring in the gloom raised chills on my back. I peered into the deeper darkness. It could have been my imagination, but something fluttered quietly. My skin prickled. A fine sheen of cold sweat popped out on my forehead.

"Hello?" I called. "Anyone there? I'm locking up. You have to leave now."

Not completely understanding the fear that skittered down my sternum, I stood stock-still. No answer. A mouse, perhaps? There must be whole nests of them in an old place like this. Drawing a steadying breath, I started for the door again. A soft, muffled thud brought me to a halt. After a moment of paralysis, I retreated to the desk and fumbled with clumsy fingers for the switches, bringing the cavernous room into light again. Screwing up my courage, I marched back to the area where I had heard the disturbance and glanced down a row of stacks. A book lay on the floor. I frowned. I would have sworn it had not been there before. Resolutely, I started down the narrow aisle, but a puckering of the flesh over the length of my body stopped me. A chill permeated the area. I stood rooted to the spot until the atmosphere grew normal again. Then, on uncertain legs, I proceeded to pick up James Baldwin's *Go Tell It on the Mountain*.

With the title came the cold again. Turning, I raced to the front, slung the book onto my desk, thumbed off the lights, and fled the

The Monk in the Stacks

building. An unreasonable panic accompanied me all the way to my dorm. It was only after I closed the door to my tiny room behind me that I took an easy breath. Rushing through my preparations for bed, I turned in immediately, although I had intended to read another chapter of Saul Bellow's *Seize the Day*.

Uncharacteristically, I tossed and turned, my mind grappling with the unsettling events of the night. The strange chill and weird noises and the dislocated book occupied my conscious mind until sleep finally claimed me, but then Andreas Mellant's broad back and trim hips invaded my subconscious. Sometime before dawn, I gave up and masturbated.

Sundays, the library observed abbreviated hours and I worked alone. I approached the Castle wishing I could linger in the beautiful sunshine of this magnificent fall day, even though at this altitude—something over eight thousand feet—the temperature was chilly despite the best efforts of a waning summer sun.

As I opened the front door, I almost stumbled across a volume lying just inside the threshold. I was surprised to note that it was Pointer's *Bawdy and Soul: A Revaluation of Shakespeare's Sonnets*. I wouldn't have thought the library would stock such a book. Homosexuality was presumably not condoned and certainly not talked about much, although in fairness, there was a sense of intellectual freedom at the school.

The library was quiet, so I glanced through the book with a keen awareness of the self-revelation I had experienced the night before. A little later, reluctantly putting the volume away in its proper place, I turned to some routine chores. Placing a small placard on the counter informing the reading public that I was working on the second floor, I made my way up the long flight of rickety stairs to shelve a couple of rare volumes.

Stepping across the threshold took me into another realm. The second story of the Castle is essentially one tremendous, high-ceilinged room with a few stacks containing the school's rarest and most valuable tomes tucked away up there to limit access. When such books were called for, the attendant librarian obtained them for the faculty member or student making the request. The remainder of the second story held worktables where Ms. Ordoñez repaired damaged volumes. Clip-on, high-intensity lamps augmented the weak light filtering through small windows clouded by decades of grime.

The wooden floor squeaked noisily beneath my sneakers. The atmosphere, while not downright cold, was chillier than that of the first floor. Despite the vastness of the room, there was a stale, dry taste to the air. I snapped on a light to dispel some of the gloom and quickly slipped the two titles back into their proper spot on the racks. As I turned to leave, the stairway to the mysterious third floor caught my eye. If the flight of steps leading to the second story was chancy, this staircase looked downright dangerous. Placed along the west wall, the steps were steep and narrow. A single plank of wood supported by two-by-four posts provided a frail banister. The top ended in a small platform that faced a stark, wooden door.

Morbid curiosity drew me forward. Up there was where the monk was supposed to have been locked away and forgotten. I placed a foot on the first step, and before I knew what I was doing, I started ascending the staircase. Despite my rising fear, augmented by squawks of protest from worn, rotting planking and tired, stressed nails, I continued upward, propelled by something I did not understand. Puffs of dust collected on the hems of my trousers with each step.

At the top, I shuffled around on the tiny landing to face the doorway. Three heavy hasps secured by huge padlocks so grimy it was obvious no one had opened them in years effectively sealed off the third floor. The door appeared to be made of slabs of heavy oak, but then everything about the Castle was heavy and sturdy. Made for the ages, they would probably say. After all, it was originally built around the turn of the twentieth century when things were made to last.

As I carefully inched around to start the shaky trip back down, a noise startled me so badly that I recoiled against the flimsy banister. It creaked alarmingly and sagged beneath my weight. Launching myself forward, I fell heavily against the locked door—and then jerked away immediately as a groan came from beyond it.

The hair on my neck and arms rose. My skin crawled. My testicles

The Monk in the Stacks

drew up, seeking protection. A chill played down the length of my back. It could have been the old door complaining when I slammed against it, but—but—

But the *first* time I heard it, I wasn't leaning against the door. Then it came again, a long, horrifying groan ending in a sigh of such pain and suffering that I panicked. The stairway might have been flimsy, but I scrambled down as nimbly as one of the mountain goats on the peaks behind the college. I don't even remember maneuvering the steps. I was just there at the bottom staring back up at that terrifying door. Regaining my senses, I raced for the stairs down to the first floor. Before I covered half the distance, the chilled air turned absolutely icy. I grew dizzy and disoriented, as if disturbed by the passage of something unseen. And then—and then the door ahead of me slammed shut. Bang! The sound was sudden and stark, drawing a shout of anguish from me.

The cold came again, pressing against me, raising a fresh wave of goose bumps. I veered away from the penetrating iciness and found myself backing toward the tall stacks of old and rare books. Abruptly, I broke for the doorway again, but an icy wave and a strong musty odor propelled me backward. Then something amorphous brushed past, and I reeled away, frightened out of my skin. Looking around wildly, I could see nothing. No one was there. I was alone. Swallowing hard, I drew a deep breath and sought to recover from my panic attack.

Movement drew my eye to the top of the first stack. As I searched for the source, a tall, slender, red-bound book slowly slipped from its place and toppled over onto one of the worktables. A fresh chill at my back and a dry, putrid stink drove me forward. As I whirled in fear at some unseen, insubstantial touch, my hand came to rest on the fallen tome. The cold retreated; a scuttling noise came from the row of stacks where the light did not reach. The air was clear and dry again.

Freed from what I had perceived to be immediate peril, I bolted for the door, tore it open, and launched myself down the stairs, not even pausing to lock the door behind me. It was only when I dropped shakily into my chair at the desk that I realized I had the book in my hand. Seeking normalcy, I glanced around the main library room. Three students occupied reading tables and peacefully studied open books, unconcerned over my thudding heart. I swallowed hard, trying to work up some saliva in my dry throat and slow my racing pulse.

The book I'd brought down from the second floor turned out to be a ledger filled with a handwritten log of daily events, or at least significant events, set down by the head of the old monastery that supposedly occupied the Castle at one time. This particular diary began in January 1925. As best I could make out from the shaky script, the writer signed himself Abbot Jonathan. Eventually, I came across a passage that drew an audible gasp from me. I bent over the faded ink and labored to make out the uncertain scrawl.

Lord God Almighty, provide me strength and wisdom. Both will be required to deal with our predicament. Brother Anthony continues to pursue his perverse ways and cannot be dissuaded. What am I to do? He is the nephew of the Bishop in Santa Fe! I have passed hints that the good brother is not happy cloistered here in the mountains, but Santa Fe does not hear. Or worse—they do but are content with the arrangement. Surely that must be the case.

Most of us can withstand Anthony's perverse pursuit, either ignoring his advances or admonishing against his wickedness. But I am fearful for Brother John. He is but a lad, and unfortunately a fair one. Oh, but that all monks were twisted and hoary, but Brother John's mere presence inflames Anthony's mad passions. From all I can determine the youth has resisted temptation, but I fear he will yield before long. I must do something, but what?

The old abbot's anguish clearly permeated the yellowing pages, but he had given me some understanding of the local myth. One of the monks was gay—and aggressively so. Amy's version of the tale claimed that one of the men posed a danger to the others and was supposedly locked away on the third floor. And now I knew who and why: Brother Anthony, because he was queer. A chill ran down my spine, although I did not know if it was fear or excitement.

The front door opened, and I lost my interest in old ledgers.

The Monk in the Stacks

Andreas Mellant strode in and by his mere appearance took possession of the room. I was inordinately pleased when he came straight
to the counter.

"Wells," he said by way of greeting.

I wondered if he knew my Christian name was Brodie. "Hi,
Andreas. You're late tonight."

"Ya. A few of us hiked up Redondo Canyon. Going again next
weekend. You can come along with us if you wish."

"Thanks, but I'll be working."

"Pity. Same arrangement as last night? You will warn me when it
is time to leave?"

"Yeah, sure. No problem."

No problem. Yeah, right! No problem except that I was hearing
and seeing things. Or more accurately, *almost* seeing things. I hadn't
actually seen anything in the dark corners upstairs; it was more like
an *impression* of something moving around. I was so engrossed in my
musings that I almost forgot to watch Andreas walk away...almost,
but not quite. I enjoyed his graceful step for a few moments until he
disappeared into the stacks housing the biographies.

Once Andreas vanished from my hot view, I sat down and finished studying the abbot's diary. It was mostly a litany of daily toil,
interspersed with threadbare economics, but there were occasional
comments on the problem of Brother Anthony. From my perspec-
tive, it was easy to see where this was leading. References to restric-
tions "for his own good" progressed to outright confinement.
Unfortunately, the tome ended before a resolution was reached.

I closed the ledger book and sat back in my chair, trying to order
things in my own mind. So far as I was concerned, the myth was
more or less confirmed. There had been an errant monk, and he
had probably been locked away in the third story of this very building. The ultimate outcome, however, was still a mystery.

But none of this explained the groan from behind the locked
door on the third floor or the weird events that had occurred on the
second. Or, for that matter, late-night happenings in the vast room
where I now sat. A science major would have concluded there were

rational laws of physics to explain things—the settling of a century-old building, the scuttling of mice or rats, even minor earth tremors tilting books off the racks.

But to my mind, which ran more to the romantic, this did not hold water. What I'd felt earlier upstairs was no ordinary occurrence. The rush of cold air was not an indoor breeze. The groans and moans did not have the timbre of settling oak. And what about that odor? Like something from an open grave. Besides, minor earthquakes did not dump select volumes at my feet. I considered the three books involved. *Go Tell It on the Mountain,* a semi-autobiographical novel about a black youth's religious conversion, was a classic. James Baldwin, the author, was an admitted homosexual whose works sometimes reflected that lifestyle. I smothered a gasp. The *Bawdy and Soul* work speculated on gay connections in Shakespearean sonnets. And the ledger documented an abbot's worries over a homosexual monk.

I shuddered as I slowly arrived at the truth—at least, *my* version of the truth. The ordinary noises of the students utilizing the library's reading room faded into the background as I grappled with the immensity of my conclusions. It had to be the monk! Brother Anthony's shade was trapped in the Castle. And he revealed himself only to other...*queers*. A sudden chill pressed upon me from behind. I shivered and stood abruptly, scooting around the counter out into the great room. Still trying to draw an easy breath, I went to the table where Andreas worked and dropped into a chair opposite him. He looked up, a fleeting frown of irritation flashing across his fine features.

"Is it time already?"

"N-not quite."

"What's the matter, man? You look like you've seen a ghost."

I blanched as he unknowingly came close to the mark. "Uh, you have a minute after I close up? I'd like to show you something and get your opinion."

"Yes, certainly."

There seemed nothing else to say, so I left him to his studies and made the rounds of the big room, reshelving the books left on reading

The Monk in the Stacks

tables. I was relieved that the eerie chill did not reappear.

Sundown comes early in these mountains, so darkness had fallen even before Sunday's short working hours lapsed. When I shooed the few remaining patrons out of the library at closing time, Andreas moseyed up and leaned on the counter while I locked the door. He studied me curiously as returned to my desk and motioned him over. He took a chair across from me.

"Tell me what you know of the old stories about the Castle," I began.

"You mean about the deranged monk locked in the attic until he died? They say his mummified body's still up there."

A distinct thud came from the back of the building. Less obvious was a swirling in the darkness.

Andreas peered over his shoulder. "What was that? I thought everyone had left."

"They have," I replied blandly. "It wasn't the attic; it was the third floor of the building. It's still locked—with three big padlocks."

"Looks like somebody was very serious about closing it up. So the story is true?"

I opened the ledger and thumbed to the proper page. A heavy sigh broke the silence. I glanced at Andreas. He had not reacted. "Did you hear that?"

"What, that thump?"

"Never mind. Here, read this."

I handed over the ledger and indicated the passage where the abbot laid out the problem of Brother Anthony.

As he bent his head to read, the chill invaded my space, causing me to shiver. My nose twitched at a sharp scent. The disturbance retreated, settling down to an excited fluttering in the dark recesses of the rear book racks.

"Damnation!" Andreas exclaimed, glancing up at me. "The old boy had a problem, didn't he? I guess the Church was hiding its deviants back then, too."

The invisible excitement in the darkness behind him increased. A low moan emanated from the corner. "Did you hear that?"

"Hear what?"

I gave one of Henri's deep shrugs. "Strange noises, stirring in the darkness, fluttering in the book stacks. Moans. Groans. Odors."

"You're nuts, Wells."

A chill signaled the approach of—something. "And you don't feel that? The cold?"

"Sure. This old building's always half cold."

"No, it's more than that." I sighed and leaned back in my seat. "I guess it's like they say. Not everybody hears it."

"Make sense, will you?"

I sat up straight and gasped aloud at a sudden epiphany. "I didn't hear it either until—" I bit down hard on my tongue to keep from betraying myself.

"Until what?"

"Until I understood." I gazed into those deep, fascinating eyes, read the unasked question, and blurted out the answer. "That I was gay. I didn't know it until the other day. I swear it."

"How did you find out?"

"Not sure I should tell you." In response to his scowl, I rushed ahead. "All right. I...I realized it yesterday...while I was watching you."

It was his turn to jerk upright. Then he settled back into the chair. "You're queer for me?"

"I guess so. I'm attracted, anyway. And that's when he revealed himself to me."

"So you're queer for me, and a dead monk's queer for you? Rich!"

A violent stirring in the darkness behind him brought Andreas upright again. He rubbed his arms against a sudden chill. "What the hell!"

"So you heard it that time? You felt the cold?"

"Y-ya," he stammered. "What does it mean?"

The answer was as clear in my mind as anything had ever been. "That you like the idea of me being attracted to you."

"Do not talk nonsense! I'm not queer."

"Maybe not. But not everybody who has a relationship with

The Monk in the Stacks

another guy is queer. Or at least that's what the books say."

"Tell me honestly, Wells. Have you ever been with a man?"

I shook my head slowly while the thing in the corner shifted restlessly. "Never."

"But you want us to get together? What is it you wish to do with me?"

The darkest corner of the room came alive for a moment. A sigh swept over us. I saw the skin on Andreas's bare arms shiver.

"I don't know. I don't have any experience."

Andreas eyed me for a long moment and then stood. "That thing...it's not going to bother us is it?" I shook my head. "Then come on."

Mutely, I followed as he walked into the darkness at the rear of the room. I noticed that he kept his distance from the unnatural darkness in the far corner. As I groped my way through the gloomy recesses between two towering stacks of books, I ran smack into Andreas. He had halted and was leaning against the wall. The touch of his body was as exciting as I had imagined it. The whole world was silent for a moment.

"You are sure you want to do this, Wells?"

I nodded, and then realized that he probably couldn't see me. "Yes. Very sure."

His hand found mine and guided me to the mound of flesh that had first sent me down this road. It was warm beneath my touch. His hands came to rest on my shoulders, and I understood what he wanted when he pressed me down. I sank to my knees.

My excited hands explored his flanks as he tore open his fly and slipped his clothing to his ankles. Contact with bare flesh energized my nerve endings. As he rose to my touch, I leaned forward and took him. Passive at first, he slowly became engaged. Eventually, a sob tore out of his throat, and he muttered my name, "Brodie. Brodie!"

And then he exploded in orgasm. After a long, wild, delicious moment, the tension drained away, leaving him slumped against the wall, enervated. I was prepared for a whole range of emotions, but not the one that came. I was inordinately proud to have done this wonderful thing for him.

Andreas pushed away from the wall and restored his clothing. The silence between us grew awkward and uncomfortable. I wanted to talk about the experience, explore it verbally. Had he liked it? He had if his tremendous orgasm meant anything. Andreas pushed past me, his hip brushing my swollen member as he fumbled his way toward the light.

I refused to let him sour the evening. I'd given this wonderful, handsome man incredible pleasure and that was enough for me. Then becoming aware of that other "presence," I whispered into the dark "Is that what you wanted?"

The answering sigh had lost some of its tortured quality. "Okay, Brother Anthony, that's all for tonight," I added in a blasé tone.

Suddenly the darkness around me exploded with energy. The cold came again, icy, penetrating, fearsome. The odor was overpowering. Frightened, I raced through the stacks and bolted to where Andreas struggled with the locked door. He spun as I approached.

"What the hell was that?" he demanded.

"I—I don't know. Let's get out of here!" Fumbling the key into the lock, I managed to turn the tumblers. We fled outside, where Andreas waited impatiently while I locked the door behind us. Then we rushed across the expanse of green to the dorm, trying not to let our panic show. Wordlessly, we parted on the first floor, and I trudged up the steps to my room. Too tired and emotionally drained to bother cleaning up, I stripped and dropped into bed. But sleep would not come until I took myself in hand and masturbated while reliving the fantastic thing Andreas Mellant and I had done back in the stacks.

Andreas avoided me for the next few days. He came to the library a couple of times, but other than flashing his dark eyes in my direction there was no greeting or acknowledgment of my existence. It saddened me beyond all reason.

There was another consequence to that beautiful but frightening night. The very next afternoon Ms. Ordoñez mildly took me to task for leaving an old ledger book open on the table upstairs.

The Monk in the Stacks

Confused, since I had shelved the ledger, I accepted the rebuke. The moment she left for the day, I made my way up to the second floor. As I neared the shelf of books containing the monastery records, I saw that, indeed, there was a ledger lying open on the nearest table.

I frowned. This made no sense. The librarian had told me she shelved the ledger "you left on the table." The answer came to me even before the cold crept up my back, raising my hackles and puckering my flesh. Slowly, I moved forward, and the chill abated. More curious than afraid, I picked up the ledger and scanned the open pages, spotting what he—it?—wanted me to find almost immediately. The old abbot's scrawl seemed shakier, as if the events overwhelming his peaceful existence had aged him considerably.

Lord God Almighty be with us and of us on this tortured day. I have made a decision, or more properly, one has been forced upon me. The Bishop refused my plea to remove Brother Anthony from our midst. I fear His Grace intends that the problem remains ours—not the Church's. Today, things reached a climax. I found the two of them together in Brother Anthony's cell, both naked and obscenely rampant. Through divine intervention I came upon them before Brother John's flesh was sullied—but only just. A moment later, and he would have been lost. Brother Anthony is shamefully evil!

Alas, such was my anger and revulsion that I made a sudden and likely unwise decision to lock him away. If my sentence was precipitous, it was nonetheless given, and I was helpless to revoke it. We locked him in that dismal space on the top floor of the monastery. Initially, all was quiet, but as I write these words, a ferocious pounding comes from above. I fear no brethren will sleep tonight, but it is the price for protecting the young man. Eventually, Brother John will come to accept that his isolation is in the best interest of his eternal Soul.

I almost dropped the book. It was *John* they locked away—for his own protection. I shivered in revulsion. That old abbot had made a political decision. He imprisoned the prey to keep away the predator. Anthony was the bishop's nephew; poor John was an innocent nobody.

I tore through the rest of the old ledgers, scanning the pages quickly until I found what I was looking for. A passage dated a year after the one I had just read gave me the end of the story. Locked away in solitude for a year, John had begun to lose his grip on reality. One night when a brother came to feed him, the deranged young man shoved past his warder, crashed through the flimsy banister on the landing, and fell to his death below. In a sort of grim amen to the entire sad story, he ended up crashing through the flimsy roof of one of the tiny cells on the second floor—Brother Anthony's room. Horrible!

My specter was strangely quiet for the rest of the week. Occasional stirrings in the dark, vague fluttering at the edge of my vision, an occasional acrid odor teasing my nostrils intruded on my thoughts, but I did not feel the icy touch of the grave. It was not that I had lost interest now that the mystery was revealed, but the worry that I had made a mistake with Andreas weighed heavily upon my mind. Any day now, I expected to hear dark mutterings that "Brodie sucks cock" or some such rumor. Why not? I deserved it. I had experienced an epiphany about my inner self and allowed the shade of a long-dead monk to goad me into acting on my discovery. I wasn't certain which was the greater irony.

That Friday night, I had snapped off the lights and was taking out my key ring when the front door opened. Andreas and I each halted dead in his tracks as we caught sight of one another. I opened my mouth to speak, but the handsome young man suddenly snatched the key ring from my paralyzed hand. After locking the door, he gazed into my eyes. Neither of us said a word as he led me deeper into the library. He carried his knapsack over one shoulder, but I was afraid to ask its purpose. My voice might break the spell. As soon as we were behind the counter, he unzipped the bag and pulled out a blanket.

I shivered at the possibilities that suggested; an excited sigh came from the stacks. Still without speaking a word, Andreas stripped off his clothing. By the dim glow of the night-lights, I feasted on the masculine beauty that had eluded my gaze in the dark. That made the moment even more magical. He was completely naked before he spoke.

"Well, what are you waiting for?"

His husky voice freed me from my paralysis. I tore out of my clothing and moved into his arms. I had not known that men kissed,

The Monk in the Stacks

but let me assure you they do. It left me weak in the knees, but that was all right because he eased me down onto the blanket. His hands roamed freely and his lips intoned a litany of endearments in a language I did not recognize. Then, at last, he lifted my legs and thrust me into the marvelous world of true man-love.

At the moment of my ejaculation, I joyfully whispered to the watcher in the shadows, "Are you satisfied now?" There was peaceful silence in the stacks, broken only by the breath of my very real lover.

About the Authors

Shane Allison is the author of four chapbooks of poetry, most recently *Black Fag*, and the editor of the erotic anthology *Hot Cops*. His poems and short stories have been published in Velvet Mafia; Suspect Thoughts; Outsider Ink; juked; Softblow; *Mc Sweeney's*; *I Do/I Don't: Queers on Marriage*; *Best Black Gay Erotica*; *Sexiest Soles*; *Cowboys: Gay Erotic Tales*; *Van Gogh's Ear*; *Chiron Review*; *Muscle Worshippers*; *Love in a Lockup*; zafusy and *S.M.U.T*. His work is forthcoming in *Best Gay Love Stories: New York City* and *Sodom and Me: Queers on Fundamentalism*. His fifth book of poems, *I Want to Fuck a Redneck*, is forthcoming. He gets e-mails at starsissy42@hotmail.com.

Tulsa Brown is an escapee from another genre of fiction, who went over the line into erotica in 2003 and never looked back. Her short stories have appeared in a host of anthologies including *Best S/M Erotica, Bear Lust, Skin and Ink, Wet Nightmares, Wet Dreams, Daddy's Boyz* and others. Tulsa has been a finalist for the Rauxa Prize for Erotic Literature in both 2006 and 2007. Her mother does not know what she is up to.

Jim Coughenour is a writer and cartoonist whose fiction, essays and illustrations have appeared in an indiscriminate variety of tawdry zines, gay rags, academic tomes and eccentric anthologies. In the 1990s he created Daimonix, a line of raw art greeting cards, an effluvia that has resurfaced on the Web as *bitternessoflife.com*. His poetry was recently displayed at Bau in the exhibition "Comedies & Catastrophe," a dual show with the painter Elizabeth Winchester. At the moment, Jim works as a user experience architect, and is an active member of the GuyWriters group in San Francisco where he participates in readings for the existentially eviscerated.

Lou Dellaguzzo's stories have appeared in *Best Gay Love Stories 2006; Inside Him: New Gay Erotica; Best Gay Love Stories 2005; Bi Guys: Firsthand Fiction for Bisexual Men; Lodestar Quarterly; Harrington Gay Men's Fiction Quarterly;* Velvet Mafia and Blithe House Quarterly. Three more of his stories—one under a pseudonym—will appear in *Best Gay Romance* (2007). A long-form work has been accepted by *Harrington Gay Men's Literary Quarterly* for Volume 9. Lou has completed a short-story collection called *Secret Shoppers.* The sixteen stories focus mostly on first encounters and beginning friendships between men who are gay or bisexual. Presently, he's at work on a novel.

Landon Dixon's writing credits include *Options, Beau, In Touch/Indulge, Three Pillows, Freshmen, Men, Mandate, Honcho, Torso,* and stories in the anthologies *Straight? Volume 2, Friction 7, Play Ball, Working Stiff,* and *Ultimate Gay Erotica 2005* and *2007.*

Stephen Greco is editor-at-large of *Trace,* the international magazine focusing on transcultural styles and ideas. A former senior editor of *Interview* magazine and *The Advocate,* Greco has contributed to numerous publications, including *New York* magazine, *The New Yorker,* and *The New York Times* online. Greco's first book, a collection of erotic fiction and nonfiction entitled *The Sperm Engine* (Green Candy), was nominated for a 2003 Lambda Literary Award and praised by *Out* magazine for its "breathless bravura." His first novel, *Dreadnought,* is currently serialized in Amazon.com's direct-download publishing program, Amazon Shorts. Greco is at work on a second novel.

Since he can only dream in black and white, **Danny Gruber** started writing stories to bring color into his world. This "color" has appeared in national magazines such as *In Touch for Men, Beau* and *Mandate* and in James C. Johnstone's anthology, *Quickies 3.* Danny grew up in the Pacific Northwest, but now lives in the Midwest and can usually be found at www.dannygruber.com.

Ron Gutierrez is a writer living in Los Angeles. Besides writing, he's passionate about his partner Mark, and long-distance cycling. He has recently completed his first novel.

Richard Labonté lives some of the time in a wee Perth, Ontario apartment, and some of the time in a sprawling ten-bedroom farmhouse on two hundred acres of land near Calabogie, Ontario. From 1979 to 2000, he helped found and then manage A Different Light Bookstores in Los Angeles, New York, West Hollywood, and San Francisco. He has edited the *Best Gay Erotica* series for Cleis Press since 1996, as well as *Hot Gay Erotica* (2006) and *Country Boys* (2007), and coedited *The Future is Queer* (Arsenal Pulp Press, 2006) with Lawrence Schimel. Contact: tattyhill@gmail.com.

Joseph Manera lives in Evanston, WY, where he is completing his internship for a doctoral degree in clinical psychology. His writing has been published in the anthologies *Boyfriends from Hell: True Tales of Tainted Loves, Disastrous Dates, and Love Gone Wrong* and *Afterwords: Real Sex from Gay Men's Diaries* as well as the *Boston Phoenix*. He is currently writing his dissertation on gay men's subjective experiences of unrequited love.

Jeff Mann's poetry, fiction, and essays have appeared in many publications, including *Rebel Yell, Prairie Schooner, Shenandoah, The Big Book of Erotic Ghost Stories, Best S/M Erotica Volume 2, The Gay and Lesbian Review, Bear Lust, Best Gay Erotica 2003* and *2004,* and *Appalachian Heritage.* He has published three award-winning poetry chapbooks—*Bliss, Mountain Fireflies,* and *Flint Shards from Sussex*—as well as two full-length books of poetry, *Bones Washed with Wine* and *On the Tongue;* a collection of personal essays, *Edge;* a novella, *Devoured,* included in *Masters of Midnight: Erotic Tales of the Vampire;* a book of poetry and memoir, *Loving Mountains, Loving Men;* and a book of short fiction, *A History of Barbed Wire.* He teaches creative writing at Virginia Tech in Blacksburg, Virginia.

Sam J. Miller is a writer and a community organizer. He lives in the Bronx with his partner of five years. His fiction and essays have appeared in numerous zines, anthologies, and print and online journals. When he's not writing or organizing poor people to fight for social justice, he's binging on silent movies and punk rock. Drop him a line at samjmiller79@yahoo.com.

Joel A. Nichols was born and raised in pre-WalMart Vermont, but has always wanted to be foreign. His fiction has appeared in Alyson's *Sexiest Soles*, *Ultimate Undies*, *Full Body Contact*, and *Just the Sex*, and will appear in Greg Herren's *Distant Horizons* (Haworth), *Second Skin*, and *Love in a Lock-Up* in 2007. He was a Fulbright fellow in Berlin and an excerpt from his novel won second place in the Brown Foundation Short Fiction Prize (2005). Joel works for a porn website, teaches college English and lives in Philadelphia.

Steve Nugent lives in Toronto and has had short fiction published in *The Church Wellesley Review*, *fab magazine*, *excalibur*, *Lichen Literary Journal*, Velvet Mafia and CreamDrops. His stories have appeared in the anthologies *Quickies 2*; *Exhibitions: Tales of Sex in the City*; *Buttmen*; *Bent*; *Afterwords: Real Sex from Gay Men's Diaries* and *Boyfriends from Hell*. A biography, *No Coward Soul* (Fire Horse Productions), was published in 2003 and his play *The Ray and Barney Visits* is in progress.

Van Scott's work has appeared in *Modern Words*, *Harrington Gay Men's Fiction Quarterly*, Velvet Mafia, *Friction Volume 7*, *Best Gay Erotic Fiction*, OpenWideMagazine.co.uk, 3AmMagazine.com, GonzoBeats.com, 400 Words, TheSubwayChronicles.com, TheAngryPoet.com and UndergroundVoices.com.

Simon Sheppard is the author of *In Deep: Erotic Stories*; *Kinkorama*; *Sex Parties 101*; and the award-winning *Hotter Than Hell*. He's also coedited *Rough Stuff* and *Roughed Up* and is the editor of the forthcoming *Homosex: 60 Years of Gay Erotica*. His work appears in over two hundred anthologies, including many editions of *Best Gay Erotica* and *The Best American Erotica*. He writes the syndicated column "Sex Talk," lives queerly in San Francisco, and hangs out at www.simonsheppard.com.

Don Shewey has published three books about theater: the biography *Sam Shepard* (1985); *Caught in the Act: New York Actors Face to Face,* a collaboration with photographer Susan Shacter (1986); and *Out Front,* an anthology of gay and lesbian plays published by Grove Press (1988). His articles have appeared in *The New York Times, The Village Voice, Esquire,* and *Rolling Stone,* and his writing has been included in a variety of anthologies including *The Politics of Masculinity; Contemporary Shakespeare Criticism; Best Gay Erotica 2000; Afterwords: Real Sex from Gay Men's Diaries* and *Boyfriends from Hell.* He grew up in a trailer park on a dirt road in Waco, Texas, and now lives in midtown Manhattan halfway between Trump Tower and Carnegie Hall.

Born and raised an Okie, **Mark Wildyr** presently resides in New Mexico, the setting of many of his stories, which explore developing sexual awareness and intercultural relationships. Approximately thirty-five of his short stories and novellas have been published in anthologies by Alyson, Arsenal Pulp, Companion Press, Southern Tier Editions of Haworth Press, and STARbooks. He also has a story in an upcoming issue of *Men's Magazine.*

About the Editor

Kevin Bentley is the author of two memoirs, the Lammy finalist *Wild Animals I Have Known: Polk Street Diaries and After* and *Let's Shut Out the World;* and editor of *Boyfriends from Hell: True Tales of Tainted Lovers, Disastrous Dates, and Love Gone Wrong; Sailor: Vintage Photos of a Masculine Icon;* and *Afterwords: Real Sex from Gay Men's Diaries.* His writing has appeared in anthologies including *Best Gay Erotica 2003* and *The Man I Might Become: Gay Men Write About Their Fathers* and in *POZ, OUT Magazine* and *ZYZZYVA.* He lives in San Francisco.